The Indian Story-Teller at Nightfall.

CRADLE TALES OF HINDUISM

BY

THE SISTER NIVEDITA
(MARGARET E. NOBLE)
AUTHOR OF "THE WEB OF INDIAN LIFE"

WITH FRONTISPIECE

NEW IMPRESSION

LONGMANS, GREEN AND CO.
HORNBY ROAD, BOMBAY
303 BOWBAZAR STREET, CALCUTTA
167 MOUNT ROAD, MADRAS
LONDON AND NEW YORK
1916

TO

ALL THOSE SOULS
WHO HAVE GROWN TO GREATNESS BY
THEIR CHILDHOOD'S LOVE OF
THE MAHABHARATA

PREFACE

IN the following stories, it may be worth while to point out, we have a collection of genuine Indian nursery-tales. The only discretion which I have permitted to myself has been that sometimes, in choosing between two versions, I have preferred the story received by word of mouth to that found in the books. Each one, and every incident of each, as here told, has one or other of these forms of authenticity.

To take them one by one, the Cycle of Snake Tales is found in the first volume of the Mahabharata. The story of Siva is inserted as a necessary foreword to those of Sati and Uma. The tale of Sati is gathered from the Bhagavat Purana, and that of the Princess Uma from the Ramayana, and from Kalidas' poem of *Kumar Sambhaba*, "The Birth of the War-Lord." Savitri, the Indian Alcestis, comes from that mine of jewels, the Mahabharata, as does also the incomparable story of Nala and Damayanti. In the Krishna Cycle, the first seven numbers are from the Puranas—works which correspond to our apocryphal Gospels—and the last three from the Mahabharata. The tales classed as those of the Devotees, are, of course, from various sources, those of Druwa and Prahlad being popular versions of stories found in the Vishnu Purana, while Gopala and his Brother the Cowherd is, I imagine, like the Judgment-Seat of Vikramaditya, merely a village tale. Shibi Rana, Bharata, and the two last stories in the collection, are from the Mahabharata. Of the four tales classed together under the group-name "Cycle of the Ramayana," it seems unnecessary to point out that they are intended to form a brief epitome of that great poem, which has for hundreds of years been the most important influence in shaping the characters and personalities of Hindu women. The Mahabharata may be regarded as the Indian national saga, but the Ramayana is rather the epic of Indian womanhood. Sita, to the Indian consciousness, is its central figure.

These two great works form together the outstanding educational agencies of Indian life. All over the country, in every province, especially during the winter season, audiences of Hindus and Mohammedans gather round the Brahmin story-teller at nightfall, and listen to his rendering of the ancient tales. The Mohammedans of Bengal have their own version of the Mahabharata. And in the life of every child amongst the Hindu higher castes, there comes a time when, evening after evening, hour after hour, his grandmother pours into his ears these memories of old. There are simple forms of village-drama, also, by whose means, in some provinces, every man grows up with a full and authoritative knowledge of the Mahabharata.

Many great historical problems, which there has as yet been no attempt to solve, arise in connection with some of these stories. None of these is more interesting than that presented by the personality of Krishna. In the cycle of ten numbers here given under his name, many readers will feel a hiatus between the seventh and eighth. Now about the year 300 B.C. the Greek writer Megasthenes, reporting on India to Seleukos Nikator of Syria and Babylon, states that " Herakles is worshipped at Mathura and Clisobothra (Krishnaputra ?). It would be childish to suppose from this that the worship of the Greek Herakles had been directly and mechanically transmitted to India, and established there in two different cities. We have to remember that ancient countries were less defined, and more united than modern. Central and Western Asia at the period in question were one culture-region, of which Greece was little more than a frontier province, a remote extremity. The question is merely whether the worship of Herakles in Greece

CONTENTS

THE CYCLE OF KRISHNA

TALES OF THE DEVOTEES

A CYCLE OF GREAT KINGS

A CYCLE FROM THE MAHABHARATA

THE CYCLE OF SNAKE TALES

A

CRADLE TALES OF HINDUISM

The Wondrous Tale of the Curse that lay upon the Snake-Folk : and first of the Serpent Realm, below the Earth

IN the world of Eternity, below the earth, lies, as is known to all men, the realm of Takshaka, the Naga king, and about him dwell mighty snakes, hoary with age, and mysterious in power. And strange and beautiful is that Snake-world to see, though once alone has the eye of man been privileged to look thereon, even in the day when the youth Utanka, having been sent abroad on his teacher's service, and having eaten and drunk unwittingly of the nectar of immortality, was robbed of the tokens he carried by Takshaka, and followed him under the earth to recover them for his master.

For fearless and strong was the youth Utanka, disciple of mighty sages, and never was he known to flinch from danger, or to turn back because the task was arduous. Passing through great hardships and many difficulties, he had fared forth to bring to his teacher's wife two jewels

3

belonging to a certain Queen. "But mind," said his master at starting, "and mind," said the Queen, when she gave them, "these ornaments are greatly desired by Takshaka, King of Serpents. See that he rob you not of them by the way."

With high resolve, then, did the youth set forth, to return to his preceptor, bearing the jewels of the Queen. But as he went by the road he saw a beggar coming towards him, who, as he came, constantly appeared and disappeared. Then being athirst, and coming to a spring, Utanka placed his casket by the roadside, and bent to drink. At that very moment, however, the strange beggar turned into the terrible Takshaka, and seizing the packet glided swiftly away. But immediately Utanka understood, and, no way dismayed, followed after him. Then Takshaka disappeared through a hole in the earth. Yet even here the mortal was resolved to follow; so he seized a stick, and proceeded to dig his way after him. And it came to pass that Indra, the King of Gods, looked on, and saw that though the youth was high-hearted yet his tool was not sufficient, and he drove the strength of his own thunderbolt into the stick of Utanka, till the earth itself gave way before the mortal, and he pressed forward through a winding tunnel, into the Serpent-world. And when the passage ended, he found himself in a beautiful region, infinite in extent, and filled with palaces and mansions and gardens. And there were towers and domes and gateways innumerable, and in the gardens were lawns and wrestling-grounds, and all manner of provision for games and sports.

And it came to pass as he went onwards, that he saw two women weaving at a loom, and their shuttle was fine, and their threads were black and white. And he went a little further, and came to a great wheel, and it had twelve spokes, and six boys were turning it. And further still he met a man clad in black, riding on an immense horse.

Now when he had seen all these things, Utanka knew that he had come into a world of magic. Therefore he began to recite powerful spells, and when the man who rode on the horse heard him, he said, "Tell me, what boon dost thou ask of me?" And Utanka replied, "Even that the serpents may be brought under my control." Then said the man, "Blow into this horse." And Utanka blew into the horse. And immediately there issued from it smoke and flame so terrible that all the world of the serpents was about to be consumed. And Takshaka himself, being terrified for the fate of his people, appeared suddenly at the feet of the youth, and laid there the jewels he had stolen. And when Utanka had lifted them, the man said,

" Ride on this horse and he will in an instant bear thee to thy master's door." And the heart of Utanka was satisfied with seeing, and he desired nothing so much as to fulfil his master's errand, therefore he leapt on the horse, and in one moment found himself in the presence of his teacher, offering to him the tokens for which he had been sent.

And now understood Utanka what he had seen in the world of Eternity, beneath the world of men. For the loom was the loom of Time, and the black and white threads were night and day. And the wheel with the twelve spokes was the Year with its twelve months, and the six lads were the six seasons. And the man clad in black was Rain, and the horse on which he rode was Fire; for only when heat is controlled by water is the world of the serpents ever in contentment. " And well is it for thee, my child," said his master to Utanka, " that thou hadst eaten and drunk of the divine nectar, for without this spell of immortality, know that no mortal ever before emerged alive from the realms of Takshaka." And the heart of Utanka rejoiced greatly, and also he desired much to find some means to put an end to the race of serpents, so full of mysterious danger to the sons of men. And he resolved to make his way to the King, and prevail upon him to undertake a warfare against them.

Now a strange and powerful curse lay upon the Snake-folk, and great fear dwelt therefore amongst them. Long, long ago, in the very beginning of time, it had happened that they increased very swiftly in numbers, and they were fierce and full of poison, and evermore at war with one another, and with the race of men. And the gods in high heaven trembled lest the Snake-folk should end forever the young race of Men-folk. And at that time it happened one day that Kadru, the Mother of Snakes, called on her children to obey her in some matter, but they, being wilful and mischievous, at first refused. Then did the heart of the Mother wax strong and full of anger, and thinking she spoke her own will, but really blinded by the fear that abode in the hearts of the gods, she opened her mouth and called down a curse on her own children. "All ye," she said, "shall perish in the fire-sacrifice that shall be made by Janamejaya, the great King!" Poor children! Poor Kadru! Surely never was anything so terrible as this, that the destruction of a whole race should be brought about by its own mother.

The awful prophecy was heard through all the worlds, and for a moment the kind gods were relieved that the race of the snakes was not to increase forever. But when they saw their distress, and when they looked also upon their beauty, their hearts were filled with pity, and they went all together to Brahma the Creator, and spoke before him of the fierceness of Kadru's anger against these dear children, the Snake-folk, and begged him in some way to soften her fearful spell. And Brahma granted them that the cruel and poisonous serpents alone should be consumed, while the others, gentle and playful and affectionate, should escape. And then very softly, so that one little snake alone was able to hear, having crept up to lie near the feet of the Creator, he whispered, as if to himself, a promise of redemption. In the lapse of ages, he said, a maiden should be born of the Naga race, who should wed with the holiest of mortal men. And of this marriage should be born in due course a son, Astika, whose love from his birth should be all with his mother's people, and he should defeat the doom that lay upon them.

Now when this promise was published abroad in the realms of Takshaka, that whole world was greatly comforted ; and patiently, and yet sorrowfully, waited the Snake-folk, age after age. For they knew that their curse was terrible, yet that it was provided in the counsels of the Creator that when their terror should be at its greatest, Astika the Redeemer also should be ready, and should arise to bid their sufferings cease.

The Story of the Doom of Pariksheet

SILENT, silent, in the forest sat the *rishi* Shamika. Long had he sat thus, motionless, in the shade of the huge trees, observing the vow of silence, and to no man would he speak, or return any answer. Only about his feet played the forest creatures, fearless and unharmed, and not far off grazed the cattle belonging to the *Ashrama*.

Now it happened one day while the *rishi* was under the vow, that Pariksheet the King came hunting through that very forest. And he was a great hunter and loved the chase. Neither had any deer, hunted by him, ever yet escaped in the woods with its life. But to-day the allurement of destiny was upon the King, so that he had been successful only in wounding a fleet stag which had fled before him. Thus, following on and on, and yet unable to overtake his quarry, he was separated from his retinue, and as the day wore on, came suddenly, in the remoter reaches of the forest, upon the hermit Shamika, sitting absorbed in meditation.

"Saw you a deer which I had wounded?"

cried the King. "Tell me quickly which way it went!" His face was inflamed with eagerness, and his clothing and jewels displayed his high rank. But though the saint evidently heard his questions, he answered never a word.

Pariksheet could hardly believe his own senses, that one to whom he addressed a question should refuse to answer. But when he had repeated his words many times, all the energy of the royal huntsman turned into bitter anger and contempt, and seeing a dead snake lying on the earth, he lifted it on the end of an arrow, and coiling it round the neck of the hermit, turned slowly about, to make his way homewards. It is said by some that ere the King had gone many paces, he realised how wrongly he had acted in thus insulting some unknown holy man. But it was already too late. Nothing could now avert the terrible destiny which his own anger was about to bring upon him, and which was already creeping nearer and nearer to destroy.

To Shamika the hermit, meanwhile, insult and praise were both alike. He knew Pariksheet for a great king, true to the commonwealth, and to the duties of his order, and he felt no anger at the treatment measured out to him, but sat on quietly, absorbed in prayer, the dead snake remaining as it had been placed by the hunter's arrow. And even thus was he still sitting, when his son Sringi returned from distant wanderings in the forest, and was derided by some of his friends and companions for the insult that the King had offered, unhindered, to his father.

Now Sringi's mind was of great power, fully worthy of Shamika's son. Not one moment of his time, not the least part of his strength, was ever wasted in pleasure. His mind and body, his words and deeds and desires, were all alike held tight, under his own control. Only in one thing was he unworthy, in that he had not the same command as his father Shamika over the feeling of anger. For he was apt to spend the fruits of long years of austerity and concentration, suddenly, in a single impulse of rage. Yet so great was he, even in this, that the words which he spoke could never be recalled, and the earth itself would assist to make good that which was uttered by him in wrath.

When, now, he heard the story of how the King, while out hunting, had insulted his aged father, the young hermit stood still, transformed with grief and anger. His love and tenderness for Shamika, his desire to protect him, in his old age, from every hurt, with his own strength, and his reverence for the vow of silence, all combined to add fuel to the fire of rage that seemed almost to consume him. Slowly he opened his lips to speak, and the words ground themselves out between his teeth. "*Within these seven days and nights, the life of the man who hath put this shame upon my father, shall be taken from him, by Takshaka himself, the King of Serpents.*" A chill wind passed over the listening forests as they heard the curse, and far away on his serpent-throne the terrible Takshaka felt the call of the young sage's anger, and, slowly uncoiling his huge folds, began to draw nearer and nearer to the world of men.

Shamika's vow of silence came to end with his son's return. But when he was told of the curse just uttered, he was full of sorrow. "Ah, my son," he cried, "our King is a great king, true to the duties of his order and the commonweal, and under his protection it is that we of the forest-*ashramas* dwell in peace, pursuing after holiness and learning. Ill doth it befit hermits to pronounce the doom of righteous sovereigns. Moreover, mercy is great, and forgiveness beautiful. Let us, then, forgive!"

The deep sweetness and serenity of the old saint flowed like a healing stream over the troubled spirit of his son, and tenderly Sringi stooped, to remove the unclean object from about his father's neck. But the words that had just been spoken had been too strong to be recalled, so when Shamika understood this he despatched a secret messenger to the King, to warn him of the danger that was hanging over him.

Then the King, Pariksheet, having heard from the messenger that the *rishi* whom he had insulted had been under a vow of silence, and hearing also that it was the sage himself who had sent him the friendly warning, was filled with regret for his own deed. Yet inasmuch as no sorrow could now avail to save him, without the utmost vigilance on his own part, he hastened to take counsel with his ministers. And a king's dwelling house was made, into which no living thing could enter unperceived, and the house was set up on a single, column-like foundation, and Pariksheet shut himself into it, determined that, until the seven days and nights had passed, he would transact both business and worship within its shelter, and seek no pleasure outside.

But now the rumour of approaching disaster to the King began to go forth amongst his people. And as Takshaka drew near to the royal refuge, he overtook a Brahmin hurrying through the forest in the same direction as himself. Recognising the Brahmin as Kasyapa, the great physician for the cure of snake-bite, and being suspicious of his errand, Takshaka entered into conversation with him. He quickly found that it was even as he had thought. Kasyapa was hastening to the court, in order to offer his services in restoring the King, when he should be bitten according to the doom.

Takshaka smiled, and laying a wager with Kasyapa that he knew not how powerful his poison was, he selected an immense banyan-tree, and rearing his head, struck at it with his poison-fang. Immediately the great tree, with all its roots and branches, was reduced to ashes lying on the ground.

But how much greater is healing than destruction! That wise Brahmin, not in the least dismayed, stept forward, and lifting up his hands pronounced strange words, full of peace and benediction. And instantly the banyan - tree began to grow again. First came the tender sprout, with its two seed-leaves, and then the stem grew and put forth fresh buds, and next were seen many branches, till at last the whole tree stood once more before them, even as it had at first been—a lord of the forest.

Then Takshaka offered great wealth and many treasures to that master of healing, if only he would desist from his mission and leave his King to die. And the Brahmin seated himself for awhile in meditation, and having learnt, in his heart, that the curse on Pariksheet would really be fulfilled, since his destiny would thereby be accomplished, he accepted the treasures of Takshaka, and consented to remain behind. And the great serpent journeyed on through the forest alone, smiling to himself over the secret bonds of Fate, spun, as these are, out of a man's own deeds.

Safe in the royal refuge the King had passed six days and nights, and now the seventh had come, nor as yet had any snake been so much as seen. For it is ever thus. Only when men have ceased to fear do the gods send their messengers.

Now, as the day wore on, the King's heart grew light, and towards the decline of the sun there came to the door of the mansion a party of strange fellows, who seemed to be forest-dwellers, bearing presents of fruits and flowers for the royal worship. And Pariksheet being graciously disposed, received the newcomers, and, asking not their names, accepted their offerings.

When they had gone away, however, the King, and his friends and his ministers who were seated about him, felt an unwonted hunger for the fruit that had just been brought, and with much laughter and mirth proceeded to eat it. And in that which was taken by Pariksheet himself he saw, when he broke it open, a tiny copper-coloured worm with bright black eyes, but so small as to be almost invisible. At this very moment the sun was setting, and the seven nights and days of the doom were almost ended. Pariksheet therefore had lost all fear, and began to regret having paid so much attention to the hermit's message. So, the infatuation of destiny being now fully upon him, he lifted the creature out of the fruit, and said to it playfully, "Unless you, O little maggot, be the terrible Takshaka, he is not here. Show us, therefore, what *you* can do!" Every one laughed at the sally, and even as the King, a week before, had placed a dead snake contemptuously on the *rishi's* neck, so now, in the spirit of mockery, he lifted the insignificant worm to the same position at his own throat.

It was the last act of Pariksheet. Instantly, challenged thus by the sovereign's own word, the seeming maggot changed its form before the eyes of the terrified ministers, becoming in one moment vaster and vaster, till it was revealed as the mighty serpent, Takshaka himself. Then coiling himself swiftly and tightly about the King's neck, and raising his huge head, Takshaka fell upon his victim with a loud hiss, and bit him, causing instant death.

The Sacrifice of Janamejaya

Now the child Janamejaya succeeded to the crown of his father Pariksheet, and wise counsellors surrounded his throne and ruled the kingdom in his name. And thus quietly passed the years in which the young man was growing to manhood. Far away in the forest, moreover, was growing up at this very time a strange and silent youth, by name Astika, whose father had been the holiest of mortal men, and his mother the sister of a king among the gentler tribes of Snake-folk. And Astika was a man, of the nature of his father, very saintly and lovable, and full of wisdom. But he had lived all his life in the snake-realm in the forest. For his father had gone away, leaving his mother, even before he was born. So all his heart was with his mother's people and with his childhood's home. Here, then, were the two children of destiny, both of the same age, both fatherless, both born to be world-changers—Janamejaya the King, and Astika the Snake-man, Brahmin, and saint. And those were the days of the power of Takshaka, the Mighty Lord of Serpents.

Now it came to pass, on a day when the young King Janamejaya had grown to manhood, that there came to him one whose name was Utanka, crying, "Avenge! avenge! the time is come! Visit on the great serpent Takshaka thy father's death." And the King began to ask eager questions as to why he was fatherless, and how his father, Pariksheet, being the noblest of kings, had met his death. But when they told him the story of the hermit Shamika and his son Sringi, and of the King's mansion built on a single column, and the copper-coloured insect concealed in a fruit, the mind of the young King put aside all the minor circumstances and fixed on the thought of the great Takshaka as the enemy of the royal house. And he began to brood over the duty of avenging the death of his father and protecting the world of men from the enmity and mischief of the whole serpent race. And behold when the King's purpose had grown deep, he raised his head, and said to his court of priests and counsellors, "The time is come! now do I desire to avenge the death of Pariksheet, my father, by causing Takshaka and all his people to be consumed together in a blazing fire, even as Takshaka himself burnt up my father in the fire of his poison. Tell me then, ye wise men, and tell me, ye my ministers, how may I proceed to carry out this vow?"

And lo, when these words were heard in the

King's court, a shudder ran through all the world of the Snake-folk. For this was the moment foretold in the curse that had lain from of old upon their race. Janamejaya was that king for whom the ages had waited. Now was the hour of their peril at hand, nay, even at the very door. And the Snake-princess began to watch for the right moment, when she must call upon her son Astika to arise and save her race. And because for the purpose of this vow had Janamejaya the King been born, therefore all power and all knowledge was found among his advisers. They questioned the scholars and consulted all the ancient books. And all was finally decided, as to the manner in which a royal sacrifice must be performed, for the purpose of burning up all the snakes including even the great Takshaka himself. All the preparations began accordingly. A piece of land was chosen and an immense altar built, and all the vessels and ornaments were brought together. A great army of priests was gathered, the fire was ready, and the rice and butter that would be thrown into the sacrificial fire were stored up. But when all things were ready, it began to be whispered that the altar-builders had noted certain omens which indicated that a stranger would come and bring about the defeat of the sacrifice. So when the King heard this he gave orders, before sitting down on his throne, that the gates were to be closed, and no stranger on any account to be admitted.

And now at last the sacrificial fire was lighted, and the priests, chanting together the proper texts and verses, began to pour the libations of clarified butter upon the flames. Oh how strange and terrible was the sight next seen! So great was the power of the minds that were concentrated upon the sacrifice, that from everywhere near and far away the snakes began to come, flying through the air, crawling along the ground, and dropping from the sky, to throw themselves of their own accord upon the fire. On and on they came, hundreds and thousands and even millions in number, writhing, struggling, and hissing in their terror ; striving to resist the terrible power that was drawing them onwards ; but all yielding to it and giving themselves to the fire in the end. And still the fires grew hotter and the flames brighter, and the chanting of the priests rose higher and higher ; for their power must go out into the uttermost parts of the universe, and lay hold on the great Takshaka himself, to draw him into the consuming flames. Keenest and most intense of all their minds was that of the King. His face was dark and sombre, and his eyes never wavered as he sat there on his throne, following with all his strength the mighty spells that the priests were chanting, in order to bring

Takshaka himself into their power, and drag
him into the midst of the fire ; for the royal
passion of blood-revenge had awakened in him,
and he thirsted for the life of his father's mur-
derer. So the priests chanted, and the King
watched, and far away the gate of the sacrificial
grounds was held by a trusted officer, whose only
fault was that he could never refuse to a Brahmin
anything he asked.

Hour after hour the sacrifice went on. But now
a strange murmur began to be heard. Takshaka,
it was said, had fled from his own kingdom and
found sanctuary in the throne of Indra, God of
the Sky, and King of all the Gods.

"I care not!" cried Janamejaya, springing to
his feet, with shining eyes. "For Takshaka there
shall be no quarter. Let the throne of Indra itself
fall into the fire and be burnt to ashes!" The
earth was thrilled to her very core, as, far up
in the skies, appeared after these terrible words,
a faint black spot, and all nature knew that the
throne of the God of Heaven was being drawn into
the sacrifice. Coiled tightly about it, and hidden
by the robes of Indra, was Takshaka, and as long
as he sheltered him, not even the King of Gods
could resist the dread sentence thus pronounced
by Janamejaya. Down and down, more and more
swiftly through space, came the divine seat, and
all eyes turned upwards, and all hearts seemed to

stand still, as they watched it drawing nearer to the royal flames. Then there was a convulsive struggle, and the throne of the Sky-father was seen to be rising again into the heavens, while suddenly the great form of Takshaka himself became visible, falling slowly but surely to his doom.

At that very moment a strange yet noble-looking Brahmin came forward to the throne of Janamejaya, saying, "O King, grant me a boon!" The King held up his hand to silence him a moment. His eyes were fixed on the mighty serpent, whirling downwards through the air. Till he was sure of victory he would grant no boons, though the gods themselves should be the suppliants. But when Takshaka had drawn so close that his end was inevitable, he turned to the stranger, according to the royal custom, and said, "Speak! for whatsoever thou askest do I grant unto thee!"

"Then," said the Brahmin, "let this sacrifice be stayed!"

The King started forward in dismay. But it was already too late. Already had the snakes ceased to fall into the fire. Already was the body of the great serpent disappearing in the distance. And the priests, finding their texts become suddenly unavailing, had ceased to chant, or to pour the sacred butter into the fire. For even as the builders had prophesied, a stranger—no other than Astika, the Snake-Brahmin—had entered the sacrificial grounds during the ceremonies, and now, by the word of the King himself, had brought to nought the intention of the sacrifice. And this entrance of the Brahmin had been the one matter in which the King's officer at the gate had had no power to obey his sovereign's orders. For, as was known to every one, the habit of his whole life had been, never to refuse to a Brahmin anything he asked.

But when Janamejaya had heard everything ; when Astika had told him of the curse of Kadru that lay upon the Snake-folk, and the promise of a redeemer who should save all but the fiercest and most dangerous of his mother's people ; when he told him, too, of his own birth for this very purpose ; of the great fear and sadness that had fallen upon the Serpent-world at the commencement of the royal sacrifice, and of his mother's calling upon him, Astika, to save her kindred, then did anger and disappointment vanish from the heart of the King. He saw men as they really are, merely the sport and playthings of destiny. He understood that even the death of his father, Pariksheet, by the poison of Takshaka, had happened, only in order to bring about the will of the gods. And he turned round to bestow on Astika rich presents and royal favours. But already was the mission of Astika ended among mortals, and he had withdrawn, unnoticed, from the court of the King, to spend the remainder of his days in the forests, among the kinsmen of his mother, in his childhood's home.

THE STORY OF SIVA, THE GREAT GOD

The Story of Siva, the Great God

In wild and lonely places, at any time, one may chance on the Great God, for such are His most favoured haunts. Once seen, there is no mistaking Him. Yet He has no look of being rich or powerful. His skin is covered with white wood-ashes. His clothing is but the religious wanderer's yellow cloth. The coils of matted hair are piled high on the top of His head. In one hand He carries the begging-bowl, and in the other His tall staff, crowned with the trident. And sometimes He goes from door to door at midday, asking alms.

High amongst the Himalayas tower the great snow-mountains, and here, on the still, cold heights, is Siva throned. Silent——nay, rapt in silence——does He sit there, absorbed and lost in one eternal meditation. When the new moon shines over the mountain-tops, standing above the brow of the Great God, it appears to worshipping souls as if the light shone through, instead of all about Him. For He is full of radiance, and can cast no shadow.

Wrapped thus into hushed intensity lies Kailash,

above Lake Manasorovara, the mountain home of
Mahadeva, and there, with mind hidden deep under
fold upon fold of thought, rests He.   With each
breath of His, outward and in, worlds, it is said,
are created and destroyed.   Yet He, the Great
God, has nothing of His own; for in all these that
He has created there is nothing—not kingship, nor
fatherhood, nor wealth, nor power—that could
for one moment tempt Him to claim it.   One
desire, and one alone, has He, to destroy the
ignorance of souls, and let light come.   Once, it
is said, His meditation grew so deep, that when
He awoke He was standing alone, poised on the
heart's centre of all things, and the Universe had
vanished.   Then, knowing that all darkness was
dispelled, that nowhere more, in all the worlds,
was there blindness or sin, He danced forward
with uplifted hands, into the nothingness of that
uttermost withdrawnness, singing, in His joy,
" Bom ! Bom !"   And this dance of the Great
God is the Indian Dance of Death, and for its
sake is He worshipped with the words " Bom !
Bom ! Hara ! Hara !"

It is, however, by the face of the Great God
that we may know Him once for all, beyond the
possibility of doubt.   One look is enough, out of
that radiance of knowledge, one glance from the
pity and tenderness in His benign eyes, and never
more are we able to forget that this whom we

saw was Siva Himself. It is impossible to think of the Great God as being angry. He "whose form is like unto a silver mountain" sees only two things, insight and want of insight, amongst men. Whatever be our sin and error, He longs only to reveal to us its cause, that we may not be left to wander in the dark. His is the infinite compassion, without one shadow or stain upon it.

In matters of the world, He is but simple, asking almost nothing in worship, and strangely easy to mislead. His offerings are only bel-leaves and water, and far less than a handful of rice. And He will accept these in any form. The tears of the sorrowful, for instance, have often seemed to Him like the pure water of His offering. Once He was guarding a royal camp at night, when the enemy fell upon Him, and tried to kill Him. But these wicked men were armed with sticks of bel-wood, and as they beat Him again and again with these, He, smiling and taking the blows for worship, put out His hand, and blessed them on their heads!

He keeps for Himself only those who would otherwise wander unclaimed and masterless. He has but one servant, the devoted Nandi. He rides, not on horse or elephant, but on a shabby old bull. Because the serpents were rejected by all others, did He allow them to twine about His neck. And amongst human beings, all the crooked and hunch-

backed, and lame and squint-eyed, He regards as
His very own.   For loneliness and deformity and
poverty are passwords sufficient to the heart of
the Great God, and He, who asks nothing from
any one, Who bestows all, and takes nothing in
return, He, the Lord of the Animals, Who refuses
none that come to Him sincerely, He will give
His very Self, with all its sweetness and illumination, merely on the plea of our longing or our
need !

Yet is this not the only form in which Siva may
come to the soul of man.   Sometimes the thing that
stands between us and knowledge is unspeakably
dear.   Yet is the Great God ever the Destroyer of
Ignorance, and for this, when our hour comes,
He will arise, as it were, sword in hand, and slay
before our eyes our best beloved.   In the middle
of His brow shines forth the great Third Eye of
spiritual vision, with which He pierces to the heart
of all hypocrisy and shams.   And with the light
that flashes from this eye, He can burn to ashes at
a glance that which is untrue.   For foolish as He
may be in matters of the world, in spiritual things
He can never be deceived.   In this aspect, therefore, He is known as Rudra the Terrible, and to
Him day after day men pray, saying, " O Thou the
Sweetest of the Sweet, the Most Terrible of the
Terrible ! "

So runs the tale.   And yet in truth this thought

of the Great God is but half of that conception which is known to the intuition of man as the divine. Two things there are which we see as God. One is knowledge, insight—*Jnanum*, as it is called in India—and this, carried to its utmost height, is Siva or Mahadeva. But some see God rather in power, energy, beauty, the universe about us. Indeed, without both of these, either becomes unthinkable. Hence Siva has ever a consort in Maha Sakti, the Primal Force. Amongst the pictures made, and the tales told, of Her, are those of Sati, and Uma, and the Great Death. She is Gouri, the Golden One, the fair, the light of the sunrise shining on the mountain snows. And she dwells ever in Kailash, as the wife and devoted worshipper of that Mahadeva, or Spiritual Insight, who goes amongst men by the name of Siva, the Great God.

THE CYCLE OF INDIAN
WIFEHOOD

C

Sati, the Perfect Wife

LONG, long ago, in the beginning of time, there was a god called Duksha, who counted himself chief of divinities and men. And it happened once that a great feast was held, and all the gods at the banquet did homage to Duksha, and acknowledged him as Overlord. Save one, Siva. He, the Great God, was present also, and was clad indeed like any beggar, in ashes and pink loin-cloth, with staff and bowl. Yet He would not bow down and touch the feet of Duksha. His motive was pure kindness. We all know that there is nothing more unlucky for an inferior than to see one greater than himself prostrated before him. It is even said in India that if this occurs to you, your head will at once roll off. So out of sheer mercy to the Overlord, Siva could not do homage, and probably afterwards forgot all about the occurrence. But the poor god did not understand His reason, and thenceforth counted Him his enemy, hating Him with all his heart. Now Duksha had had many daughters, but they were by this time all married, except the youngest, who was so good that she was known as *Sati*. (For the word *Sati* means *being, existence*, and nothing really, you know, exists but goodness!)

In secret Sati's whole soul was given up to the worship of the Great God. She adored the image of Siva day after day, and offered before it water and white rice, praying that her whole life might be passed in loving Him, and Him alone.

In the midst of all this, Duksha declared that it was time for her to be married, and announced a *Swayamvara,* or feast of the Bride's Choice. Poor Sati! How could she marry any one else when her whole heart was given to the Great God? But the fatal day arrived. In a vast court, on splendid thrones, sat all the kings and gods who had been invited, in a great circle. Sati came in, with her wedding garland in her hand. All round she looked. She could tell which were gods, because they were lighted from within, so they neither winked nor cast shadows, and which kings, for they did. Both were there, and she might choose any one of them. He would be happy, and her father would be glad. They glittered with jewels and were gay with gorgeous-coloured robes. Again and again she searched the place with her eyes, but He whom she looked for was not there. It was a terrible moment.

Then in her despair, Sati stood still in the midst of the hall, and threw her flowers up into the air, saying, " If I be indeed Sati, then do thou, Siva, receive my garland ! " And lo ! there He was in the midst of them, wearing it round His neck !

Her father, Duksha, was choking with rage, but what could he do ? The choice of a princess was final. So the wedding ceremonies had to be completed. When that was done, however, he called her to him. " Undutiful child ! " he cried, " you have yourself chosen this beggar for your husband. Now go and live with Him, a beggar's wife, but never come back to me or look upon my face again ! "

So Siva took her away to Kailash, and she was happier there than, in all the dreams and prayers of her girlhood, she had ever imagined. One day, however, the sage Narada, clothed in his pink robes and looking big with important news, came to call. He went up to Siva, sitting on a tiger-skin, deep in meditation, and sat down near Him to have a chat. " H'm ! " he said, as soon as he thought he had Mahadeva's attention, " your father-in-law, Duksha, is arranging for a fine festival. There's to be a fire-sacrifice with full state-ceremonies, and all his family are invited."

" That's good ! " said Siva, rather absently.

" But he hasn't asked you ! " said Narada, eyeing him curiously.

" No," said Siva ; " isn't that fine ? "

" What ! " said Narada, beginning to look

puzzled ; " don't you mind the insult, the terrible
sacrilege, of offering royal worship without calling
for the presence of the Great God ? "

" Oh ! " said Siva wearily, " if only people would
leave me out of everything, perhaps I could get
rid of this burden of making and destroying
worlds, and lose myself in one eternal meditation ! "

Evidently it was impossible to get any fun out
of a gossip here. Mahadeva was too grateful to
His father-in-law for leaving Him in peace.

So Narada turned to tell the news to Sati. All
her woman's curiosity was roused at once. A
thousand questions had to be answered. She
wanted to know about the preparations, and the
guests, and exactly how the sacrifice and banquet
were to be arranged. Finally saying, " But I
must go too ! " she turned to find her Husband,
and Narada, feeling sure that events were afoot,
hastened away.

Alone, in Kailash, Sati stood before Siva. " I
want to go and see the feast ! " she said.

" But," said He, " you are not asked ! "

" No daughter could need an invitation to her
father's house ! " pleaded Sati.

" Yes," said Siva, " but you, My beloved, *must*
not go. I fear for you the dreadful insults of those
who hate Me."

Then, before the eeys of the Great God, the

very face and person of Sati began to change. He had said "must" to her, and now she would show Him who and what she was, who loved and worshipped Him. So she assumed some of her great and terrible forms. She appeared to Him ten-handed, standing on a lion — Durga, the Queen and centre of the Universe. She showed herself as the gentle foster-mother of the worlds. She became the black and awful Goddess of Death. Till Mahadeva Himself trembled in Her presence and worshipped Her, in turn, as His own equal. Then she was the tender and devoted Sati once more, pleading with Him as a mortal wife with her husband. "Even as you declare," she said, "we are about to go through terrible events. But these things must be, to show mankind what a perfect wife should be. Moreover, how could harsh words hurt Her, who bears all things and beings in Her heart?"

So He yielded, and she, attended by the one old servant, Nandi, riding on their old bull, and wearing the rags of a beggar's wife, set off for the palace of her father, Duksha.

Arriving there at last, and entering the Hall of Sacrifice, she—the young and beautiful Sati of a few short years before, still young and even more beautiful, but arrayed in such strange guise—was greeted by peals of laughter from the assembled guests. They were her sisters, resplendent in silks and jewels, each seated on the throne of her husband, on his left side.

There at the end of the hall, amongst priests and nobles, she saw Duksha about to begin the sacrifice. Sati went up and stood reverently before her father. When he saw her, however, Duksha became furious. " Ho, beggar's wife!" he said. "Why come you here? Did I not curse you, and drive you from my presence?"

" A father's curses are a good child's blessings," replied Sati meekly, stooping to the earth to touch his feet.

"Good children do not choose to marry beggars!" he replied. "Where is that Husband of yours? Thief, rascal, evil dishonest daughter-stealer that He is!"

He was going on to say more, but even he could not finish, for Sati, blushing crimson, had risen to her full height, and her beauty and sorrow made her wonderful to look upon. One hand was raised, as if to say, "Hush!"

" Words such as these, my father," she was saying, "the faithful wife must not even hear. These ears that have listened are yours. You gave them to me, for you gave me life, and all this body. Then take it back. It is once more your own. Not for one moment shall I retain it, at the cost of such dishonour."

And she fell dead at Duksha's feet. Every one

rose in horror, and the father himself stood as if
turned to stone, aghast at the consequences of
his own words.   But there was no hope.   The
beautiful and faithful soul of Sati had indeed fled.

Then Nandi, her old attendant, set out swiftly
for Kailash, to report to Siva what had happened.
But as he did so, shaking in every limb, he turned
round in the doorway and said, " If you, O Duksha,
survive these deeds at all, may it be only with
a goat's head on your human body ! "   In such
great moments men see truly, even into the
future.

Up in Kailash, Siva was hard to waken from
His meditation.   But when at last He heard and
understood what Nandi had to tell, His wrath and
grief were without measure.   Putting His hand up
to His head He pulled out a single hair, and cast
it on the ground before Him.   Up sprang a giant,
armed for war.   Him Siva made generalissimo of
His hosts.   Then He shook His matted locks, and
out of them leapt a whole army of dwarfs, giants,
and soldiers.   These ranged themselves in order
behind their leader, he behind Mahadeva, and all
turned to march down upon the abode of Duksha.

When they reached it, the forces set to work,
cutting off the head of the King and wrecking the
palace.   But Siva made His way straight to the
body of Sati, and taking it reverently on His
shoulders would have left the place.

At this moment, however, came a woman, weeping and worshipping His feet. At length the sound of her voice penetrated to the ears of the grief-intoxicated God.

"Speak! Who worships Me?" He said.

"It is I, the mother of Sati!"

"Mother, what would you have?" said He very gently.

"Only that of your mercy; you will give back the life of my husband, Duksha."

"Let him live!" said Mahadeva at once, and His servants obediently restored the life taken.

But Duksha had no head, and his own could not be found. "This will do very well," said the general of the army, pointing to the head of the goat that had been slain for sacrifice; and some one seized it and put it on the body of Duksha. So there he really was, even as Nandi had said, surviving, but with a goat's head on his human body.

But Siva, bearing the body of Sati, strode forth in the grief of a God. To and fro over the earth He went. His eyes shot forth volcanic fires, and His footsteps shook the worlds. Then Vishnu, to save mankind, came behind Siva, and hurled His discus time after time at the corpse of Sati, till, falling piece by piece, with fifty-two blows it was at last destroyed, and Siva, feeling the weight gone, withdrew to Kailash, and plunged once more into His solitary meditation.

But of how Sati was born again as Uma in the house of Himalaya the king, of how she strove once more for the love of the Great God ; and of how Siva, with His whole heart on Sati, refused to be won, and burnt Eros to ashes with a glance, are not these things told, by Kalidas the poet, in his great poem of "The Birth of the War-Lord"?

The Tale of Uma Himavutee

Now Sati was born again on earth as the Princess Uma. In the divine regions, long periods of
our time pass like a single day, and the years that
were spent in becoming a baby and growing up
into a woman seemed to Uma a very little thing.
She knew well who she was, and remembered that
she had come into the world only that she might
win Siva once more for her own, and be with Him
forever.

This time she had chosen as her father one
who loved Mahadeva, and would feel deeply
honoured by having Him for his son-in-law,
Himalaya, the Mountain-king. Uma was extraordinary from her earliest years for her goodness. It was not only that every duty was
faithfully performed, and those rites of purification
that Siva loves carried out to the last letter, but
such long hours were spent in worship and in
fasts of terrible rigour, that her mother often
implored her to stop, fearing that she would
lose health, or even life itself. But the Princess
persisted, for she knew that beautiful as she was,
her great difficulty in this life would be to make

Siva forget Sati long enough even to look at her.
She must therefore devote all her energy to the
training of soul and will. Notwithstanding this,
however, she grew daily more and more lovely.
And this was not surprising, as you would say, if
you could have seen those wonderful mountains
that were her home. There the dark cedars toss
their heads all night long against the sky, and
wild roses and red pomegranate blossoms fill the
summer with their beauty. There graceful trees
and delicious fruits abound, and wild flowers
bloom in profusion. There birds and beasts
give thanks continually that they exist, and on
the rugged mountain-tops the snows are as grand
as the forests below are beautiful.

With eyes and ears always filled thus, what
could a maiden do but drink in loveliness and
draw closer to its spirit day by day?

But greatest of all her charms was that pale
golden tint of skin that is so admired by Hindu
women. Indeed, she was so renowned for this,
that to this day only queens in India may wear
anklets and ornaments of gold upon the feet.
Subjects wear silver, because yellow is Uma's
own colour, and to touch it with the foot is
sacrilege.

Now when Uma was about eighteen, all the
gods became as anxious as herself for the grant-
ing of her desire. Their interest in the matter

came about in this way :—Sometime before,
Brahma, the Creator, had shown great favour
to one of the demons, and granted him an
unusual degree of power. In the strength of
this gift the recipient had greatly exalted himself,
and was threatening to usurp the thrones of all
the lesser divinities. They appealed to Brahma,
and told their story. The great four-headed
Father listened to their woe, and smiled indul-
gently. " I cannot myself avenge your wrongs,"
he said, " upon one who has received my friendship. Do you not know the proverb, ' Even a
poisonous tree should stand uninjured by him
who planted it ' ? But as I look into the future,
I see that when Siva marries the Princess Uma—
and he can wed no other—he will become the
father of a son who shall lead the armies of heaven
to victory. Do what you can, therefore, to hasten
the marriage. You are thereby bringing nearer
the Birth of the Divine War-Lord."

The thunder-like voice of the Creator died away
in space, and the gods consulted as to what
could be done. In the end, Indra, chief of the
lesser gods, went to visit Modon, the Indian God
of Love.

He and his wife Roti had, living in their
home, a faithful friend and soldier called Spring,
and all three listened to the request that Indra
had come to make. He wished Modon to shoot

one of his invisible arrows into the heart of Siva.

The tall and graceful young god turned pale when he understood at last what was wanted. It was believed in the divine world that the Great God was proof against mortal weakness, and the impertinence of attempting to inflict on Him the wound of human love was almost too much, even for these merry-hearted souls. They feared failure, and discovery, with the anger of Mahadeva.

Yet they had a strong affection for Indra, the God of the Sky. They owed him much. They were eager to serve him. At last said Modon, " If Spring will go before, and help me, as he has always hitherto done, I am willing to try," and this promise being extorted, Indra arose and left them ; but he told them first of the grove in which Siva would be found.

Now when Modon set forth to find Mahadeva, Spring went before. At his approach and the waving of his wand, all the trees in the forest broke into blossom without ever a green leaf. Then entered Modon, with his beautiful wife, Desire, and the world became warm with the friendship of the creatures. Birds warbled to each other, the wild deer drank out of the forest pools side by side ; the hum of insects rose on the breeze ; even the flowers seemed to pass under the gracious influence, and bend buds and bells a little nearer.

On came the Archer, Love, in the footsteps of his friend, till, near the heart of the wood, he found what he sought—a magnificent old cedar, and spread beneath its shade a black leopard-skin for meditation. The next moment an old man appeared, and held up his hand, saying, "Hush!" It was Nandi. Instantly, perfect silence fell upon everything. The forest stood as if painted on the air. No breeze stirred a single leaf. The birds remained on the boughs, with throats opened to sing, but no sound came forth. The insects hung on the wing motionless, and the bees, drawing near to sip honey from the flowers of Modon's bow, made a thick line like a black arch above it, or covered the quiver, made of blossoms, like a veil, as still as death.

Then Modon saw a white form shine forth and take shape beneath the cedar. It was Siva Himself, whom he awaited. Motionless, under the tree, sat the Great God, lost in His reverie. In the middle of His forehead was a faint black line, like a wrinkle, but slightly tremulous. And Modon's heart beat faster, for he realised that this was the great Third Eye of Mahadeva, capable of flashing forth fire at any time, and he knew not when it might open. Here was the opportunity that he wanted, but even now he dared not shoot, since there was none near by on whose behalf to awaken love. Gradually, however, the forest was returning to life from the long swoon imposed on it by Nandi, and as it did so, the very helper that Modon needed came in sight, for the most beautiful girl that he had ever seen entered the wood. Her manner and bearing were royal, and she wore the silken robe of prayer. It was Uma, the Princess of the Mountains, come to offer her morning worship to Siva.

The slender form of the young Archer was hidden amongst the trees as she passed on to the feet of the Great God. Absorbed in His presence, she knelt before Him, and He opened His eyes and smiled upon His worshipper.

At this moment the audacious Modon drew his bow and made ready to take aim. Scarcely a second was it, yet the thought entered the mind of Mahadeva that the lips of this maiden were very red, and then, ere the idea was fully formed, a mighty wave of horror swept over him, the great Third Eye had opened and sought the source of the vain impulse, and where the too venturesome God had been on the point of sending forth his dart, lay now, only a handful of ashes, in the form of a man.

A second later the luminous figure of Siva had faded out from beneath the cedar, and Uma knelt alone to make her offerings.

D

But the grove was filled with the voice of lamentation. Desire, the beautiful wife of Love, was not to be consoled, that one flash of anger had not destroyed her with Modon. And she called on Spring, as her husband's friend, to build the funeral-fire in which she might die and follow him. At this moment, however, the voice of Indra rang through the wood. "Sweet lady!" it pleaded, "do nothing rash! It is true that you are separated from your husband for a while. But in a few months the work he began here will be completed, and when Mahadeva weds Uma, He will of His free grace restore the life of Modon also. Only wait patiently." And Spring prevailed upon Roti to rely on the promise of Indra and wait.

[True enough, certain months afterwards, the spirit of her husband was given back to her. But his body had been destroyed. So, since then, walks Love invisible amongst men and gods.]

And Uma, left alone in the forest, realised that all her beauty had failed to prevail upon her Husband to forget her as Sati for one moment. Now, therefore, she must make a stronger appeal, and of a strangely different kind.

Then she left her princely home and went away to a hermitage, far from the dwellings of men, to live. A rough grass girdle and the covering of birch-bark became all her clothing. She slept on

the bare earth, in the little time when she was not
telling the name of Siva on her beads, and her
right arm grew marked and worn with the constant pressure of her rosary. Her hair was matted,
and for food she seemed to take no thought.

How long this course of life had lasted, she
herself knew not, when one day a Brahmin beggar
passed that way, and stopped at her door to beg
for food.

Uma, always pitiful as a mother to the needs
of others, though she appeared to have none of
her own, hastened to give him alms. But when
he had received her dole, the beggar seemed
desirous of lingering awhile to chat.

"Lady, for whose sake can you be practising
such a course of penance?" he asked. "You are
young and fair. Methinks this is the life of one
old or disappointed that you lead. Whose love
draws you to live thus?"

"My heart," she replied, "is all for Siva."

"Siva!" said the beggar, "but surely He is a
queer fellow! Why, He seems to be poorer than
poverty, and a dreamer of dreams. I trust indeed,
Lady, that your heart is not given to that Madman!"

"Ah," said Uma, sighing gently, "you speak thus
because you do not understand! The actions of
the great are often unaccountable to the common
mind. The ways of Mahadeva may well be beyond
your ken!"

"But," he persisted, "believe that I speak wisdom! Spend your life no longer in a vain effort to reach One who is not worthy of your love. Give up the thought of Siva. Even if He be what you say, He does not deserve——"

"Stop!" said Uma, "I have let you speak too long. I cannot listen to one word more," and she turned to go.

She was just lifting her foot, had not yet quite turned her eyes away, when a strange change began to steal over the Brahmin's features, and the Princess Uma, watching it, stood rooted to the spot. She held her breath. Surely there must be some mistake. Indeed, she could not believe her eyes. But at last she had to believe. For fasts and vigils had done what beauty alone could never have accomplished. The Brahmin who stood before her was none other than— Mahadeva Himself.

Savitri, the Indian Alcestis

THERE are few of the Greek stories that we love so much as that of Alcestis. Every one remembers how Admetus, her husband, was under a curse, and unless one could be found to die for him, he must, on a certain day, give up his life and betake himself to the dark realms of Pluto. And no one can forget that there was one to whom death seemed a little thing to suffer, if only thereby Admetus might be saved. This was his wife, Alcestis. So she, the brave woman-heart, left the light of the sun behind her, and journeyed alone to the under-world and the kingdoms of the dead.

Then was there sorrow and mourning in the halls of Admetus, until evening, when, as we all know, there came thither a guest whose strength was beyond that of mortals, and whose heart was open to the sadness of all. And he, the mighty Herakles, taking pity on the sorrow of Admetus, went down into Hades, and brought forth the soul of the faithful wife. Thus was the curse removed, and Death himself vanquished by men. And Alcestis dwelt once more with her husband Admetus, and after many years, as ripe corn into the garner, so passed they away, and were both together gathered to their fathers.

In this story we learn a great deal of the thought of the Greeks about women. We learn that they knew that woman, though usually so much weaker than man, and needing his protection, could yet, in the strength of her love for another, become brave as a lion, and face dangers gladly from which a man might shrink in terror.

In India also, amongst her gentle white-veiled women, with all their silent grace, there is the same courage, the same strength. There also it is known that a timid girl—a very daughter of men, not like Sati or Uma, some divine personage veiled in flesh—though utterly unaccustomed to the touch of the rough world, will become suddenly brave to protect another. The Indian people know that there is no darkness that a true wife will not enter at her husband's side, no hardship she will not undertake, no battle that on his behalf she will not fight. And yet their story of the ideal woman is curiously different from this of Alcestis. Different, and at the same time similar. Only listen, and you shall judge for yourselves.

Beautiful and gifted was the royal maiden, Savitri. And yet, at the mention of her name, the world thought only of her holiness. She had come to her parents as the Spirit of Prayer itself. For the marriage of her father Aswapati and his queen had for many years been blessed with no children, which thing was a great sorrow to them. And they were now growing old. But still, daily, the King lighted with his own hands the sacrificial fire, and chanted the national prayer *Savitri*, and begged of the gods that even yet he might have a child. It was in the midst of his worship one day, as he sang *Savitri*, and brooded deep on the divine will, that suddenly in the midst of the fire, he saw the form of a woman, that very goddess who was guardian spirit of the Indian prayer, and she blessed him and told him that his wife and he would yet have a daughter, whose destiny was high and whose name was to be that of the prayer itself. Thus, out of the devotion of two royal lives, was born the Princess Savitri.

Oh how good she was, and at the same time how strong! Full of gentleness and pity, there was yet nothing wavering or foolish about her. True to every promise, faithful to all who were in need, fearless and decided when difficult questions came up, she was a comfort to her parents and to all their people.

At last her father began to feel that it was time to think of her marriage. She was now seventeen or eighteen, and as yet no proposal had been made for her hand. Nor had her parents any idea to what prince to send the cocoanut on her behalf, as hint that a princess waited for his wooing. At this point, however, Savitri herself made a suggestion. Before making any attempt to arrange the marriage, let her go on a long pilgrimage; pray at one holy shrine after another; take the blessings and listen to the words of many holy men; enter deep into communion with her own Guardian Spirit; and on her return, if no direction had been vouchsafed her, it would still be time enough to deal with the question of her marriage. For these things are guarded by destiny, and it is not well to meddle hastily with high matters. Every one thought this idea admirable. To some of her father's councillors it may have seemed that in this way Savitri would receive an education fit for a great queen. She would see the country and do homage to its holy and learned men. Others may have thought of the advantages in health and beauty. But to her parents it seemed that even as she had come to them, so also she would enter her husband's home, out of the very heart of prayer.

So great preparations were made. Grey-headed old courtiers were told off to watch over the Princess, and numbers of servants were sent to attend on her. She was to drive in a carriage, gilded all over, and surrounded by curtains of scarlet silk, through which she could see everything without being seen. And a long train of men and elephants were to follow, bearing tents and furniture and food, as well as a palanquin for Savitri to use, instead of the car, when she should be travelling in the forest. They started early one night when the moon was new, that they might cross the hot dry plain in the dark hours, and reach the forests before day. The Princess had never gone so far before. She had wandered about the royal gardens all her life, and she had driven about the city and parks in a closed carriage. But this was quite different. She was setting off on an adventure, alone, free. She felt that she was being led somewhere. Every step was the fulfilment of a delightful duty. It was her first long separation from her father and mother. Yet she was happy, and the tossing trees and howling jackals and midnight sky filled her with joy, even at moments when the torch-bearers, at the head of the train, were startled at the roar of a tiger in the jungle. On such a journey the starlit night becomes like a great mother-heart, and one enters it, to listen to a silence deeper than any voice.

The march had lasted till long after daybreak, when they reached the edge of a forest beside a stream, where Savitri could bathe and worship, and cook her own simple meal. They stayed there the rest of that day, and resumed their pilgrimage early next morning.

This life continued for many months. Sometimes they would encamp for a whole week within reach of a certain hermitage. And Savitri would enter her palanquin every morning and have herself carried before the hut of the holy man, to offer gifts and request his blessing. Then she would sit on the ground before him, closely veiled, ready to listen if he chose to speak, but if not, content only to watch, since blessed are the eyes that look upon a saint.

And all the time she was drawing nearer and nearer to the great day of her life, that was to make her name dear to womanhood throughout the ages.

Journeying one day in the forest she saw, through the curtains of her litter, a tall, strong young man. There was something about him that made her hold her breath. Across one shoulder he carried an axe, and in his other hand he held a bundle of faggots. He was evidently a forester. Yet his bearing spoke of courage and gentleness, and the courtesy with which he helped some one of her train, and then stood aside for them to pass, told of high breeding and great gentlehood of heart. Inquiries were made as to the name and parentage of this young man. And then the Princess and her train turned homewards. For Savitri knew that to-day her destiny was come upon her. Here stood that soul to whom through endless births she had been united.

He might be a forester or he might be a king. In any case she, with her mind's eye cleansed by pilgrimage and prayer, had recognised him to whom in all her past lives she had been wife, and she knew that what had been should again be. Here was he whom she should wed.

Aswapati was in his hall of state, when at last his daughter entered his presence. Savitri would have liked to see her father alone, but beside him sat the holy man Narada, clad in his pink cloth, and the King bade her speak freely before him. " Has my child determined where she will bestow herself ? " he asked gently, when the first warm greetings were over.

Savitri flushed crimson as she replied.

" Tell me all about this youth," said Aswapati the King eagerly.

" In a certain woodland, my father," said the Princess timidly, "we met a young man who is living the life of a forester. His father is a blind king who has been driven from his throne in his old age, and is living in the forests in great poverty. This youth have I determined to marry. He is gentle, and strong, and courteous, and his name is Satyavan."

As soon as Savitri had begun to describe her choice, Narada had looked startled and interested. But now he held up one hand suddenly, saying, " Oh no ! not he ! "

Aswapati looked at him anxiously. "Why not?" he said. "My daughter has wealth enough for two."

"Oh, it is not that!" said Narada; "but if Savitri weds this youth she will certainly become a widow, for Satyavan is under a curse, and twelve months from this day he is doomed to die!"

The Princess had grown very pale. For every Hindu woman prays to die before her husband. But when Aswapati turned and said to her, "This is sad news, my daughter! you must choose again," she said, "No, my father. One gives one's faith but once. I cannot name a second as my husband. It is sad to be a widow, but having taken Satyavan, I must face whatever comes to me with this husband of my choice."

Both the King and Narada felt that these words were true, and messengers were sent next day, bearing a cocoanut from Aswapati to the young prince dwelling in the forest. This meant that the King desired the youth to marry his daughter, and Satyavan and his parents gladly accepted, with the one stipulation that Savitri should come and live in their home, instead of taking her husband away from them in their old age.

So the wedding was proclaimed. The fire was called to witness their union. The iron ring was bound on Savitri's left wrist, and Satyavan and she had the veil and cloak knotted together, and hand in hand walked seven times around the sacred fire, while the priest at each circle chanted the ancient prayers of their people that that stage of life might be blessed to them both.   Then they went away into the forest to live, and Savitri put away all the robes and jewels of a princess, and set herself to be a faithful and loving daughter to her new parents.   Only she could never forget the terrible doom that had been pronounced upon her husband, and she never ceased to bear in mind the secret date on which Narada had said that he would die.   For Yama, the God of Death, is the only being in all the worlds, perhaps, who never breaks his word, and "as true as Death" has become such a saying in India, that Yama is held to be also the God of Truth and Faith.

This was the thought that made poor Savitri's heart beat fast.   She knew that there was no hope of the curse being forgotten.   She could see quite plainly, too, that no one but herself knew anything about it.   It remained to be seen whether she could find a way to save her husband or not.

The dreadful moment drew nearer and nearer. At last, when only three days remained, the young wife took the terrible vow that is known as the *three vigils*.   For three nights she would remain awake, in prayer, and during the intervening days she would eat no food.   In this way Savitri hoped

to reach a state of the soul where she could see
and hear things that commonly pass unknown to
mortals.

The blind King and his aged Queen implored
their new daughter to relax this effort, but when
she made the simple answer, " I have taken a
vow," they could say no more. In that case her
resolution was sacred, and they could only help
her to carry it out. At last the fourth morning
dawned, but still Savitri would not touch food.
" No," she said, "it will be time enough at nightfall. Now I ask, as the only favour I have yet
begged, that you should allow me also to go out
into the jungle with your son, and spend the day."
She was careful not to mention Satyavan's name
to his parents, for that would have been forward
and ill-bred. The old couple smiled gently. "The
girl is a good girl," they said to one another, " and
has yet asked for nothing. We certainly ought
to allow her to go. Satyavan, take thou good
care of our daughter." At these words Savitri
touched their feet, and went out with her husband.

She had calculated that the blow would fall at
midday, and as the hour drew near she suggested
that they should stop in a shady spot and wander
no further. Satyavan gathered grass and made
a seat for her. Then he filled her lap with wild
fruit ; and turned to his work of hewing wood.

Poor Savitri sat and waited, listening breathless

for the strokes of his axe upon the trees.   Presently they rang fainter and feebler, and at last
Satyavan came tottering up to her, with the words,
"Oh, how my head pains!"   Then he lay down
with his head on her lap, and passed into a heavy
swoon.

At this moment the wife became aware of a
grim and terrible figure advancing towards them
from the jungle.   It was a stately personage, black
as night, and carrying in one hand a piece of rope,
with a noose at the end.   She knew him at once
for Yama, God of Truth and King of the Dead.

He smiled kindly at Savitri.   "My errand is not
for you, child!" he said to her, stooping at the
same time and fixing his loop of rope around the
soul of Satyavan, that he might thus drag him
bound behind him.

Savitri trembled all over as he did this, but when
the soul of her husband stood up to follow, then she
trembled no longer.   She also stood up, with her
eyes shining and her hands clasped, prepared to go
with Satyavan even into the realms of Death.

"Farewell, child," said Yama, turning to go,
and looking over his shoulder ; "grieve not over-
much!   Death is the only certain guest."

And away he went, down the forest-glades.
But as he went, he could distinctly hear behind
him the patter of feet.   He grew uneasy.   It was
his duty to take the soul of Satyavan, but not that

of Savitri. What was she doing now? Could she be following him? Why, in any case, had she been able to see him? What power had sharpened her hearing and cleared her sight? To most mortals, Death was invisible. Patter! patter! Yes, that certainly was a footfall behind him. Foolish girl! Was she striving to follow her husband? She must go home sooner or later. Still he would try to soothe her grief by gifts. "Savitri," said Yama, suddenly turning round on her, "ask anything you like, except the life of your husband, and it shall be yours. Then go home."

Savitri bent low. "Grant his sight once more to my father-in-law!" she said.

"Easily granted!" said the Monarch of Death. "Now, good-bye! This is not the place for you."

But still the footsteps followed Yama. The forest grew denser and more gloomy, yet wherever he could go, Savitri seemed to be able to follow.

"Another wish, child, shall be yours!" said Yama. "But you *must* go!"

Savitri stood undismayed. She was beginning to feel herself on good terms with Death, and believed that he might give way to her yet. "I ask for the return of my father-in-law's wealth and kingdom," she answered now.

"It is yours," said Yama, turning his back. "But go!"

Still the faithful wife followed her husband, and Yama himself could not shake her off. Boon after boon was granted her, and each time she added something to the joy of the home in which she had not yet passed a year. At last Death himself began to notice this.

"This time, Savitri," he commanded, "ask something for yourself. Anything but your husband's life shall be yours. But it is my last gift! When that is given, you are banished from my presence."

"Grant me, then, that I may have many sons, and see their children happy before I die!" said Savitri.

Yama was delighted. So Savitri was willing to flee from him, he thought! "Of course! Of course! A very good wish!" he said.

But Savitri was standing still before him, as if waiting. "Well," he said, "have I not granted it? That is all."

At these words Savitri raised her head and smiled. "My Lord," she said, "a widow does not remarry!"

The dread King looked at her for a moment. As God of Death, how could he give up the dead? But as God of Truth, could he urge Savitri to be untrue? A moment he hesitated. Then he stooped and undid the noose, while the whole forest rang with his laughter.

E

"Peerless amongst women," he said, "is that brave heart that follows the husband even into the grave, and recovers his life from Yama himself. Thus do the gods love to win defeat at the hands of mortals."

An hour later, under the same tree where he had swooned, Prince Satyavan awoke, with his head on Savitri's knee. "I have had a strange dream," he murmured feebly, "and I thought that I was dead."

"My beloved," answered Savitri, "it was no dream. But the night falls. Let us hasten homewards."

As they turned to go, the jungle rang with the cries of a royal escort, who had come out to seek them. For that very day, Satyavan's father had received word of the restoration of his kingdom, and the life of hardship and poverty was behind them all forever.

Nala and Damayanti

ONCE upon a time there was a king named Nala, who ruled over a people known as the Nishadas. Now this Nala was the first of kings. In person he was strong and handsome, full of kingly honour, and gracious in his bearing. He loved archery and hunting, and all the sports of monarchs. And one special gift was his, in an extraordinary degree, the knowledge, namely, of the management of horses. Thus in beauty, in character, in fortune, and in power, there was scarcely in the whole world another king like Nala.

If there were one, it could only be Bhima, King of the Vidarbhas, a sovereign of heroic nature and great courage, deeply loved by all his subjects. Now Bhima had three sons and one daughter, the Princess Damayanti. And the fame of Damayanti, for her mingling of beauty and sweetness, and royal grace and dignity, had gone throughout the world. Never had one so lovely been seen before. She was said to shine, even in the midst of the beauty of her handmaidens, like the bright lightning amidst the dark clouds. And the hearts of the very gods were filled with gladness whenever they looked upon this exquisite maiden.

It happened that constantly before Damayanti, the minstrels and heralds chanted the praises of Nala, and before Nala those of Damayanti, till the two began to dream of each other, with an attachment that was not born of sight. And Nala, conscious of the love that was awakening within him, began to pass much of his time in the gardens of his palace, alone. And it came to pass that one day he saw there a flock of wild swans with golden wings, and from amongst them he caught with his hands one. And the bird was much afraid, and said, "O King, slay me not! Release me, and I will go to Damayanti and so speak to her of thee, that she will desire to wed thee, and no other in the world!" Musing, and stroking the wings of the swan, Nala heard his words, and saying, " Ah, then do thou indeed even so!" opened his hands, and let him go free.

Then the swans flew up and away to the city of the Vidarbhas, and alighted in the palace gardens before Damayanti and her maidens. And all the beautiful girls scattered immediately, to run after the fleeing birds, trying each to catch one. But that after which Damayanti ran, led her away to a lonely place, and addressed her in human speech. " Peerless amongst men, O Dama-

yanti!" it said, " is Nala, King of the Nishadas.
Accept thou him! Wed thou with him!
Ever happy and blessed is the union of the
best with the best!" The Princess stood with
head bowed and folded hands, as soon as she
understood what the swan would say ; but when
he ended, she looked up with a smile and a sigh.
"Dear bird!" she said, "speak thou even thus
unto him also!"

And the handmaidens of Damayanti, from this
time on, began to notice that she grew ab-
stracted. She wandered much alone. She sighed
and became pale, and in the midst of merriment,
her thoughts would be far away. Then, deli-
cately and indirectly, they represented the matter
to Bhima, and he, reflecting that his daughter
was now grown up, realised that her marriage
ought to be arranged, and sent out messages
all over the country, that on a certain day her
swayamvara would be held.

From every part, at this news, came the kings,
attended by their bodyguards, and travelling in
the utmost splendour, with horses and elephants
and chariots. And all were received in due state
by Bhima, and assigned royal quarters, pending
the day of Damayanti's *swayamvara*. And even
amongst the gods did the news go forth, and
Indra, and Agni and Varuna, and Yama himself,
the King of Death, set out from high Heaven

for the city of the Vidarbhas, each eager to win the hand of the Princess.

But as the proud gods went, they overtook a mortal wending his way on foot, and his beauty and greatness, of mind as well as body, were such that they immediately determined to leave their chariots in the skies, and tread the earth in the company of this man. Then, suddenly alighting before him—for the gods know all—they said, " Nala ! thou art a man to be trusted. Wilt thou promise to carry a message for us ?"

Nala, seeing four luminous beings appear before him, and hearing them ask him to be their messenger, answered immediately, "Yea ! That will I !" and then, drawing nearer, he added, " But tell me first who are ye who address me ? and what is the message, further, that I should carry for you ?" Said Indra, "We are the Immortals, come hither for the sake of Damayanti. Indra am I. Here at my side is Agni, God of Fire. There is Varuna, Lord of Waters. And next to him stands Yama, destroyer of the bodies of men. Do thou, on our behalf, appear before Damayanti, saying, 'The Guardians of the World are coming to thy *swayamvara*. Choose thou, I pray thee, one of the gods for thy lord !'"

" But," said Nala, "I myself am come hither with the self-same object. How can a man plead with the woman whom he loves on behalf of others? Spare me, ye Gods! Send me not upon this errand!"

"Then why, O King!" answered the gods gravely, "didst thou first promise? Why, having promised, dost thou now seek to break thy word?"

Hearing this, Nala spoke again, saying, "But even if I went, how could I hope to enter the apartments of Damayanti? Is not the palace of Bhima well guarded?"

But Indra replied, "Leave that to us! If thou wilt go, thou shalt have the power to enter!" and saying "Then, O Gods, I obey your will!" Nala found himself, on the moment, in the presence of Damayanti, within the private apartments of the palace of Bhima.

Damayanti sat amongst her ladies. The next day was to be her *swayamvara*, and feeling sure that Nala would attend it, the smiles had come back to her lips, and the colour to her cheeks. Her eyes were full of light, and the words she spoke were both witty and tender. Seeing his beloved thus for the first time, Nala felt how deep and overflowing was his love for her. Truly, her beauty was so great, that the very moon was put to shame by it. He had not thought, he had not heard, he could not even have imagined, anything so perfect. But his word was given, and given to the gods, and he controlled his own feeling.

This determination did not take even so much as that instant which it required for him to become visible to the assembled maidens. As he did so, they sprang to their feet in amazement, feeling no fear, but struck with wonder at the beauty of the spirit who appeared thus before them, and full of the question, "Who can it be?" Yet were they too shy to venture to speak to him. Only Damayanti came forward gently, and smilingly addressed the heroic vision, saying, "Who art thou? And how hast thou contrived to enter unperceived? Are not my apartments well guarded, and the King's orders severe?"

Hearing these words, the King answered, "My name, O Princess, is Nala. I have entered here undiscovered, by the power of the gods. I come as their messenger. Indra, Agni, Varuna, and Yama, all alike desire, O beauteous one! at the morrow's *swayamvara* to be chosen by thee. As their messenger, I say, 'Choose thou one of them for thy lord!'"

Damayanti bowed as she heard the names of the gods. Then, with a smile, she turned herself to Nala. "Nay, O Hero!" she answered, "it is not the gods, but thee thyself whom I shall choose. Thy message reached me, borne hither by the swans. Thee have I accepted in my heart. For thee has the *swayamvara* been

called. Failing thee, I refuse to be won by
any!"

"Nay," answered Nala, "in the presence of
the gods, wouldst thou choose a man? Ah, for
thine own sake, turn thy heart, I pray thee, to
those high-souled lords, the creators of the worlds,
unto the dust of whose feet I am not equal!
Misguided is the mortal who setteth them at
nought. Be warned, I beg of thee. Choose
thou one of these heavenly beings. What woman
would not be proud, to be sought by the Protectors of Men? Truly, do I speak unto thee,
as thy friend!"

Tears were by this time running down the
cheeks of Damayanti. Trembling, and standing
before Nala with folded hands, she answered,
"I bow to the gods, but thee, O King, have I
chosen for my lord!"

"Blessed one!" answered Nala gently. "Do even
as thou wilt. How dare I, having given my word
to another, turn the occasion to my own profit?
Yet, if that had consisted with honour, I would have
sought my will! Knowing this, do thou decide."

The face of Damayanti had changed as Nala
spoke these words. Under the tears were now
smiles. For his secret was told. A moment she
stood and thought, and then she raised her head.
"I see a way, O monarch," she said, "by which
no blame whatever can attach itself to thee.

Come thou to the *swayamvara* with the gods. Then, in their presence, shall I choose thee. And the choice will be mine alone. Thou shalt be without sin."

Nala realised nothing, save the promise that Damayanti on the morrow would give herself to him. With throbbing pulses, but quiet manner, he bowed his head in farewell, and, immediately becoming once more invisible, returned to the presence of the gods and told them all that had happened. "The maiden said to me, 'Let the gods, O Hero, come with thee to my *swayamvara*. I shall, in their presence, choose thee. Yet shalt thou be without sin.'" And the gods accepted the report of their messenger, for he had been faithful to his trust.

.   .   .   .   .   .

The morning of the *swayamvara* dawned brightly, and the kings entered the lofty portals of the amphitheatre, even as lions might enter into the mountain wilds. The scene was all magnificence. Amongst the great pillars sat each royal guest on a shining throne. Each bore his sceptre and turban of state. Each was surrounded by his own heralds and minstrels, and amongst the blaze of silks and banners and jewels shone the flowers and foliage that decorated the hall.

At the appointed hour, preceded by her trumpeters, and surrounded by her escort, the Princess

Damayanti entered. And her loveliness was such that, to the assembled monarchs, she seemed to be surrounded with dazzling light. All drew in their breath, and remained almost without stirring, at the sight of such matchless beauty. One by one the names and achievements of each monarch were proclaimed. The heralds of the Princess would challenge, and those of each king in turn would reply, and Damayanti stood listening, ready to give the signal, when her choice should be made.

But when the name of Nala was called, and she raised her head and looked up, before stepping to his side, what was not the terror of Damayanti to find that there, seated side by side on different thrones, all equally splendid, all equally noble, were no less than five Nalas, and she had no means of distinguishing him whom she would choose?

The Princess looked and tried to choose. Then she hesitated, and stepped back. Then she tried again, but all to no purpose. She knew of course that this was a trick of the gods. Four of these five were Indra, Agni, Varuna, and Yama. One was Nala. But which one? She tried to remember the marks of the celestial beings, as they had been told to her in her childhood by old people. But none of these marks did she see on the persons before her, so exactly had they all reproduced the form of Nala. What must she do? At this supreme moment of her life she dared not make a mistake.

Pondering deeply in her own mind, it suddenly occurred to Damayanti that she should appeal for protection to the gods themselves! Immediately, bowing down unto them in mind and speech, and folding her hands reverently, she tremblingly addressed them :—

"From that moment, O ye Gods, when I gave ear to the words of the wild swan, did I choose Nala, the King of the Nishadas, to be my lord. That I may be true to this, let the gods now reveal him to me! Inasmuch as neither in thought nor word have I ever yet wavered in that resolve, oh, that I may hereafter be true to it, let the gods now reveal him to me! And since, verily, it was the gods themselves who destined the King of the Nishadas to be my lord, let them now, that themselves may be true to themselves, reveal him to me! To Nala alone did I vow to give myself. That I may be true to this vow, let them now reveal him to me! I take refuge in the mercy of the exalted Guardians of the Worlds! Let them now resume their proper forms, that I may know my rightful lord!"

Touched by these pitiful words of Damayanti, and awed by her fixed resolve and her pure and womanly love, the gods immediately did what they could, in that public place, to grant her prayer, by taking back, without change of form, their divine marks. And straightway she saw that they were not soiled by dust or sweat. Their garlands were unfading, their eyes unwinking. They cast no shadows. Nor did their feet touch the earth. And Nala stood revealed by his shadow and his fading garlands; the stains of dust and sweat; his standing on the ground, and his human eyes. And no sooner did Damayanti thus perceive the difference between him and the gods, than she stepped forward eagerly to fulfil her troth. Stooping shyly, she caught in her left hand the hem of Nala's garment, and then raising herself proudly, she threw round his neck a wreath of beautiful flowers. And all present, seeing her thus choose the one human Nala for her husband, broke out into sudden exclamations, and the gods themselves cried, "Well done! Well done!"

And Nala stepped down from his high place, and said, "Since thou, O blessed one, hast chosen me, a mortal, from the midst of the Immortals, know me for a spouse to whom shall thy every wish be sacred. Truly do I promise thee, that as long as life lasts I shall remain thine and thine alone!" And so with mutual vows and homage, they both sought and received the protection of the gods. Then did all guests, royal and divine, depart; and the marriage of Nala and Damayanti was performed; and they went, in great happiness, to the city of the Nishadas.

Now as the gods were returning to their own regions, they met Koli, the King of Darkness, and Dwapara, Spirit of Twilight, coming to the earth. And when they asked where they were going, Koli replied, "To Damayanti's *swayamvara*. My heart is fixed on wedding with that damsel." Hearing this, Indra smiled, and answered, "But her *swayamvara* is already ended. In our sight she hath chosen Nala for her husband." To this said Koli, that vilest of the celestials, in great wrath, "If, spurning the Immortals, Damayanti in their presence hath wedded with a mortal, then is it meet she should suffer a heavy doom!" But the gods answered, "Nay, with our sanction was it that Damayanti chose Nala. And what damsel is there who would not have done the same? Great and manly and learned, that tiger amongst men, that mortal who resembles one of the Divine Protectors, has truthfulness and forbearance and knowledge, and purity and self-control, and perfect tranquillity of soul. Whoever, O Koli, wisheth to curse this Nala, will end in cursing and destroying himself by his own act!"

Having spoken thus solemnly, the gods turned, leaving Koli and Dwapara, and went to heaven. But when they had gone, Koli whispered to Dwapara, "I must be revenged! I must be revenged! I shall possess Nala, and deprive him of wife and kingdom. And thou, entering into the dice, shalt help me to do this!"

Yet was it twelve long years ere Koli, watching Nala, could find in his conduct any slightest flaw by which he might be able to enter in and possess him. At last, however, there came an evening when he performed his worship without having completed all his ablutions. Then, through this error, Koli took possession of Nala. Also he appeared before his brother, Pushkara, tempting him to challenge Nala to a game of dice. And Dwapara also, at the same time, placed himself in the hands of Pushkara as the principal die. Such was the beginning of that terrible gambling that lasted month after month, and ended by depriving Nala of all that he had.

Many times, in the course of that play, came Damayanti and the citizens and subjects of Nala, and begged him to desist. But he, maddened by the indwelling Koli, turned a deaf ear to his queen, and grew only the more intent upon the dice. Till she, seeing that evil was about to come upon them, sent for the royal charioteer. "O charioteer," she said, "I seek thy protection. My mind misgiveth me. The King may come to grief. Take thou therefore these my children, my son Indrasen and my daughter Indrasena, and carry them to my father's house. And when thou hast given them into the care of my kindred, do thou even as thou wilt." And when the royal councillors had been consulted, they found the bidding of the Queen to be good, and the children were sent to the care of Bhima.

And when the charioteer had gone, Pushkara won from Nala his kingdom and all else that was left to him. And laughing he said, "O King, what stake hast thou now? Damayanti alone remaineth. Let us play for her!" And Nala gazed at Pushkara in anguish, but spake never a word.

Then, taking off all his ornaments, and covered only with a single garment, leaving behind him all his wealth, the King set out to leave the city. But Damayanti, clothing herself also in one long scarf, followed after him through the gates. And for three days and nights they wandered together, without food and without rest. For Pushkara had made proclamation that any who gave help to Nala should be condemned to death ; so that, partly for fear of the sentence, and partly lest they should bring further harm on their king himself, none of his subjects dared to offer them anything.

At last, on the fourth day, wandering in the

forest seeking for roots and fruits, Nala saw some
birds of golden colour, and thinking, "Here is
food!" snatched off his one piece of clothing, and
threw it over them to catch them. But lo! the
birds rose upwards to the sky, bearing the garment with them! And then, looking down and
beholding the once mighty lord of the Nishadas
standing naked in the forest, his mind full of gloom,
and his gaze rooted to the earth, the birds spake
mockingly, and said to him, "Oh thou of little
wit, we are none other than the dice with which
thou playedst. We followed thee to take away
thy garment. For it pleased us not that thou
shouldst take with thee even a single cloth!"
Hearing these words, and realising his terrible
plight, since he had, it was evident, mysterious
beings for his foes, Nala turned himself to Damayanti, and said over and over again, "Yonder,
my gentle one, is the road to thy father's kingdom. I have lost all, Damayanti. I am doomed
and deprived of my senses. But I am thy lord.
Listen to me. Yonder is the road to thy father's
kingdom."

But Damayanti answered him with sobs. "O
King, how could I go?" she asked him, "leaving
thee in the wild woods alone, deprived of all
things, and worn with hunger and toil. Nay,
nay, whenever, in these ill-starred days, thy heart
may turn to the thought of thy former happiness,

thou shalt find me near thee, to soothe thy weariness! Remember what the physicians say, 'In sorrow is there no physic equal to the wife'! Is it not true, O Nala, that which I say unto thee?"

"O my gentle Damayanti," answered Nala, "it is even as thou sayest. Truly there is no friend, no medicine, equal unto the wife. But I am not seeking to renounce thee. Why dost thou tremble so? I could forsake myself, beloved, but thee I could not forsake. Wherefore, my timid one, shouldst thou dread this?"

But on Damayanti lay the prevision of the wife, and she answered, "I know, O King, that thou wouldst not willingly desert me. Yet maddened and distracted, many things are possible. Why dost thou repeatedly point out to me the way to my father's home? Or if thou really desirest to place me with my kindred, then let us wend together to the country of the Vidarbhas. Thou shalt there be received with honour by the King, and, respected by all, shalt dwell happily in our home." "Surely," answered Nala, "thy father's kingdom is to me even as my own. Yet could I not by any means go there at such a crisis. Once did I appear there in fortune, bringing glory upon thee. How could I go in this misery, causing thee shame?"

Talking together in this fashion, Damayanti had contrived to share her own clothing with her husband, and thus wandering slowly on together, they came to a shed reserved for travellers. Here they sat down on the bare earth to rest, and then, worn out with hunger and weariness and sorrow, both, unawares, fell fast asleep.

But Nala, whose mind was distraught by Koli, could not rest. As soon as Damayanti slept, he woke, and began to turn over in his mind all the disaster he had brought upon her. Reflecting on her devotion, he began to think that if only he were not with her, she would surely find her way to her father's kingdom. And out of the very honour in which he held her, it was unimaginable to him that she should be in danger on the way. Thinking thus, the question occurred to him, how could he cut their common garment without her being awakened by his act? and with this question in his mind, under the influence of Koli, he strode up and down the shed. At that very moment, he caught sight of a sword lying a step or two away, unsheathed. Seizing this, he cut the veil in half, and then, throwing the sword away, he turned and left Damayanti, in her sleep, alone.

Yet again and again, his heart failing him, did the King of the Nishadas return to the hut to look once more, and yet once more, at his sleeping wife. "Dragged away," says the chronicler, "by Koli, but drawn back by love," it seemed as if the mind of the wretched King were rent in twain, and one half fought against the other. "Alas! alas!" he lamented, "there sleepeth my beloved on the bare earth, like one forlorn! What will she do when she awaketh? How will she wander alone through the perils of these woods? May the Sun himself —thou blessed One!—and the Guardian Spirits, and the Stars and the Winds, be thy protectors, thy womanly honour being its own best guard!"[1] And addressing thus his dear wife, peerless in beauty, Nala strove to go, being reft of his reason by Koli. Till at last, stupefied and bereft of his senses, Nala forsook his sleeping wife. In sorrow departed he, maddened and distraught, leaving her alone in that solitary forest.

    .   .   .   .   .

Three years had gone by, and once more Damayanti was dwelling,—but now with her children by her side,—in her father's house. For Bhima had sent out messengers in all directions to seek for her, and by them had she been found and brought back to her own people. But always she wore but half a veil, never would she use ornaments, and ever she waited sorrowfully for the coming again of her husband, Nala. For in all this time he had never been heard of.

Now it had happened to Nala that on finally leaving Damayanti he saw a mighty forest-fire,

---

[1] *Lit.*—Adityas, Vasus, Ashwins, and Maruts.

and from its midst he heard the voice of some creature crying, "Come to my aid, O mighty Nala!"

Saying, "Fear not!" the King stepped at once within the circle of fire, and beheld an enormous snake lying there coiled up.

And the snake spoke, saying, "I have been cursed, O King, to remain here, unable to move, till one named Nala carry me hence. And only on that spot to which he shall carry me can I be made free from this curse. And now, O Nala, if thou wilt lift me in thy hands, I shall be thy friend, and do to thee great good. Moreover, there is no snake equal unto me. I can make myself small and light in thy hands. I beseech thee to lift me and let us go hence!"

Then that great snake made himself as small as the human thumb, and taking him in his hands, Nala carried him to a place outside the fire. But as he was about to place him on the ground, the snake bit him, and Nala perceived that as he was bitten, his form had been changed.

And the snake spoke, saying, "Nala, be comforted! I have deprived thee of thy beauty, that none may recognise thee. And he who has wronged and betrayed thee shall dwell in thee from this time in uttermost torture. Henceforth art thou in peace, and that evil one in torment from my venom. But go thou now to Ayodhya, and present thyself before the king there, who is skilled in gambling. Offer him thy services as a charioteer. Give to him thy skill with horses, in exchange for his knowledge of dice. When thou dost understand the dice, thy wife and children will be thine once more. And finally, O King, when thou desirest to regain thy proper form, think of me and wear these garments." And saying these words that lord of Nagas gave unto Nala two pieces of enchanted clothing, and immediately became invisible.

And Nala made his way to Ayodhya, and entered the service of Rituparna the King, receiving great honour as the Master of the Horse. And all the stables and their attendants were placed under him; for Rituparna desired nothing so much as that his steeds should be fleet.

But night after night the fellow officers of the charioteer—who was known in the palace of Ayodhya as Vahuka—would hear him alone, groaning and weeping, and listening they distinctly heard the words: "Alas! where layeth she now her head, a-hungered and a-thirst, helpless and worn with toil, thinking ever of him who was unworthy? Where dwelleth she now? On whose bidding doth she wait?" And once, when they begged him to tell them who it was that he thus lamented, he told them in veiled words his whole story. "A certain person," he said, "had a beautiful wife, but little sense. The wretch was false. He kept not his promises. Fate came upon him, and they were separated. Without her, he wandered ever to and fro oppressed with woe, and now, burning with grief, he resteth not by day nor night. At last he has found a refuge, but each hour that passes only reminds him of her. When calamity had overtaken this man, his wife followed him into the wild woods. He repaid her by deserting her there! Abandoned by him, lost in the forest, fainting with hunger and thirst, ever exposed to the perils of the wilderness, her very life was put by him in danger. Yea, my friends, it was by him —by him that she was thus deserted, by him, that very man, so foolish and ill-fated, that she was left thus alone in the great and terrible forest, surrounded on every side by beasts of prey, by him, by him!"

With his mind dwelling thus on Damayanti, did Vahuka the charioteer live in the palace of Rituparna. And Damayanti, sheltered once more in her father's house, had one thought, and one only, and that was the possibility of recovering Nala. Now it was the custom amongst the Vidarbhas to send out Brahmins periodically, who, bearing the King's orders, wandered from town to town and from country to country, telling stories to the people from the holy books, and giving religious instruction wherever it was needed. It had indeed been by the aid of these strolling

teachers that Damayanti herself had been discovered, when she was acting as lady-in-waiting
to a foreign princess.   Now, therefore, it was decided that she should give them their directions,
and try by their means to trace out her long-lost
husband.   They came to her therefore for instructions, and she gave them a song which they
were to sing in all the assemblies that they should
come to in every realm.

> " Whither, beloved Gambler, whither art thou gone,
>   Cutting off one half my veil,
>   Abandoning me, thy devoted wife,
>   Asleep in the forest ?
>
> Ever do I await thee,
> As thou wouldst desire me,
> Wearing but half a veil,
>   Enwrapt in sorrow.
>
> Relent, O King ! O Hero !
> Relent and return thee,
> To her who weepeth incessantly
>   For thy departure ! "

"Crying thus, add to the part your own words,"
she said to the Brahmins, "that his pity be
awakened.   Fanned by the wind, the fire con-
sumeth the forest ! "

Again—

> " Surely a wife should be protected
> And maintained by her husband.
> Strange that, noble as thou art,
> Thou neglectest both these duties !

Wise thou wast, and famous,
High-born and full of kindness.
Why didst thou then deal to me this blow?

Alas, the fault was mine!
My good fortune had departed from me!
Yet even so, thou greatest, thou noblest
Amongst men, even so, have pity,
      Be merciful to me!"

"If, after ye have sung in this wise," said Damayanti to the Brahmins, "any should chance to speak with you, oh, bring me word of him! I must know who he is, and where he dwelleth. But take ye great heed that none may guess the words ye speak to be at my bidding, nor that ye will afterwards return to me. And do not fail, I beseech ye, to seek out all that is to be known regarding that man who shall answer to your song!"

Having received these orders, the Brahmins set out in all directions to do the bidding of Damayanti. And their quest led them far and near, through cities and villages, into strange kingdoms, amongst forests, hermitages, and monasteries, and from one camp of roving cowherds to another. And wherever they went they sang the songs and played the part that Damayanti had laid upon them, seeking in every place, if by any means they might bring back to her news of Nala.

And when a long time had passed away, one of these Brahmins returned to Damayanti, and said

to her, "O Damayanti, seeking Nala, the King
of the Nishadas, I came to the city of Ayodhya,
and appeared before Rituparna. But though I
repeatedly sang thy songs, neither that King nor
any of his courtiers answered anything. Then,
when I had been dismissed by the monarch, I was
accosted by one of his servants, Vahuka the
charioteer. And Vahuka is of uncomely looks
and figure, and possessed of very short arms.
But he is skilful in the management of horses,
and is also acquainted with the art of cookery.

"And this Vahuka, with many sighs and some
tears, came up to me and asked about my welfare.
And then he said, 'She should not be angry with
one whose garment was carried off by birds, when
he was trying to procure food for both! The
honour of a woman is its own best guard. Let her
not be an-angered, against one who is consumed
with grief. Noble women are ever faithful, ever
true to their own lords, and whether treated well
or ill, they will forgive one who has lost all
he loved!' Hearing this, O Princess, I hastened
back to tell thee. Do now what seemeth best
unto thyself."

Words cannot describe the joy of Damayanti as
she heard this news. She knew now where Nala
was, and the task with which he was entrusted.
It lay only with her woman's wit to find some
means of bringing him to her father's house.

Having pondered long and carefully over the matter, she went to her mother, and in her presence sent for the same confidential servant —a kind of chaplain to the royal household— who had found herself and brought her back from exile to the city of the Vidarbhas. Having her mother's full sanction, but keeping the matter secret from Bhima, Damayanti turned to this Brahmin, Sudeva, and said, "Go straight as a bird, Sudeva, to the city of Ayodhya and tell Rituparna the King that Bhima's daughter, Damayanti, will once more hold a *swayamvara*. Kings and princes from all parts are coming to it. Knowing not whether the heroic Nala lives or not, it is decided that she is again to choose a husband. To-morrow at sunrise, say thou, when thou seest him, the ceremony will take place." And Sudeva, bowing before the Queen-mother and her daughter, left the royal presence, and proceeded to Ayodhya.

When Rituparna heard the news, he sent immediately for Vahuka, the charioteer. If he desired in one day to reach the city of the Vidarbhas, there was only one driver in the world who could enable him to do so. "Exert thyself, O Vahuka!" he exclaimed. "Damayanti, daughter of Bhima, holds to-morrow a second *swayamvara*, and I desire to reach the city this very day!"

Hearing these words Nala felt as if his heart would break. "What!" he thought to himself,

" is this the madness of sorrow? Or is it perhaps a punishment for me? Ah, cruel is this deed that she would do! It may be that, urged by my own folly, the stainless Princess cares for me no longer. Yet I cannot believe that she, my wife, and the mother of my children, could possibly dream of wedding any other. In any case, however, there is but one thing to be done. By going there I shall do the will of Rituparna, and also satisfy myself." Having thus reflected, Vahuka answered the King, saying, "O monarch, I bow to thy behest. Thou shalt reach the city of the Vidarbhas in a single day."

Wonderful and eventful was the driving of Vahuka the charioteer that day. Never had Rituparna, or the servant who attended him, seen such skill. The servant indeed remembered, as he watched it, the fame of Nala. But he turned his eyes upon the driver, and seeing his want of beauty, decided that this could hardly be he, even though he should be disguised and living as a servant, in consequence of misfortune. Every now and then the chariot would rise into the sky, and course along with the fleetness of the wind. Like a bird would it cross rivers and mountains, woods and lakes. In a few seconds it would speed over as many miles. And Rituparna knew not how to express his delight in the skill of his charioteer. Words could not speak his anxiety to reach the city of the Vidarbhas before nightfall; and more and more, as the hours went on, did he become convinced that only with the help of Vahuka was this possible. But about noon the two became involved in a dispute about the number of leaves and fruits on a certain tree. Rituparna, who was a great mathematician, said there were so many, and his officer insisted on stopping the car, cutting down the tree, and counting, to see if the King's words were true! Rituparna was in despair. He could not go on without Vahuka, and Vahuka was intent on verifying the numbers. However, the charioteer was sufficiently amazed and respectful to the King's knowledge when he had counted the fruits and found them to be correct. Then, in order to coax him onwards, Rituparna said, " Come on, Vahuka, and in exchange for thy knowledge of horses, I will give thee my knowledge of dice. For I understand every secret of the gaming-table. This was the very moment for which Nala had waited and served so long! However, he preserved his composure, and immediately the King imparted to him his knowledge. And lo! as he did so, Koli, the spirit of darkness, came forth, invisible to others, from within Nala, and he felt himself suddenly to be released from all weakness and blindness, and to have again all his old-time energy and power. And radiant with renewal of strength, the charioteer mounted once more on the chariot, and taking the reins in his hands, drove swiftly to the city of the Vidarbhas.

As Rituparna, towards evening, entered the city, the sound of the driving of his chariot fell on the ears of Damayanti in the palace, and she remembered, with a thrill, the touch of Nala on a horse's reins. But, mounting to one of the terraces, she looked out, and could see only one who drove like Nala, but none who had his face and form. "Ah!" she sighed, "if he does not come to me to-day, to-morrow I enter the funeral fire! I can bear no longer this life of sorrow!"

The King of Ayodhya meanwhile, hastening to call on Bhima, began to think there must have been some mistake. He saw no other kings and princes with their chariots. He heard no word of any *swayamvara*. He therefore said that he had come merely to pay his respects. This, thought the King of the Vidarbhas, was a little strange. A man would not usually come so far and in such hot haste, in a single day, merely for a passing visit of courtesy. However, feeling sure that the reason would reveal itself later, he proceeded to offer Rituparna the attentions due to his rank and importance.

Nala, however, had no eyes for anything about him. Buried in thought, he gave orders for the disposal of the horses, and having seen them duly

carried out, sat down with arms folded and head
bent.   At the sound of a woman's voice he looked
up.   A maid sent from within the palace was asking him, in the name of Damayanti, why and
for what purpose had he and Rituparna come.
"We came," answered the charioteer bitterly,
"because the King heard that the Princess of
the Vidarbhas would for a second time hold a
swayamvara!"   "And who art thou?" again
asked the maiden.   "Who art thou?   And who
yon servant yonder?   Might either of ye by
chance have heard aught of Nala?   It may even be
that thou knowest whither King Nala is gone!"

"Nay, nay!" answered Vahuka.   "That King
in his calamity wanders about the world, disguised,
and despoiled even of his beauty.   Nala's self only
knoweth Nala, and she also that is his second self.
Nala never discovereth his secret to any!"

"And yet," replied the maid, "we sent a
Brahmin to Ayodhya, and when he sang—

> 'Ah, beloved Gambler, whither art thou gone,
>   Taking with thee half my veil,
>   And leaving me, who loved thee,
>   Sleeping in the woods?
>   Speak thou, great King, the words I long to hear,
>   For I who am without stain pant to hear them!'

When he sang thus, thou didst make some reply.
Repeat thy words now, I beseech thee.   My
mistress longeth again to hear those words!"

At this Nala answered in a voice half choked—
"She ought not to be angry with one whose
garment was carried off by birds, when he was
trying to procure food for both! The honour
of a woman is its own best guard. Let her not
be angered against one who is consumed with
grief. Noble women are ever faithful, ever true
to their own lords, and, whether treated well or
ill, they will forgive one who is deprived of every
joy!" As he ended, the King could no longer
restrain himself, but burying his head in his arms,
gave way to his sorrow; and the girl, seeing this,
stole away silently to tell all to the Princess.

News was brought also to Damayanti of the
greatness and power of Rituparna's charioteer.
It was told her how on coming to a low doorway
he would not stoop down, but the passage itself
would grow higher in his presence, that he might
easily enter it. Vessels at his will filled themselves
with water. He needed not to strike to obtain
fire, for on holding a handful of grass in the sun,
it would of its own accord burst into flame in his
hand. Hearing these and other things, Damayanti became sure that the charioteer Vahuka was
no other than Nala, her husband. Yet, that she
might put him to one more test, she sent her
maid, with her two children, to wander near
him. On seeing them, Nala took them into his
arms and embraced them, with tears. Then,

realising how strange this must seem, he turned to the waiting-woman and said apologetically— "They are so like my own! But do not thou, maiden, come this way again. We are strangers here from a far land. We are unknown, and I would fain be alone."

And now, having heard this, Damayanti could wait no longer, but sent for the permission of her father and mother, and had Nala brought to her own apartments. Coming thus into her presence, and seeing her clad just as he had left her, wearing only half her veil, the seeming charioteer was shaken with grief. And Damayanti, feeling sure that he was Nala, and seeing him as a servant, whose wont it was to be a king, could scarcely restrain her tears. But she composed herself, and said quietly, "Well, Vahuka, did you ever hear of a good man who went away and left a devoted wife, sleeping alone, in the forest? Ah, what was the fault that Nala found in me, that he should so have left me, helpless and alone? Did I not choose him once in preference to the very gods themselves? And did he not, in their presence, and in that of the fire, take me by the hand, and say, 'Verily, I shall be ever thine'? Where was that promise, do you think, when he left me thus?"

And Nala answered, "In truth, it was not my fault. It was the act of Koli, who hath now

G

left me, and for that only, have I come hither! But, Damayanti, was there ever a true woman who, like thee, could choose a second husband? At this moment have the messengers of thy father gone out over the whole world, crying, ' Bhima's daughter will choose again a husband who shall be worthy of her.' For this it is that Rituparna is come hither!"

Then Damayanti, trembling and affrighted, folded her hands before Nala, and said, "O dear and blessed lord, suspect me not of evil! This was but my scheme to bring thee hither. Excepting thee, there was none in the whole world who could drive here quickly enough. Let the gods before whom I chose thee, let the sun and the moon and the air, tell thee truly that every thought of mine has been for thee!" And at the words, flowers fell from the sky, and a voice said, "Verily Damayanti is full of faith and honour! Damayanti is without stain!"

Then was the heart of Nala at peace within him. And he remembered his change of form, and drawing forth the enchanted garments, he put them on, keeping his mind fixed on the great Naga. And when Damayanti saw Nala again in his own form, she made salutation to him as her husband, and began to weep. Then were their children brought to them, and the Queen-mother gave her blessing, and hour after hour passed in recounting the sorrows of their separation.

The next day were Nala and Damayanti received together in royal audience by Bhima. And in due time, Koli being now gone out from him, Nala made his way to his own kingdom of the Nishadas and recovered his throne, and then, returning for his queen, Damayanti, and their children, he took them all back to their own home, and they lived there happily together ever after.

THE CYCLE OF THE RAMAYANA

As Mary the Madonna to the women of Christendom, so is Sita, Queen of Ayodhya, to them of Hinduism. Hers is indeed a realm beyond the aspiration of merely earthly sovereigns. For she is the ideal of womanhood itself, and she wields undisputed sway, in millions of hearts, over the kingdoms of love and sorrow, and stainless womanly honour and pride. Though beautiful and a queen, she never chose ease. To her the simple lives of saints and scholars were more joyous than all the luxuries of courts. She knew every mood of the forests, joining in their praise in the early morning, when birds wake and blossoms open and the dew is fresh ; and bowing her soul with theirs in the evening adoration. She shared a throne, yet never forgot that for their people's good, and not for their own pleasure, do sovereigns reign. She knew the highest human happiness, and was not blinded by happiness. She knew the deepest and bitterest sorrow, and lived serene amidst her sorrow. Such was Sita, Queen of Ayodhya, crowned of love, veiled in sorrow, and peerless amongst women.

The City of Ayodhya

To the north of Benares, between the Himalayas and the Ganges, stretches the country now known as Oudh, whose name long ago was Kosala. In the whole world, perhaps, can be few other lands so beautiful as was this, for it abounded in corn and in cattle and in forests, and all its people were prosperous and in peace. Kosala had great rivers, and fair places of pilgrimage, and noble cities, many and great. And she was surrounded on every hand by strong kings and powerful kingdoms. Yet was she the jewel amongst those kingdoms, and the centre of the circle. And, like a queen amongst cities, walled and moated, adorned with towers and stately buildings, and with numberless banners and flags and standards, stood Ayodhya, the capital of Kosala. And she was wonderful to behold. Thronged by the kings of neighbouring kingdoms was she, coming to her to pay their tribute; frequented by the merchants and craftsmen of many lands; full of palaces and parks, and gardens and orchards. And Ayodhya was famous, both for her wealth and for her learning. She abounded in rice and in jewels, and the waters of her wells and streams were sweet as the juice of sugar-cane. And her streets were thronged with heroes, and her cloisters with scholars and with saints. Her roads, moreover, were broad, and kept constantly watered, and strewn with flowers. Verily, like unto the sovereign city of Indra's heaven, was the city of Ayodhya, in the land of Kosala.

Beautiful and beloved as she was, however, of her citizens and children, Ayodhya had yet one thing which they prized above all others. This was the memory of how once upon a time she had been ruled by a divine king. For the story went that long ages ago there had sat on her throne one Rama, who was the Lord Himself. It was said that Vishnu, being desirous of showing unto men what an ideal king should be, bodied Himself in this form, and Lakshmi, the divine spouse, dwelling from all eternity in the heart of God, took shape as Sita, the consort of Rama, and for one short generation of mortals, perfect manhood and womanhood were seen on earth, in these two royal lives.

The ways of fate are mysterious, and the lives of men and gods how strangely different! Surely for this it was that these sovereign careers were so full of sorrow. Yet never for one moment did Sita or Rama fail to remember that the well-being of their people is the highest good of monarchs

And the peasants of Oudh remember to this day "the kingdom of Rama," and pray, with longing in their hearts, for its return.

Rama the Prince was the eldest son of the King Dasaratha and his wife Kausalya. He was highly trained and proficient in all the sports and accomplishments of knighthood ; and along with his half-brother Lakshmana he had won his spurs, by making an expedition,—under the guidance of one of the greatest scholars of the age,—in which he had been able to survey the whole of his dominions, and had also rooted out and extermin- ated in their own strongholds certain notorious demons and outlaws, who had long troubled the peace of cities and *ashramas* in Kosala. It was at the end of this victorious journey that Rama and Lakshmana had been received with great honour by Janneka, King of Mithila, and given his daughters, Sita and Urmila, in marriage. The princes had been joined at Mithila on this occasion by their father Dasaratha, who was present at their twofold wedding, and took them back with him in his train to Ayodhya.

What a dream of happiness had been the years that followed ! Bending their will in all things to that of their father, the princes had discharged with brilliance the duties of their high station. Rama especially, having truth and justice for his prowess, became the joy of the whole people. Making their pleasure and welfare his sole object, he administered the affairs of the city heedfully. And bending his wise mind to his young wife, Sita, and dedicating to her his whole heart also, Rama passed long hours of delight in her sweet company. She charmed him, say the old records, as much by her loveliness as by her dignity and nobleness, and still more by her goodness than by her loveliness. And she in her turn, by her perfect sympathy and graciousness, was able to enter into every thought and feeling of Rama, so that the bond of her wifehood was one of joy as well as duty. And those who saw Sita and Rama together, felt them to be in truth one soul, and inseparable, even as Vishnu, the Divine Lord, cannot be separated in the thoughts of men from Sree, the divine grace.

Now seeing his son Rama so full of virtues and accomplishments, there arose a desire in the heart of the old King Dasaratha to have him made king before he himself should die. And being much troubled by certain inauspicious omens observed by the royal astrologers—omens which were apt to portend trouble, and even to bring about the deaths of kings—he felt that the coronation would be well made without delay. Therefore he called to his presence a royal council, and when the nobles and ministers were all assembled, he told them his whole mind, and asked advice. "It may be," said he gently, ending his statement and appeal, "that my longing desire, and also my weariness, obscure my judgment. Well do I know that from the voices of many in conference is truth brought forth." As the King ceased speaking, there arose the sound of a restrained resonance, as of many talking softly together. The nobles and the Brahmins, the ministers and great citizens, discussed quietly amongst themselves the new proposal. At last, having come to a common decision, they appointed their own spokesman, and announced to Dasaratha their sympathy and agreement with all his wishes. And when the whole assembly, at the end of this address, raised their clasped hands to their heads like so many lotuses, in token of their acquiescence, the King felt an inexpressible relief and joy. He sent messengers for Rama, summoning him to appear before the council, and these, receiving homage from him, acquainted him with his intention of installing him on the morrow as his immediate successor. Then, having again received the homage of his son, Dasaratha dismissed the assembly, and began to make preparations for the forthcoming ceremony.

Scarcely had the counsellors and officers of the household dispersed, when the King, retiring to his own apartments, sent once more for his son, and talked with him long and quietly regarding his own wishes, the ceremony of the morrow, and the possibilities of his future policy. Reminding him, at last, of the necessity that both Sita and himself should pass the night in prayers and austerity, Dasaratha dismissed him, and Rama sought the presence and blessings of his mother, Kausalya, before returning finally to his own palace. There he was followed almost immediately by the priest of the royal family, with minute instructions for the evening observances, and the hours that remained were spent accordingly.

Now the news of the installation had gone out through all Ayodhya. The streets and thoroughfares were thronged with excited people. Every house was decorated with raised flagstaffs and flying pennons. The terraces and verandahs of the city were filled with groups of watchers. Garlands and incense and great branching lampstands had been brought out for the adorning of the roadways. Even frolicsome lads, playing about the city, knew only one theme, and stopped their games to talk eagerly together of the anointing of the prince that would take place on the morrow.

Yet amidst all this joy, the heart of Dasaratha the King was filled with a strange unrest. He could not forget that his dreams of the night before had been ill-starred. And he had a feverish desire to hurry on the installation, for his mind turned, with a curious foreboding, to his second son Bharata, now absent from the city, as the source of some possible ill to Rama. Bharata had never failed in the course of duty, nor did the King in any way suspect his motives. Yet something, he knew not what, whispered to him that it would be well to crown Rama in the absence of Bharata.

There lived in the palace of Dasaratha, in the apartments of the youngest queen, Kekai, a certain humpbacked woman, of malicious temper, who acted as an attendant. This woman, returning from a journey, and making her way into that palace whose splendour was like that of the moon, found all Ayodhya at work, having the streets watered, strewn with lotus-petals, and ornamented with pennons. She saw too the crowds of freshly-bathed worshippers, heard the chanting of music of rejoicing, saw the thresholds of the temples sprinkled with white powder, and perceived the fragrance of sandal-wood in all the water. There could be no doubt, in fact, that the city was keeping some unexpected festival, and she was not slow to acquaint herself with the reason.

Through this woman, then, came to Kekai the news of the approaching coronation of Rama.

On first hearing it, the young Queen was filled with delight, and tossed a costly and beautiful jewel to her handmaid, in token of her pleasure. But the woman knew how to poison the mind of her mistress, and an hour or two later, when Dasaratha came to call on Kekai, in order to acquaint his youngest wife in person with his plans regarding Rama, the servants told him, to his consternation, that if he would find her, he must follow her to the anger-chamber.

There, in truth, lay the King's wife—even, if the truth were known, his favourite wife—on the bare floor, like a fallen angel, having cast away her garlands and ornaments. Clad in garments that were not fresh, her countenance clouded with the gloom of wrath, she looked like a sky enveloped in darkness, with the stars hidden.

Like unto the moon rising in a sky covered with fleecy white clouds, so did Dasaratha enter into the mansion of Kekai. Like a great elephant in the midst of a forest, did he seek her out, in the anger-chamber, and, gently carressing her brow and hair, ask what he could do to comfort her. Again and again did he promise that nothing she could ask would be in vain.

At this Kekai rose, and called upon sun and moon, night and day, the sky, the planets, and the earth, to witness to the King's words. And having done so, she reminded him of how she had once nursed him back to life, in his camp, in time of war, and how he had then promised her two boons, which it would lie with her to name. To-day, at last, she would claim these boons. She desired that her husband should banish Rama to the forests, sentencing him to live for fourteen years the life of a hermit. And she desired further that her own son Bharata should be installed and crowned in his stead as heir-apparent.

At first the King indignantly refused Kekai's absurd requests. Then, comparing her habitual sweetness and nobility with her present extraordinary conduct, he wondered if she had suddenly become insane. Finally, he pleaded and remonstrated, striving to make her withdraw her request. The affection he had hitherto felt for this youngest and most charming of his three queens began now to seem to him like a disloyalty to Rama's mother. He wondered if he had caused her pain and loneliness. He saw his whole life as an error, and he prayed for mercy.

But Kekai, in her present strange and cruel mood, was inflexible. She spoke only to remind the King of the heinousness of a broken promise. Again and again she insisted that the word had been given, and it must be kept. And in the morning it was she who sent messengers to summon Rama to an early audience of his father, to be given in her presence. It was she also, standing behind the seat of the afflicted monarch, who fixed piercing eyes on the kneeling prince, and asked whether he had strength to fulfil a vow taken by his father.

Rama answered in surprise, that for Dasaratha, his father and his king, he would leap into the fire, or swallow deadly poison. And when his mind was thus prepared, amidst the groans and sighs of her husband, she commanded the prince that day to leave the kingdom, and withdraw to the forest for fourteen years, there to live the life of the most pronounced ascetic, while her own son Bharata would ascend the throne and reign in his stead.

Not a shadow passed over the face of Rama as he listened to this demand. Nor did those outside the palace, who saw him a few minutes later, perceive in him the slightest sign of mental trouble. Fully agreeing with Kekai that the King's word must at all costs be kept, touching his father's feet with his head, and seeking in vain to offer him consolation, he cheerfully gave the pledge his stepmother required, and turned away, as happily as he had come, to make preparations for the day's departure.

He had recognised in his own mind, the moment he heard the words of the young Queen, that she was merely voicing the will of some power behind herself. Never before had he had to make any distinction between the honour due from him to his own mother and to her. Nor had she ever before distinguished, in her affection, between himself and her own son Bharata. Yet here was she, the daughter and wife of kings, ordinarily possessed of an excellent disposition and highly accomplished, speaking harshly and cruelly in the presence of her husband, like the most ordinary of women! To the mind of Rama, this was incomprehensible. Therefore he put it aside, as the working of destiny, over which neither Kekai nor he could have any control, and set himself to fulfil it. He laughed quietly with Lakshmana at the jars of water, standing in rows, which had been carried by the servants for the coronation ceremony. " Verily," said he, " water drawn with my own hands from the well, would be more fit for the ceremonies that will to-day accompany the vows of a hermit ! "

But he knew well that of the two things, the forest-life or a throne, the forest was more glorious. And with a glad heart he made preparations to leave without delay. Lakshmana would fain have led an armed rebellion against Dasaratha, in favour of Rama. Kausalya would willingly have measured forces with Kekai for the protection of her son.

H

But Rama, whose mind did not waver for a moment, soothed and calmed all opposition, and made it understood that his decision was final. The King's word must be made good.

Sita, in the inner apartments of her own palace, had spent many hours in the morning worship, and stood now, waiting for the return of her husband. She half-expected him to return to her, duly installed and anointed, covered with the white umbrella of state, and surrounded by innumerable attendants. Instead of this, he entered her presence with a look of hesitation, showing signs, with regard to her, of uncontrollable emotion. Reluctantly he told her that this meeting was their farewell. He must wend his way to the forest, and live for fourteen years in banishment.

Tears had sprung to the eyes of the princess at the thought that they must be parted, but when she heard the reason, she recovered all her gaiety. Life in the forest had no terrors for her ; the loss of a throne occasioned her no regret ; if only she might follow her husband, and share his life and its hardships with him. And so at last it was arranged. Rama, Sita, Lakshmana, presented themselves before Dasaratha in full court, and there doing homage and saying farewell, they received from the hands of Kekai the dress of ascetics, and set out immediately for the life of exile in the forest.

And it came to pass that some days later, when Bharata, the son of Kekai, returned to Ayodhya, he found that his father, Dasaratha, had died of grief. And when he discovered why and by whom this had been caused, he fell upon the hump-backed serving-woman, and in his wrath, although she was a woman, had almost slain her, till she, in her despair, took refuge in the name of Rama, and was spared. And when they told the young prince that the kingdom was his, he could hardly speak for wrath and shame. For in the eyes of Bharata there was none so beloved as his elder brother Rama. Likewise to him was his allegiance sacred, for he regarded Rama as his King.

Bharata, therefore, withdrew from Ayodhya—leaving the sandals of Rama on the throne of the King, under the shadow of the royal umbrella—and stationed himself at Nandigrama, to rule the kingdom in his brother's name. Thus Kekai had not even the satisfaction of acting as the mother of the sovereign, for by Bharata's own orders all men continued to regard Rama as the monarch, and Kausalya his mother as the Queen-mother.

The Capture of Sita

How delightful to Sita, Rama, and Lakshmana were the years of their forest-exile! Wherever they went they were welcomed by companies of hermits, and admitted to the forest ways of life. Thus they were quickly established in huts made of leaves, and carpeted with the sacred grass, like other ascetics. Quickly, too, had they arranged their accessories of worship, and gathered together their small stores of necessaries. And without loss of time Sita fell into the habit of cooking for her husband and brother, like any peasant-woman, and serving them with her own fair hands. Now and then it would happen, during their first years in the forest, that they came upon some great saint, who would recognise Rama at the first glance as the Lord Himself. But more often they met with ascetics of a commoner mould, who understood the personal prowess of the royal brothers, and begged them, with folded hands, to rid the forests of the demons and brigands who were apt to make the life of the *ashramas* one of danger.

So Rama and Lakshmana, armed with royal

weapons, ranged through the forests, slaying and maiming the demon-races everywhere. For this reason, all evil beings became their foes. And far away, in the Island of Lanka, Ravana, the ten-headed king of demons, determined to compass the death and destruction of Rama.

While these royal anchorites, therefore, sat in the evening shadows of the forest, watching the last low rays of the setting sun, and talking together on high themes ; while Sita fed the birds and called the squirrels to eat from her hands or her lips ; or while they all watched the green steeds that go in the dawn before the chariot of Indra, evil was brewing for them in the distant south. One of the kindred of Ravana had been scarred and disfigured by Rama, and not by any means could the Ten-headed forget.

One morning Sita was busied in little household offices, going to and fro about the hermitage, gathering flowers for the day's worship here, or fruits for the noonday meal there. Suddenly she noticed, at some distance, a small and very beautiful deer, feeding and playing in the shadows of the trees. In colour this deer was bright golden. Its hair looked strangely soft and thick, and it was near enough for the Queen to observe the exquisite fineness of its hoofs, and the delicacy of ears and eyes.

Some strange enchantment had surely, that

morning, fallen upon Sita, for she, who was usually so merciful to all living things——pleading for their lives with her husband and his brother ——was now all eagerness that this deer should be caught. She foresaw long years in Ayodhya, when she would keep it as a palace pet. And when at last it should die, its skin should be used, by Rama or herself, as the seat of worship.

Shamefacedly, and in a whisper, she called her husband and brother-in-law to see the little creature and hear her wishes. Lakshmana was by no means taken by the animal. He suspected some magic spell, and warned both Sita and Rama to be on their guard. But these suspicions seemed groundless ; Sita's longing to possess the deer continued ; and Rama was so desirous of giving her pleasure that, without loss of time, he attired himself for the chase, and seizing his weapons, and commending his wife to his brother's care, sallied forth.

The deer had a curious way of leading him near enough to take aim, and then vanishing, only to reappear in some unexpected direction. This it did time after time, and Rama was led far afield in pursuit. The sun had already passed noon, and the shadows were beginning to grow long, when, at last, the hunter succeeded, and an arrow was lodged in the heart of the quarry. Then the form of the deer dropped away, and out of it rose the fiend-wizard Maricha, who exclaimed loudly three times in Rama's own voice, "O Sita! O Lakshmana!" and vanished.

Far away in their distant cottage Sita heard these cries of Rama, and shivered with terror, for she knew not what might have happened to her lord. She turned, therefore, and entreated Lakshmana to leave her and go and seek for Rama. All through the hours of that terrible day, she had dimly felt that evil was drawing nearer and nearer to them all, yet not so distinctly could she foresee its nature as to be able to ward it off. Now, however, all these fears and vague presentiments were concentrated in her anxiety about her husband's fate. Lakshmana, too, had not been without forebodings, but these made him extremely averse to leaving Sita alone. He could not imagine Rama at a loss and requiring his assistance, but he felt gravely responsible for the safety of the young wife. So keen, however, grew the trouble of Sita, and so insistent was her urging, that at last there was nothing for it but to go. So, warning her not to leave the shelter of the cottage during his absence, Lakshmana went forth to seek for Rama.

Scarcely had he gone, when a holy man appeared at the door, asking alms. Dreading to be uncharitable, Sita turned to speak with him and offer him the usual hospitality. She felt ill at ease, however. She could not forget that she was alone. And above all, she little liked the looks that the mendicant cast at her from time to time. Trying to conceal her agitation, she looked out in the direction whence she might expect to see Rama return from his hunting, together with Lakshmana. But on all sides she beheld only the yellow forest-lands. Neither Rama nor Lakshmana was in sight.

Soon she discovered that the Brahmin who stood before her was not what he seemed. The rags and matted locks of a holy man were only a disguise adopted by Ravana, the ten-headed Demon-King, who had come, in the hope of carrying her away. Horrified at the dilemma in which she had so rashly placed herself, the courage of Sita, and her confidence in her husband, never wavered for an instant. She warned the Demon-King that he might more safely offer violence to the wife of Indra himself, the Wielder of the Thunderbolt, than to her, the wife of Rama. For an insult done to her, none, she said, should escape death, not though he drank the nectar of immortality.

At these words, Ravana suddenly assumed his proper form, vast, and having ten heads and twenty arms. Having done this, he seized Sita by force, and rose, carrying her, into the sky.

Weeping as she went, Sita cried aloud, charging

everything around her, the rivers, lakes, and trees—nay, the very deer who must be moving beneath her—to tell Rama, on his return, that she had been seized by Ravana. At her cries, it is said, the king of the eagles awoke from his agelong slumbers in the mountains, and flung himself at Ravana, for the rescue of Sita. Nor was it till every ornament had been riven from Ravana's person, his weapons broken, and his flesh made torn and bleeding—nay, not till the lordly eagle himself had received his death-wound, that the king of birds desisted from that fierce encounter. Then Sita darted towards the prostrate body, and, stroking it with her hands, wept in the midst of the forest, calling on Rama and Lakshmana to save her.

Suddenly Ravana swooped down on her once more — as she stood, with her faded garlands falling backwards, vainly clasping a friendly tree —and seizing her by the hair, rose again, bearing her into the sky.

And the veil of yellow silk that she wore streamed in the wind, looking like sunset clouds against the sky. And when the invisible beings of the upper air saw this sight, it is said that they rejoiced, for to them the capture of Sita meant the death of Ravana, and they regarded the release of the world from his terror, as already accomplished.

But the daughter of Janneka, being borne through the air by Ravana, looked like lightning, shining against dark clouds. Like stars dropping from the sky, because their merit is exhausted, so did her golden ornaments begin to fall to the earth. And the anklets flashed as they dropped, like the circling lightning. And her chains shone, even as the Ganges throwing herself from heaven. And showers of blossoms fell from her head to the earth, and were drawn up again by the whirlwind of Ravana's swift passage, so that they studded the space about him as he went, in a ring, and looked like rows of burning stars, shining about a sombre mountain.

And the trees, waving their branches in the agitation of this flight, strove to whisper, " Fear not ! Fear not ! " And the mountains with their waterfalls and their summits towering upwards like uplifted arms, seemed to lament for Sita. And the lotuses faded in the pools, and the fish became troubled, and all the creatures of the forest trembled, for wrath and fear. And the wind wailed, and the darkness deepened, and the world wept, while Sita was borne away by Ravana to his island-kingdom of Lanka in the south.

But she, as she went, seeing five great monkeys seated on the top of a hill, conceived a sudden hope that by their means she might send news to Rama, and flung down amongst them, unseen by

Ravana, certain ornaments, and also her yellow veil.

And Rama, wending his way homeward through the distant forest, after the slaying of the deer, noticed that the jackals were howling behind him, and had not a doubt that some ill had befallen him. A moment later he met Lakshmana, and knew Sita to be alone.

But when the two heroes, shaken with anxiety, reached their cottage, and found that she had vanished, the anguish of Rama was impossible to describe. At first, hoping against hope, he refused to believe that she was lost. But when at last there was no conceivable hiding-place that had not been searched and found empty, when the silent forest had failed to answer his despairing questions, when every call had been echoed back from the desolate wilderness, then Rama came to the conclusion that Sita had been devoured by demons, and with the bitterest self-reproaches, he fell into a stupor of grief.

The Conquest of Lanka

Now when the morning had come, and Rama
and Lakshmana, ranging the forests, had found
some of the flowers and jewels of Sita, it appeared
as if Rama, calling up his divine energy, would
annihilate the world. Filled with rage, girding
himself tight with bark and deerskin, his eyes
red with anger and his matted hair pulled up
short, he stood in the forest, shortening his bow
and taking out flaming arrows with which to
shoot, even as Siva, the Destroyer, in the act to
destroy. But Lakshmana, overcome with pity
for a sorrow that could so move his brother to
a wrath never shown before, soothed him, and
spoke to him words of patience and encourage-
ment. Let him first try caution and energy. Let
him strive for the recovery of Sita. Only if he
should fail in this, would there be need, with his
arrows of celestial gold, flaming like the thunderbolt of Indra, to set himself to uproot the world
from its foundations, scattering its fragments
amongst dead stars.

Being thus calmed, and following the marks
of conflict,—drops of gore, jewelled arrows, and

pieces of golden armour,—they came gradually
nearer and nearer to the scene of the battle
between Ravana and the eagle. At last they
reached the spot itself, to find the king of birds
with both his wings cut off in the encounter,
breathing his last. Between laboured gasps he
told them of the struggles he had witnessed, and
the cries he had heard. He was able also to
utter the name of the Demon-King. But when
he would have told them more, he died. And
the Lord, filled with gratitude and compassion
for this feathered hero, performed over his dead
body those ceremonies of piety which lift the
soul to the higher regions. And then, making
their way from point to point, the two brothers
persisted in their quest of Sita.

It was in the forest that bordered the beautiful
lake of Pampa, with its red and white lotuses,
that they met with a band of monkeys whose
chieftain, Sugriva, was mourning the capture of
his own wife at the hands of an enemy. Strange
to say, it had been into the midst of this very
Sugriva's council that Sita had dropped her scarf
and ornaments, and these were now brought forth
for Rama's inspection. At sight of them he was
overcome, for the things were undoubtedly Sita's,
though Lakshmana was able to recognise only
his anklets. Then the monkeys created branches
of fragrant and beautiful blossoms to shade their

king and his guests, and all sat down and entered
together into consultation.   But first the great
monkey, Hanuman, son of the Wind God, produced a fire by means of two pieces of wood.
Then, worshipping the flame with flowers, he
placed it carefully between Rama and Sugriva,
and they went round it together, and so were
fastened in friendship.   And it is said that at
that moment, in her distant prison, the left eye
of Sita throbbed for joy at that alliance between
her lord and the monkey-chief.

It was agreed between the two sovereigns—
Sugriva and Rama—that the King of Kosala
should first slay Vali, the enemy of the monkeys,
and restore his own wife to Sugriva.   This
having been done, Sugriva, on his side, would
undertake to discover the hiding-place of Sita,
and to furnish troops for the conquest of Ravana
and the destruction of his strongholds.   This
expedition could not, it was determined, be
undertaken in the rainy season, but immediately
on the setting in of autumn, it should be carried
out without fail.

Scrupulously did the two human allies fulfil
their share of this treaty.   Within a few days
Sugriva's enemy was slain, and his wife restored
to him.   But alas, for the instability of the
monkey-nature!   He became straightway im-
mersed in woodland frolics, and Rama saw the

precious days and weeks slipping away from him, while, as far as he could see, no preparations whatever were being made. This, it must be said, was not literally true; for Hanuman, the monkey general and councillor, had already remonstrated with his sovereign regarding this unseemly delay, and had been despatched by Sugriva to collect an army. So when Lakshmana at last went, with manly directness, to protest against perfidy and want of faith, their ally was able to point to the gatherings of hundreds of thousands whom he could see about him, and to assure him that in many other parts of the forests formidable monkeys and bears would be found stationed, each with another army in his keeping, waiting to receive their marching orders.

The first point was to find out the whereabouts of Sita, and for this purpose Sugriva divided the hosts of monkeys, ordering some to search in the north-east, others in the north-west, and still others again in the distant south. His own reliance, however, was placed mainly on the prowess and energy of the great Hanuman, who was going with the southern army; and when he said so to Rama, the King gave this emissary a ring engraved with his own name, to be a token to Sita, should he find her, of whence he came.

But many weeks of unavailing search went by before Hanuman, Son of the Winds, swelling

himself to a vast size, and concentrating all the
energy of his mind, leapt at one bound across
the sea, and landed in Lanka, the island-kingdom
of Ravana. Having done so, the powerful
monkey paused. High on a mountain-top before
him, gleaming in inconceivable loveliness of level
terraces and soaring spires, he saw the famous
city of Lanka ; and he took counsel with himself
as to the means by which he might enter her.
Finally he determined to wait for sunset, and
when that hour came, he reduced himself to the
size of a cat, and so entered the city.

It was, in truth, like some dwelling-place of
the gods. Its many-storied buildings and fretted
screens were studded with crystal. Great arch-
ways and splendid gates lent it their grandeur
in all directions. Its streets and roadways were
broad and well-cared for. Magnificent were its
towers of victory. Beautiful were its lantern-
pillars. Its houses were like palaces, and its
tombs like dainty marble canopies. Wonderful,
verily, was this Lanka, famous throughout the
world, ruled over by the might of Ravana, and
vigilantly guarded by night-rangers of terrible
strength. Oppressed by the thought of this
glory, the spirit of Hanuman became sunk in
gloom ; when suddenly, as if on purpose to
comfort him, the full moon arose in all her
splendour with the stars. And the great monkey

looking up, saw her, lovely with the sheen of a white conch-shell, wearing the tint of a white lotus, arisen and afloat in the heavens, like a beautiful swan swimming in a lake.

Hour after hour of that night did Hanuman range, without success, through the mansions of the great lords of Lanka. In and out of their halls and apartments he went; not a single sleeping-chamber did he leave unexplored. Even the palace of Ravana saw him enter it, and the ten-headed king, sleeping off the night's intoxication, knew not that a little monkey, whose visit boded no good to him or his, drew near in the small hours of the morning, and peered at him, as he lay on his great sleeping-dais of polished crystal. But nowhere, in any of those mansions or great houses, did Hanuman find Sita.

The Queen of Ayodhya, in fact, within a few hours of entering Lanka, had been banished to a park of asoka-trees, and placed there in charge of demon-women, powerful to look upon, and instructed to torment her. Ravana had quickly realised that favours could have no influence over his proud captive, and had determined to try on her the effect of harsh treatment. Now Sita was the daughter of the Earth-Mother. It was told of her that her father in her babyhood had found her in a ploughed furrow. To her, therefore, the open grove, and the wide air, and running streams

I

were more bearable than the close walls of the palace, with its luxuries, had been. She was too deeply wrapped in sorrow to notice the faces or the treatment of her women guards. She had not even tasted food while in captivity For on the first night of her imprisonment the God Indra, casting the people of Lanka into an enchanted sleep, had appeared before her, bringing in his hands the food and drink of Heaven, which take away from mortals all hunger and thirst. And when the Queen was afraid to touch his gifts, lest he should prove in truth to be some other, wearing the guise of the King of Heaven, he shone forth before her for a moment with his divine attributes, and then she ate and drank fearlessly from his hands of the food of the Immortals. Thus had she lived in her garden-prison during the weary weeks and months of her separation from Rama, and here, as the dawn approached, did Hanuman find her, feeling sure that his quest was ended.

Seated beneath a tree beside the river was a woman weeping. Pale and worn she was, and clad in threadbare silken garments of worship. But the bent head had about it something queenly, and the veil was worn with a grace unknown to the demon-women of Lanka. The monkey could see, moreover, that this woman before him was fair of tint, and very beautiful. Her air, with all its grandeur, had also in it something that was dainty and gentle. He held his breath, for he could hardly doubt that this was that Sita whom he sought, the captive wife of Rama. As he waited and watched, however, quivering with the excitement of his discovery, whom should he see enter the garden but the great ten-headed Ravana himself! Bowing low before the prisoner, the Demon-King took a seat at some distance from her, on the grassy bank, turning himself to face her, and the monkey bent his ear to a level with the branch on which he sat, the better to hear each syllable that might pass.

At the approach of Ravana the pale Queen had grown still more pale, and Hanuman could see that she was trembling with fear, like a green plant in the wind. But when her visitant began to speak, a red spot burnt on her cheeks and a light in her eyes, and she raised her head haughtily, as if it could hardly be to *her* that he presumed to address himself. To most of what he said, she listened as if she scarcely heard. Once, indeed, her captor waited, as if expecting some reply. But she answered only, " I have warned you already, O Demon-King! that the deeds you have done, and the words you now speak, will be punished with death. Only one who desired to mock the gods, and bring ruin upon him-self, could act as you have the daring to do "

Then again she sat, looking before her into space, as if she neither saw nor heard.

When Ravana at last left the garden, in rage and disgust, he sent back into it the demon-guards, and they encircled the beautiful Sita, tormenting her. And she, finding herself in the midst of them, like a fawn encircled by wolves, burst into tears, and sobbed to herself, with broken words of sorrow and endearment, for the loss of Rama. At this the demon-women drew back somewhat, finding little amusement in their sorrowful prisoner. But though this was the very opportunity that Hanuman had waited for, yet he was afraid to address the Queen suddenly, lest she should be startled and call her guards. To avoid this, therefore, he began to run about, talking to himself about Rama, in order to attract her attention.

At last his mistress looked up. "Oh, dear Brother of the Woods," she said, "do you also know the beloved name?"

"Madam," answered the monkey very quietly, "I think that you are she whom I was sent to find. If so, tell me what is your state here."

"I am Sita," answered the captive, in a low, subdued voice, "daughter of Janneka of Mithila, and wife of the son of Dasaratha. And I am imprisoned here, under sentence of execution. Two moons hence, I am condemned to die."

Then Hanuman hastened to tell her all he

could of Rama : that he was well ; that day and night he brooded on the thought of her rescue ; that he had gathered together a great army for the overthrow of Lanka ; and finally, that he himself had been deputed by him to find out, and report on, her place of concealment.

At all this news Sita was overjoyed. Yet she was not without doubt also. For Ravana had the power of taking other shapes at will. Already he had approached her as her own mother, and again he had appeared before her as Rama himself, in the hope that she would at least speak kindly to him, which only a miracle had prevented her doing. Now, therefore, she could not even be sure that this monkey was what he seemed to be. She dreaded another of the demon's tricks.

Then Hanuman came forward and placed at her feet the engraved seal of Rama, that he had sent her as a token.

Hurriedly Sita lifted the jewel and concealed it in her hair. Tears broke from her eyes, and she sobbed with joy. Then, with nervous, trembling fingers she took from some part of her dress a charm that her husband had given her, and told her messenger at the same time to remind the King of a certain great hawk who had wounded her and been slain by him, as they sat together one afternoon in the gardens of Ayodhya. By

the twofold token of the talisman and the memory,
she knew that her place of imprisonment would
stand accredited.

"Lady," said the monkey, as he put his cold
nose down on the earth to salute her, before
leaving the garden, "how easily could I carry
you home to Rama on my back! I am larger
and stronger than you think. The matter to me
would be a small one!"

The Queen had drawn herself back as he spoke,
and a change had come over her face, as though
she remembered that other wild flight through
the evening shadows, when Ravana, like some
gigantic bird of prey, had carried her through
the skies to Lanka. "Oh no!" she said, half
hesitating, lest she should hurt her servant, yet
wholly firm, "I could not let any one take me
home except my husband himself!"

"And that is well!" said Hanuman, feeling deep
satisfaction within himself at her reply. "For I
think that my master also would desire for himself the honour of liberating you. It will not be
long till he reaches you, and then you will be
royally avenged. But now I feel my wild monkey-
nature hot within me, and I have it in mind to do
Ravana some mischief ere I leave this place."

A whisk of his tail, and another salutation, and
he was gone, leaving the captive lonely indeed,
but full of hope. Next day she remembered his

parting words with secret smiles—for news was brought to her that in the orchards of the demons all the young fruit had been destroyed in a single night, by a terrible monkey, who had slain num berless guards, and had been seen at one bound to leap across the sea.

Rama, meanwhile, had ranged his army in order, and tested his command. When Hanuman, therefore, returned with his welcome news, he was ready to order the march upon the seashore. The next problem was that of taking the troops across the straits. At the fiercely-impatient prayer of Rama, Ocean himself now appeared to him, and reft his own bed upwards to form the basis of a bridge from the mainland to Lanka. Then all the hosts of monkeys came forward with branches and logs and trunks of trees, and built the whole into a firm and lofty structure, steady enough to withstand the tides of the salt sea. And the people tell how even the little squirrels helped in the building of the bridge to Lanka, bringing stones and shells and broken nuts to make it smooth. And for this, when the work was ended, the Lord took one of these smallest workmen in his hand, and stroked him, blessing him, from head to tail. And because of this blessing of Rama it is that the Indian squirrel wears three white stripes on his dark fur—they are the finger-marks of the blessing of the Lord of the Universe.

Thus was built the bridge that spans to this day, the straits beside the great pearl-fisheries of Manaar. And when it was finished, the troops were brought safely across it ; and all knew that the very next step would be the seizing of Lanka, the destruction of Ravana, and the release of Sita.

All this time Mandodari, the wife of Ravana, had been imploring her husband to set his prisoner free. But he had answered only with expressions of contempt for Rama, and boasts of his own power. When the forces of the enemy had been brought across the sea, however, everything was changed. Ravana himself, it was said, had leapt to his feet in consternation when the news was heard. The hostile army was now at their very gates; and the prospects that only the day before were still unclouded, looked very grave. For in Lanka, by this time, they judged of the power of each one of Rama's soldiery by that of Hanuman, who in a few hours had destroyed, unaided, all their orchards.

Mandodari now, therefore, was joined in her pleadings by her husband's own brother. " Set the stranger free," they entreated, " while yet there is time to save the city ! Rama is in the right, and fate itself must fight upon his side ! "

To his brother, Ravana gave some curt reply, that drove him in anger out of his presence. But to his wife he was exceedingly gentle. "My beloved," he said, "it is the enemy's duty to avenge himself upon us, if he can. Would you rather that your husband and sons died, if die they must, whining for mercy, or bravely, as good knights should, contending for their prize?"

Then Mandodari felt that her husband had spoken his secret thought, that he and her boys would die, and she be left childless and a widow. But she uttered no cry, nor shed even a tear, for she knew that her work now must lie in strengthening, not in making them afraid.

Some hours later Rama and Lakshmana, in their camp, saw an officer with soldiers drawing near to them under a flag of truce. He dismounted on reaching them, and said, "Gentlemen, we, the people of Lanka, are entirely in the wrong in this matter. I have come to offer you my alliance." It was Vibhishana, the brother of Ravana, with his men-at-arms.

The princes received him as an honoured guest, and proclamation was made, that on the taking of Lanka he should be appointed governor.

Almost immediately after this the storming of the city began, and it is told in an old book that during the course of the siege Lakshmana saw an archer on the walls take aim at Vibhishana to shoot him. The brother of Rama remembered only, in that moment, that the deserter was their guest, and ran forward to receive the arrow, says the teller of the tale, as a man might run to embrace his beloved. Thus was the life of Vibhishana saved, though that of Lakshmana himself was well-nigh lost. The siege lasted many days, but the town finally fell, and only the fortress remained to be attempted.

And now, at last, did Rama achieve his heart's desire, for he engaged in single combat with Ravana, and slew him with his own hand. Then the great doors of the castle were flung open, and the moment had come for the return of Sita.

The Ordeal of Sita

RAMA'S whole heart was filled with the longing to see Sita, and renew once more the life-sweetness which had been broken that morning when he left her to catch the golden deer. Yet he was no mere mortal, full of blind impulse, a prey to the chance-born desires of the passing moment. He foresaw that if their reunion was to be secure, it must take place in public, and must be accompanied by some proof of his wife's honour and devotion which could never be shaken in the popular mind. There could be no happiness for Sita if her subjects did not love her and trust her implicitly. There could be none for him if her name were not lifted high above the stain of suspicion or reproach.

But the first duty that awaited him had nothing to do with these questions. He was at this moment at the head of a conquering army. His first responsibility lay in protecting the city, with its women, its children, and its treasures, from his own forces. He hastened, therefore, to crown and proclaim Vibhishana King of Lanka. This done, he called Hanuman secretly, and, bidding him obtain the permission of the new King to enter the city, sent him to Sita to acquaint her privately with his victory.

Publicly he proffered a formal request to Vibhishana that he would personally escort the Queen of Kosala to his presence. She was to come, moreover, wearing the robes and jewels proper to occasions of state. The loving heart of the woman would have prompted her to fly to the shelter of her husband just as she was, in the mourning garments of her captivity. But Vibhishana reminded her gently of the sacredness of a husband's expressed wish, and she submitted immediately to the tiring which this imposed. Hard, verily, are the roads that princes walk! Treading at each step on her own heart, must Sita make her way to her husband's side.

At last the Queen was ready and entered the closed palanquin, with its hangings of scarlet and gold, in which she would be borne into the presence of Rama, Vibhishana himself riding before her to announce her coming. At the city gates, however, came the request that she should alight and proceed through the open camp on foot. Scarcely understanding, and so absorbed in the thought of seeing the King that she had little care for any minor detail, Sita rose from her seat in the covered litter and stepped out on the broad road. Round her, to right and left, were the soldiery. In front was seated Rama, in full audience, with grave and solemn air. All eyes were on Sita, who had never, since her childhood to this hour, been seen in public. Instinctively the knightly Vibhishana realised the embarrassment this must cause to the shrinking and sensitive Queen, and he was in the act of ordering the dispersal of the crowds, so as to leave the meeting of the royal pair unwitnessed, when Rama put up his hand and stopped him. " Let all stay ! " he commanded. " This is one of those occasions when the whole universe becomes the veil of woman, and she may be seen by all without sin ! "

Nearer and nearer came Sita meanwhile, with slow and regal step. Her eyes were drinking in every line, every movement of her husband's face. He rose to receive her ; but all men saw that he looked not towards her, but stood with head bowed and downward-gazing eyes. How beautiful was the Queen ! How stately and full of grace she looked ! And yet, decked as she was in royal ornaments, there was that about her which spoke more plainly still, assuring all who looked on her that here was a woman of true and noble heart, a humble and loving wife, fit to be, as she was, the crown and support of all the happy homes throughout her land. Every man in the hosts that day held his breath in

awe and reverence, at the revelation seen in her
of what great womanhood should be.

At a sign from her husband, and a few paces
away, the Queen stood still, and Rama looked
up and addressed her in thick, constrained tones.
"Ravana has been duly defeated and slain," he
said. "Thus has the honour of Ayodhya been
vindicated to the utmost. It is for the Queen,
whom he separated from her husband, to say in
what guardianship, and with what establishment,
she will now choose to live. Thy wishes, O
gentle one!" he added, addressing her for a
moment directly and swept away by his own
tenderness, "shall be carried out in full. But
it is not seemly or possible to restore to her old
place one whose fair fame has been sullied by
residence in the palace of Ravana."

At these words the Queen stood, in her sudden
astonishment and pain, like one who had been
stabbed. Then she raised her proud head to its
proudest height, and, though her lips quivered
and the tears fell, without her will, her wonderful
voice rang out untremulous. "My character,"
she said, "must indeed be misconceived. Even
Rama, it seems, can mistake my greatness, and
truly then am I undone! Yet if my lord had
but told me, while yet I was imprisoned in Lanka,
that it was for the honour of Ayodhya he would
recover me, I would indeed have spared him all

his labours. How easy had it been to me to die there, only I supposed that other motives moved him! Go, Lakshmana, and make for me here a funeral pyre! Methinks that is the only remedy for the disaster that has come upon me."

This, then, was Sita's desire for guardians and establishment! Lakshmana looked towards his brother in anger and surprise, but, receiving only a quiet gesture, hastened to have the funeral pyre prepared. The face of Rama was like that of Death himself in the hour of the final destruction of all things, and none present dared to speak to him. As for Sita, her tears were now raining down; but still she stood there, waiting patiently.

When the wood had been piled and the fire set blazing, Sita walked three times round her husband, standing in his place, with head bowed, and it was evident to all that her heart was full of sweetness. Then, coming forward to the fire, and standing before it with her hands folded as for prayer, she said, "Do thou, O Fire, the witness of the worlds! protect me, whose heart has been ever true! Take me to yourselves, O ye pure flames! for unto the Lord of Purity the pure fleeth."

Saying this, and walking three times round the pyre, the Queen, having bidden farewell to the world with undaunted heart, entered into it. Like gold being set upon a golden altar was the stepping of Sita into that flaming fire. And lamentations arose on all sides from amongst the lookers-on. But lo, as her foot touched the pyre, voices of angelic sweetness were heard from heaven chanting the glory of Rama, and the mystery of the ineffable union of the Divine Being with His own divine grace. And there advanced from the heart of the fire to meet Sita, Agni, the God of Fire, Himself. Supporting her with his right arm, and stepping out from amongst the flames, the divinity bore her forward to Rama, whose face had suddenly become radiant with joy, and gave her to him, joining them together.

"She is thine own, O Rama!" he said; "she is thine own—ever faithful and true to thee, in thought, word, and deed. Lo, at my command is it that thou takest her back unto thee. For I have spoken, and she is thine own!"

And Rama said, receiving her, "Verily, my beloved, no doubt was in my mind concerning thee. Yet was thy vindication needful, in the presence of all our people. Truly art thou mine. Think not thou canst be divided from me. Thou art mine, and I could not renounce thee, even as the sun cannot be separated from his own rays."

And as they stood thus, wedded once more—as in their youth by man, so now by the God of

Fire Himself—it seemed to all present as if the gates of heaven were suddenly swung backward above them, and they saw Dasaratha, seated in his car, blessing Sita as well as Rama, and hailing them King and Queen of Ayodhya.

It was true that the fourteen years of their exile were ended, and as Rama understood from this vision that the soul of his father would not be in peace till his coronation was finally accomplished, he did everything that was possible to hasten their departure. A day or two passed, distributing wealth and rewards amongst the soldiers, and then mounting with Sita into the royal car, drawn by white swans, they coursed swiftly through the sky, and arrived at Ayodhya.

It is told of the days that followed that, Rama governing that kingdom, widows were not distressed, nor was there fear from wild beasts nor from disease. The people were safe from robbers, and there was no other trouble. The old were not called upon to perform the funeral ceremonies of the young. All were happy together, nor did they envy one another. And the trees bore fruits and flowers perpetually. Showers fell whenever they were desired. And the winds blew pleasantly. And all men became pious and truthful under the rule of Rama, and his kingdom was blessed with all the marks of fortune.

How happy would have been the story if it had ended thus! So did the great poet Valmiki intend it. And so for hundreds of years must men have known it. But in some later age, by an unknown hand, a sequel was written, and this sequel is strangely sad. It tells how the terrible ordeal of Sita had not after all been enough, or perhaps had taken place too far away, to satisfy her people. The murmuring and suspicion that Rama had foreseen, did, after all, break out, and when he heard this the King knew that it was useless to fight against the inevitable, Sita and he must henceforth dwell apart. For the good of his subjects a king must be willing to make any sacrifices, and it could never, he felt, be for their well-being that their sovereign's conduct should be misunderstood. But though his will was thus heroic, Rama could not trust himself to see Sita and say his last good-bye to her, face to face. He sent her, therefore, in the care of Lakshmana, to make a long-desired pilgrimage to the hermitage of Valmiki, on the far side of the Ganges. There Lakshmana was to give his parting messages, and take farewell of her.

Oh how terrible was the desolation of Sita on this occasion! There was, indeed, the consolation that she understood her husband, and he her. The last words of each for the other made this separation of theirs like the plighting

of a solemn troth. Yet she knew that their parting
was to be for ever. She would be always with
him in spirit, but neither might hope to look
upon the other's face again.

Twenty years passed in this retirement, under
the guardianship of the wise and fatherly Valmiki,
whom the twin sons of Sita regarded as a kind
and beloved grandfather. But when twenty
years had gone by there came to Valmiki's hermitage the news of a royal sacrifice at Ayodhya.
Now the saint had already composed *Ramayana*,
and taught it to Lava and Kusa, the sons of
Rama. He determined, therefore, to take the
boys to Ayodhya and let them sing the poem
before their father, on the occasion of the
sacrifice.

Long before it was finished, Rama had realised
that the lads before him must be his own. It
took many days to chant the poem, but the King
and his counsellors listened greedily to the end.
Then, with a sigh, Rama turned to the great
Valmiki and said, " Ah, if only Sita were here !
But she could never consent to a second trial of
her honour ! "

" Let me ask her ! " answered Valmiki, who
longed above all things to bring this husband
and wife together once more, for the happiness
of both.

To the surprise of Rama, word was brought

that Sita would consent next day to go through a second public trial, this time by oath instead of by the fiery ordeal.

The morning came. The King and all his ministers and attendants were seated in state, and vast crowds, of all ranks and from all parts of the country, were admitted to see the trial of Sita. In came the Queen, following after Valmiki. Closely veiled, with head bent, hands folded, and tears in her eyes, she walked ; and it was easy to see that all her mind was meditating upon Rama. A murmur of praise and delight broke from all the spectators. Little did any one there dream of what they would shortly see happen !

As Valmiki presented the Queen to Rama and to the assembly, and as Rama turned to call upon her to swear to her own faithfulness and sincerity, before all their people, every one noticed that a cool and fragrant breeze began to blow, as if betokening the nearness of the gods. No one, however, was prepared for the effect of Rama's words on Sita.

That proud though gentle soul had borne all that was possible to her. Perfect in sweetness and perfect in submission, she had endured twenty years of loneliness without murmuring. But all now had come to an end. " O divine Mother ! " she cried, " thou great Earth-Goddess, if it be true that in my heart I have never thought of any other than Rama, then for my wifely virtue take me to Thyself! If constantly, by thought, word, and deed, I have prayed for his welfare, then for this great virtue do Thou give me refuge!" And as the weary cry rang out, a wonderful thing happened. The earth opened, and a great jewelled throne rose up, carried on the heads of Nagas, lords of the underworld. On the throne sat the Earth-Goddess, stretching out her arms to take to herself this child of hers, who had cried to her for refuge; and celestial flowers rained upon both, as the throne re-entered the earth. At the same time voices were heard from the heavens, saying, "Glory, glory unto Sita!" And as the Queen and the Earth-Mother passed out of sight of men, the whole universe passed, for one moment, it is said, into a state of holy calm.

One heart, however, did not share this peace. The mind of Rama was torn with grief. And true as Sita had been to him, so true was he ever after unto her. For the performance of those ceremonies in which the help of a queen was necessary, he had a golden image made of his wife, and went through his official actions by its side. So passed all things, until that hour had struck, beyond which no man may delay, and when that came, Rama and his brothers bade farewell to the world, and going out of Ayodhya to the river-side, they entered into their divine bodies, and were seen no more in the world of men.

And ages passed by, and the story of their days became a memory, for there were none left on the earth, of all those who had lived beneath their sway.

THE CYCLE OF KRISHNA

The Birth of Krishna, the Indian Christ-Child

"Thou Supreme bliss of Devaki!"

KANSA, the tyrant king of Mathura, was wicked and oppressive beyond the power of men to bear. The very earth cried out against his injustice and evil deeds. And then, for the comforting of those who could endure no more, a prophecy began to be whispered about, regarding the slaying of the tyrant. And the origin of this prophecy was indeed most strange.

Kansa had a great love for his sister Devaki and also for Vasudeva, one of his nobles, and his friend. He exerted himself, therefore, to bring about a marriage between the two, and when the wedding was over, he himself acted as charioteer, to drive them both to the home of Vasudeva. But lo! on the way, a voice spoke to him from heaven, saying, "The eighth child of this couple, O Tyrant, shall be a boy, who in his twelfth year shall slay thee with his own hands!" At these words, all Kansa's love for the bride and bridegroom turned to hatred. Swiftly he turned the horses' heads, and driving back to Mathura, whence they had come, cast Devaki and Vasudeva into the dungeons underneath his palace, there to endure imprisonment for life, that he might the more easily slay each child of theirs at birth. And now this had happened seven times, that a child had been born, and Kansa had destroyed it—save indeed once. For one child, the boy Bolarama, had been carried away secretly, and the King had been told that he was already dead. Now, however, had the time come for the fulfilment of the prophecy. And Devaki and her husband waited in their prison for the coming of that child who should be the deliverer of His people.

Outside, the wind wailed, and the rain fell, and the waters of the Jumna rose, as if in flood. The night was wild, whereon would come to earth Krishna, the Holy Child. Within, in the dungeons of Mathura, Devaki and her husband Vasudeva waited, trembling; for they knew that to-night, of a truth, would be born as their son that soul of whom it had been foretold that he, and no other, was the destined slayer of Kansa. Was it not for that very reason that they at this moment were in prison? And their hearts were sore within them, for what welcome could they offer to the coming child? Knew they not, only too well, that with the morning Kansa himself would visit them, to kill the babe with his own hands? Terrible was the time of watching, while the storm howled without, round them rose the bare forbidding walls of the prison, and in the heart of poor Devaki the hope and love of a mother struggled with sadness and fear.

Slowly, slowly the hours went by, till midnight. And then, just as the bell of the great water-clock outside the palace began to boom out the hour, the hearts of the mother and father were filled with joy, for at that very moment, their Babe had come to them. In that one brief instant, as she held Him in her arms, Devaki forgot the ordeal of the morrow, forgot the cruel death that awaited her Child, and knew only the bliss of the mother, who welcomes the newly-born.

At the moment of His birth, the prison was filled with a soft light, streaming out from the Babe Himself, and as He lay back in His mother's lap, they saw shining out from behind Him four arms. One hand held the *shank* or battle-trumpet; another the discus; a third the mace; and in the fourth was a lotus on its stem. Then Devaki and Vasudeva knew these for the signs of Vishnu, and they worshipped the Child, saying the salutations, as Narayan, Saviour of the World. But as the salutations ended, the veil of Maya descended upon them once more, and the Child appeared to them as their own babe. All about them now, however, they heard voices. At first they did not trust to their own ears, thinking the sounds were of the wind and rain. But presently, listening, they heard distinctly the words, "Arise! Take the young Child, and leave Him in the house of Nanda, Chief of the Cowherds, in the village of Gokool, and bring hither the girl-child who has just been born there."

What could be meant by telling a prisoner, unable to leave his prison, to rise and carry a baby to a village on the far side of the Jumna? How could Vasudeva open the dungeon doors? How could he pass the guards? How, if he did all this, would he be able to cross the Jumna itself on coming to it at this late hour? Yet the feeling of some incomprehensible power was strong upon them, and they were full of terror for the fate of the Child on the morrow. So Vasudeva yielded himself to the bidding of the unknown. He arose, lifted the Babe, covered Him with his own garment, and, staff in hand, went forward to the prison-entrance. To his amazement the bolts slid back, the locks turned, the chains fell softly, and the heavy doors swung outwards of their own accord before him. Outside, the guards and soldiers slumbered heavily, and no one woke, as Vasudeva, with the Babe Krishna hidden beneath his robe, passed into the open road.

Here the storm was even worse than it had

sounded from within the prison. Heavily the
warm rain fell, and the winds raged, and the man's
heart was heavy with foreboding, as he listened to
the rushing of the great river in the distance, and
wondered how he should reach its further bank.

At this very moment, in the darkness before
him, he saw a jackal, and silently resolved to take
the wild creature as his guide. On went the
animal ; on followed the man, until they came to
the river-side. Then the jackal plunged in at a
certain place, and proceeded to make his way
over, and Vasudeva, seeing that here there must
be a ford, step after step went across in his wake.
And men say that in the guise of this jackal, for
protection of the Divine Child, it was Durga,
Queen of Heaven and Mother of the Universe,
who had come to earth that night.

But it is told that, as they went, the Babe grew
heavier and heavier in His father's arms, till all at
once He slipped and would have drowned, only
just in time he caught Him back and bore Him
safely on. For Mother Jumna also longed to take
the Lord into her keeping, and fold Him for a
moment to her breast.

At last came Vasudeva with his precious burden
to the village of Gokool, and to the dwelling-place
of Nanda, the King of Cowherds. Softly the door
of the great farmhouse opened before him, and, still
obeying the same gentle guidance that had led him

forth from the prison, he entered, and saw a light burning in the first room within the doorway. The lamp stood by the bedside of a sleeping mother and a new-born child. Quietly, quietly Vasudeva bent down and exchanged the children. To the farmer-chieftain's wife he gave the Babe he carried, and from her side he took the little daughter who slept there. Then, without a word, he turned and went back by the way he had come, to the dungeons of Kansa, in the city of Mathura, and gave the girl-child of Nanda to his own wife, Devaki.

Great was the rejoicing amongst the cowherds when they all woke up in the morning and found that the child whom they remembered as a girl was really a boy. For this was the only explanation of the mystery that occurred to them. It is said indeed that that morning there was no food to eat in the house of Nanda, for all the pots of milk and curd fell from the hands of the women when they heard the news, in their astonishment and delight. Then thousands of people came, and every one was fed, and wealth was distributed and there was great rejoicing. So this is always kept in India as Nanda's Feast, and on the day before, as the people believe, there is always rain.

But in the stronghold of Kansa, it was told that morning that a child had been born in the night to Devaki and Vasudeva. Then was the heart of the tyrant hot within him, and he came down into the dungeons in person, attended by all his guards, that he might with his own hands slay this child, who, it was said, had been born to be his destroyer.

To the King's amazement, however, he found that the child was not a boy at all, but a girl. Had Kansa been less wicked and tyrannical he would have rested here. A girl could hardly, at the age of twelve, be the slayer of a man. And the prophecy had pointed distinctly to a boy. But evil men are blinded by their own wickedness. The very unexpectedness of the event enraged him, and he put out his hand to seize the babe by the foot, and dash it to pieces against the prison walls. As he touched it, however, to the astonishment of all present, the seeming child slipped from his grasp, and high above their heads rose the shining form of a goddess. "He who shall slay thee, O King, is even now growing to manhood," she said, mockingly, "in the village of Gokool on the far side of the Jumna," and then, as they looked, the radiant being faded away, and none could tell even the direction in which she had disappeared.

But wrath and mortification filled the heart of Kansa the Tyrant, and for many a long year thereafter he knew no rest, in his burning zeal to outwit the gods, and end the life of the Child Krishna, ere yet He should be old enough to become his slayer.

The Divine Childhood

BY the advice of his counsellors, the Tyrant Kansa, knowing that his future slayer had been born, and was living somewhere within the dominions of Mathura, determined now to send out his emissaries for the killing of all new-born children, everywhere. And he had under his command powerful beings of his own kindred, known as demons, or Asuras, who were able to assume any shape at will, and could fly through the sky.

Some of these therefore he sent forth secretly for the slaughter of innocent babes, throughout his dominion. And it came to pass that one evening, as the shadows grew long, the Vampire-nurse Putana, who was one of them, having wandered through cities, villages, and forests, destroying infants, arrived at Gokool. And the form which she assumed to enter the place was that of a woman so resplendent in beauty, that the people supposed her to be some goddess, come to offer worship and benediction at the cradle of their chieftain's son. Going hither and thither as she would, secretly observing the youngest of the children, Putana came finally to the great house

of the village, that of Nanda, and entering found
the Child Krishna. As she bent over Him, to
take Him into her arms, the Babe saw and understood her real nature, and closed His eyes; and in
that moment she lifted Him. But the women
who were sitting or standing near suspected no
evil. They noticed only the apparent sweetness
and beauty of the stranger, and never dreamt
that this was in truth the dreaded Vampire-nurse,
whose caress was death to all babies, and her
heart like a sharp sword encased in a hard scab-
bard. A moment later, and with many endear-
ments, she had begun to feed the child. Now
the breast of Putana was full of deadly poison.
But the Babe only touched her with His little
mouth, apparently giving a single gentle tug, as
babies do, and lo! the very life of the witch was
drawn out of her. With a loud cry of rage she
fell to the earth, and as she did so, all her beauty
dropped away from her, and showed itself to have
been only a disguise. Every one, hearing the yell
of the dying Vampire, hastened to the spot, but
there lay the Divine Child laughing and kicking,
as if He never guessed that by a touch of His
mysterious strength, the enemy of children had
been slain ! But when the news reached Kansa,
of the death of his messenger, and the Child that
could not be killed, he became sure that Krishna
was that very Babe of whom the voice had spoken,

and he determined to leave no stone unturned to compass His death.

Never was mortal woman happier than Yasoda, wife and queen of Nanda, and foster-mother of Krishna. Day after day, as the months went by, she held Him in her lap, and fed and played with Him, or soothed Him gently to sleep. For what was He, after all, but a baby? Not even by her, as yet, was it suspected what was His great strength, or Who He was. One day she was called away for something, and before going, she turned and laid the Child down on the ground, in the shadow of a disused bullock-cart. It had long stood idle, and had come to be used as a sort of dairy-table, for it was covered now with great jars containing milk for butter and curds. These in their turn were protected from dust with grass and leaves, and over the whole were the bamboo mats that acted as the waggon hood. Here, then, in the shadow lay the Babe, and about Him, in the farmyard, played other children. And now did the Demon Shakat enter into the cart, thinking it would be easy to fall and crush the Infant, by a seeming accident. But the little one who lay there was the Lord Himself! Nothing could deceive or baffle Him. At the very instant when the waggon began to break, He gave a kick with His tiny foot, and lo! the cart, with all that stood on it, was thrown to the other side of the farmyard, and Shakat-Asur, the demon, was killed.   Hearing the noise, people came in astonishment from every part of the farm, and great was their happiness to find the Babe still living.   But when they heard from the rest how it had happened, what were they to believe? He was as yet too young even to creep about. Only Yasoda, clasping her Heart's-Joy tight between tears and laughter, felt that there was something here beneath the surface, that they none of them understood.   Strange dangers threatened the life of her little one.   Wondrous wisdom and strength were hidden within Him. These things to her, His mother, it was easy to accept.

One day, as she nursed Him with all her tenderness, she suddenly felt Him grow as heavy as a mountain, and was obliged to lay Him on the ground.   At that very moment, a great black cloud enwrapped them both for an instant, and when it passed on, she saw the Babe Krishna rising higher and higher above her, clinging, as it seemed, to the very throat of a whirlwind.   In agony watched the mother, while all about Gokool the air grew black with storm and dust.   On swept the hurricane, yet with course impeded, as it seemed, by the weight of the Being it struggled to carry. Moments passed of terrible suspense, in which the distracted mother and weeping women of the village ran hither and thither, as if to find or catch the Boy. Then there came a lull, and down, down, down, into the midst of Gokool, fell the Demon of the Hurricane, with his Baby-Destroyer still holding him by the throat!

Yasoda, indeed, had many curious experiences, and found much to ponder over. When her little Son was old enough to crawl about on all-fours, He became very difficult to keep in order. He would constantly besmear Himself with mud, and even put earth to His lips and eat it. So His gentle foster-mother was compelled to be angry and punish Him. Then the Child cried, but as He opened His mouth, she, watching Him, seemed to be smitten into a trance, for she saw there revealed, as if within Him, all the worlds, in all their manifold gradations of existence. The whole infinite Universe within that one Babe Krishna! And the mortal, unable to bear the revelation, closed her eyes, trembling, till the kind gods drew over her sight once more the veil of illusion, and she was able to look upon the Divinity before her as if He were nothing but her Son.

The little hands were busy with everything. There was no keeping this rogue out of mischief. So one day, when Yasoda was at work about the house, she tied about the Child a long rope, which was attached, at its other end, to an old and broken axle of a cart-wheel, and thus protected, left Him to play alone.   Not far off stood two ancient trees, with a tiny gap between them. But Yasoda, leaving Him, had no fear for her Baby, for His tether was long and the axle heavy. He could play and scramble and crawl, she thought, to His naughty little heart's content, and yet never be able to move very far from where she had put Him.

This was reckoning, however, without her host ; for when no one was near, crawling here and crawling there, the child actually managed to creep between the two great trees !   Then on and on He went, dragging His rope and its axle after Him, till at last the weight was wedged tightly in the gap.   At this He gave a slight jerk, and suddenly, without more ado, those two lords of the forest fell with a crash, and Krishna near by, on His hands and knees, was found laughing quietly, not the least afraid !

But now a strange thing befell.   Out of those trees, in the presence of every one—for all had run to see what was happening, thinking, in fact, that a thunderbolt had fallen—came two bright spirits, telling how for ages they had lain imprisoned there beneath a spell, that could only be lifted by the touch of the Lord.   Then they offered salutations, and worshipped the Liberator of Souls, before they disappeared.

Another day, after the Child had begun to

toddle, a woman came to the farmstead with fruit to sell, and Krishna, desiring to have some, ran into the house, and returned to her, carrying the necessary handful of rice, but letting it stream out in all directions between His open fingers. The fruit-seller was so pleased with the look of the Child, and so touched with His feeble effort to pay her justly, that she insisted on giving Him all the fruit He wanted, and could hardly be persuaded to take anything in return. Her scruples, however, were overcome, and she consented to accept the little one's offering, when behold, as He poured the remaining rice into the knotted corner of her veil——tied like a bag for the carrying of it——each grain, touching the cloth, became a jewel!

Another of the little fellow's tricks was to make His way into the dairies of His village friends and help Himself, on behalf of His friends the monkeys and birds, to cream and butter and other good things. Every one liked Him to do this, yet they felt that it would never do to let Krishna grow up a thief! So the dairy-wives came in a body, and complained to Yasoda. Then Yasoda scolded Him, and at last took her churning-rope to tie the little hands together. But her whole churning-rope was two finger-lengths too short to make a knot about the wrists of her Boy! Then she found another, and tying them together, tried

again, then another, and another, and another.
But it was all to no purpose. All the ropes of
the farmhouse, added to one another, were not
long enough to tie the hands of the Lord of
the Universe. Then a great awe fell upon
Yasoda, and she began to feel the vision of the
Universe stealing over her again. But the Child,
seeing that His mother was tired, hunting here
and there for ropes, and trying to tie His hands,
submitted Himself, and became good, and immediately one rope was found enough with which
to fasten the little wrists.

And so the time passed, till He was seven or
eight years of age. Then the cowherds moved
away from Gokool to the forests of Brindaban.
And Krishna, being now joined by His elder
brother Bolarama, was allowed to go daily to the
pastures with the other lads tending their father's
herds.

Krishna in the Forests

How happy were the years that Krishna and His brother spent in the forests, for the herd-boys and herd-girls of Gokool and Brindaban! To the herd-girls especially,—the Gopis, as they were called,—He was at once play-fellow and pet ; and Indian poetry is full, to this day, of the memory of His pastimes with them, in those beautiful woods and meadows. There, when the trees were covered with blossoms, and the south wind blew, they would put up swings and play at swinging all day long. Or there would be a game at hide-and-seek amongst the cows and buffaloes feeding quietly ; and those who were to be caught would draw attention to their hiding-places, by imitating the cries of peacocks or the quacking of ducks. Sometimes the lads would leap streams with the motions of a frog, or play the game of leap-frog on dry land. Or they would all make a ring about some great tree, and try to capture Krishna, as He darted in and out under their arched arms. Even the grazing animals had a special love for the Lord, and lowed happily, whenever He caressed them, or came near, gathering about Him in a ring, to listen, whenever, — standing with feet crossed beneath the beautiful *kodumbha*-tree,—He played upon His flute.   Some say, indeed, that at such moments the lotus - buds lying on the Jumna waters opened, and the river itself bent out of its straight course.   And it is said that in Brindaban, owing to the presence of the Lord Krishna, the weather never grew too hot, nor did the grass grow thirsty.   It was always cool and fragrant ; the trees were always in blossom ; and a gentle breeze played always upon the foreheads of the cowherds.

One game was played there regularly once a year.   It was a game of triumph over Kansa. For the Tyrant of Mathura had not forgotten his old eagerness to slay the future Avenger of his People, and he continued now and again to despatch his malicious emissaries to Brindaban, there to work the death of the young Krishna. Once he sent Bak-Asur, the great Crane ; and once it was Metrasur, the Demon-Sheep.   It was the death of the latter of these which caused such great rejoicing throughout the whole country-side, that its anniversary has been kept every year, from then till now.

When the spring was at its loveliest, on the eve of the full moon of Phalgun—that most beautiful month of all the twelve—when the fragrance of

mango-blossoms filled the air, and red flowers
covered the asoka-tree, and the long delicate buds
of the leaf-almond were about to burst into tender
green, on this very day, a large ram that had
seemed to be feeding quietly in the meadow, saw
Krishna coming, and, lowering its head, ran
forward to butt Him with its horns. So large
was the animal, and so vicious and determined
his onset, that the Lord must have been killed on
the spot, had He succeeded in touching Him.
But that Divine Intelligence was never baffled.
Even in the height of a frolic, He could not be
found off guard. The young Cowherd waited till
the great sheep had almost reached Him. Then,
seizing him easily by the neck, He swung him
round and round, and finally dashed him against
a tree. Possibly the garments of those standing
near were stained with the blood of the demon, or
it may be that the fury of the hunter came upon
them, and they " blooded " one another. However this was, the night is yearly celebrated,
by burning a rude image of the demon, put
together with sticks and knots of grass. And
water coloured with red powder is taken to
represent the blood of Metrasur, and all the
members of the family receive this, in blessing,
on their heads ; and next day in the streets, it is
thrown by the boys on the garments of passers-
by. Thus is commemorated the rejoicing of the

Gopis over the escape of Krishna from the Demon-Sheep.

Many wonderful tales are told of this time in the life of the youth Krishna. One of these is His Victory over the Snake Kaliya. Another is the story of the Lifting of the Mountain. But most wonderful of all was the love that the Gopis had for Him, as they romped and frolicked and tended the herds in the beautiful forests of Brindaban. It was a love without any selfishness. When Krishna was near, they felt themselves lifted into a golden atmosphere, where all was gaiety and lightness of heart; nothing seemed serious or troublesome; and their happiness bubbled over in the form of gentleness and play. If one were eating some delicious fruit, and suddenly saw the luminous form of Krishna, she would unconsciously offer it, for the next bite, to His lips, instead of to her own.

Yet each was only kinder and more faithful to all others, by reason of this wonderful play. For it is written that the homes of the Gopis never suffered, their husbands and their children never cried on them in vain, they never fled from any duty, in order to indulge in the company of Krishna. And not those of the Gopis only, but also all the humble homes about Brindaban, were made happy by His presence. In truth, Krishna

the Cowherd,—or Hari, as He was called,—was
the Lord Himself, and this love of peasant-folk
for Him was neither more nor less than the love
of human souls for the Divine. None who had
ever sported with Him, or listened to His playing
of the flute beneath the trees, could bear thereafter to leave that Presence. The souls of all
such were bathed in holy peacefulness and joy.
But their hands were rendered only the more
helpful, their hearts more tender, their feet more
eager to run on swift errands of mercy to others,
for the fact that in mind and spirit they knew
themselves to be playing always with the Divine,
in the beautiful form of the Cowherd of Brindaban.

Leader of all the Gopis was Radha, and to her
specially was it given to realise this intensity of
sweetness. Hers was the frank and instant
recognition, the deep understanding, and the
constant vision of His glory. And she it was
who reached the unutterable depths of sorrow,
when the simple joys of that peasant-world could
hold Him no longer, and He left Brindaban for
ever, to return to the life and responsibility of
kings, freeing His people from the Tyrant of
Mathura. Wherefore, because of this wondrous
union between the human soul of Radha and
the Divine in Krishna, all love has come to be
summed up in Their love. And when the Infinite

whispers Its secrets to the finite — as happens sometimes to all of us in loving—the moment is expressed, in Indian poetry, as the speech of Krishna the Cowherd with Radha, leader of the Gopis

The Dilemma of Brahma

A CURIOUS miracle was performed by the Lord Krishna. Having gone to the forest one morning with His companions and their herds, He and they wandered from one beautiful part to another. The sun had not long risen, and the young cowherds were full of happiness. Some played with the dancing shadows, others with the echoes. Some climbed with the monkeys, others stood still like storks or herons, deceiving the very birds themselves, by the perfection of their gestures. Above all, wherever Krishna announced His intention of going, a hundred voices rose in emulation, shouting, "Let me be first ! Let me be first !" Suddenly, the cows began to disappear into the mouth of a great open cave, and the boys, as was their duty, when they came up to it, followed them. Krishna was the last to reach the place, but no sooner had He done so, than He saw that what had seemed like a cavern was nothing of the sort, being in reality the mouth of a great serpent-demon, by whom His friends and their cattle had all been swallowed. He further understood that the great jaws remained still motionless and open, because the real object of the demon was to devour Himself, and thereby avenge the deaths of those whom He had already defeated. The lad stood a moment, wondering what to do. His companions and the herds must be delivered. But how? It was only a moment, and He stepped boldly inside the mouth of the monster, and stood there, in front of its throat. The great teeth made to snap down upon Him, and the muscles hastened as though they would contract. But this was not so easy. By dint of His mysterious power, the Lord of the Universe, calling all His concentration to His aid, began to expand and expand within the serpent's mouth. Taller and taller, larger and larger He grew, and with each accretion of size, the demon became fainter and fainter, and the hopes of His comrades entangled within waxed higher. There He stood in the very mouth of the dragon, and fought for His friends with invisible weapons. The crowning moment came at last. His power reached its zenith. The demon was suddenly disrupted and without strength, and the cowherds with their cows walked back out of the jaws of this living death. And then, before all their eyes, the soul of that evil being arose, and did obeisance to the feet of Krishna, before it passed away, a purified spirit, to the far-off regions of blessedness. For the touch of the Lord ever brought salvation, even though to the body He might mete out death.

Some hours had passed away in this struggle and the consequent rejoicing of the cowherds. Hence, finding a place full of clear sands, near running water, where the black bees hovered over the lotuses, and beautiful birds flew about amongst the branches, and the air was filled with drowsy humming, some one suggested that here they should take their morning meal. The proposal met with acceptance from all, and they sat down on the sands to eat. But, since none could bear to take his eyes off Krishna, the assembly, when it was ranged for eating, looked like a single great lotus, with Him as its centre ; and so seated, using flowers and leaves and pieces of fruit and bark as plates, they all, with much merriment, began to feast.

All unknown to them, they were being watched by the God Brahma, who had seen the miracle of the morning, and was minded to play them a trick. He wanted to find out whether the Boy Krishna, who could do such extraordinary things, was in reality human or divine. He suspected Him of being an Incarnation of the God Vishnu, and intended to put the matter to proof.

When the boys, therefore, sat down to eat the God Brahma quietly drew away their herds of cattle, and shut them up in deep sleep in a mountain cave. The lads looked up suddenly, and saw to their terror that all the cows had disappeared. But Krishna, jumping up, said that He would find them and drive them back, if only the rest would not disturb themselves. He had no sooner left them, however, to seek for the missing cows, than Brahma took all the herd-boys and herd-girls, and throwing them into the same deep sleep, shut them up also, along with their cattle, in the same cave. And Krishna, returning disappointed, could find no one.

A few moments passed in perplexity, and then He who could see all things, determined that this must be some dilemma proposed by the Creator, and resolved on a course of action.

That night the same number of cows and bullocks and calves were driven into the village as had left it for the forest in the morning. The herd-girls, also, and herd-boys went home, all in their own places. But never had the people loved their children and their animals as they now began to do. It was wonderful, this love that was drawn out by the herds and their keepers. Hitherto, people had been tempted to love the Lord Krishna, and even His brother Bolarama, more than their own children. But now, all their hearts were centred in their own homes, and for

M

love of their own children and their own cows, it seemed almost as if they would forget the Lord Himself. In fact, Krishna had made all these out of Himself. All alike were His special manifestation. And He, the Lord, was now present in His own form, in every household and cattle-pen. So matters continued for a whole year.

Now a day of the gods is a year of men, and Brahma, coming at the end of the day, to see what Krishna had done to meet His trick, found, to His amazement, that there were now in the forest as many herds-folk and animals as before. But drawing nearer still, it appeared to Him as if each of these were clothed in the yellow garb, and carried the flute, and wore the circlet with the peacock's feather, just like Krishna. Behind each, moreover, to His piercing sight, shone forth the four arms, with the hands holding discus and mace and conch and lotus. Then was He satisfied that the young Cowherd was indeed the God Vishnu Himself, and when He had worshipped Him, and Krishna had resumed into Himself all these His manifestations, He released from the cave, where He had hidden them, the sleeping herdsmen and women and their cattle. And they awoke, knowing not that even a moment had passed. They found themselves seated at their forest-meal, as they had been when they dis-

appeared.   And   each   remembered   only   the
words that had been on his lips, or the food
that had been in his hands, at the moment
of the vanishing of the cows a whole year
before.

Conquest of the Snake Kaliya

IT happened one morning that Bolarama was unwell, and could not go to the forest with the cows. Now Yasoda in the night had had a dream that Krishna was drowned in the lake Kaliya. She begged Him therefore for that day to stay at home. But His companions were so loth to go without Him, and He pleaded so hard to be allowed to accompany them, that at last her resolution gave way, and she allowed Him to go.

The day was hot, and the cows wandered further afield than usual, and must be followed by the cowherds. Behind all came Krishna, Who had been resting with His friends under a shady banyan tree. In this way they arrived at the shores of a certain great lake, and being thirsty, all alike, save Krishna, Who had not yet reached them, bent down and drank its water. Now the lake was the Lake Kaliya, made venomous by the poison of the hundred-headed snake Kaliya, who dwelt in it, and when Krishna left the banyan's shade and came up to His comrades, they all lay apparently dead on its shores. A few minutes passed, however, and the tears of Krishna brought them all back to life. For His mercy and love could not fail to give life and strength, and He poured them out in abundance over His fainting friends.

Now such was the poison of the Lake Kaliya that nothing could remain alive near its banks. The very birds, as they flew across it, fell down dead. The grass and the plants in its neighbourhood became withered and burnt up. The forest appeared to have retreated from its edge. And the only living thing to be seen was a vigorous *kodumbha* tree, on whose branches an eagle—the Bird of God—had once perched. Even the mist and spray that might rise from the lake had the effect of poison. As Krishna therefore looked on the surrounding desolation, and realised the danger from which His friends had just escaped, His heart grew hot within Him, and the thought arose in His mind that He would rid the world of the poisonous serpent Kaliya, with his hundred heads, and deliver men and animals and plants from his terror. He climbed, therefore, to the top of the *kodumbha* tree, and making His way out to the end of a long branch, He stood there a moment, and then, with a great leap, dived into the lake. His friends the cowherds stood breathless on the shore as He splashed about in the water, striking it with His fists and creating whirlpools, in order to attract the attention of the snake. It was not long before He succeeded, and Kaliya, greatly enraged at this agitation of the waters, raised his terrible cluster of heads to see who it was that troubled his peace. No sooner did he see Him, than with coil after coil of his huge body he wrapped the youthful swimmer round, and drew Him down to the bottom of the lake, there to sting Him to death at leisure. Holding Him thus in his embrace, and darting his heads here and there at the body of Krishna, he gave bite after bite. But a strange thing happened. Instead of entering the flesh of the Cowherd, whatever poison-tooth touched His skin would immediately break!

The minutes as they went by seemed to those on the shore like hours, and still the combatants remained under water, and the Lord had not once appeared to His friends. At the same time terrible omens began to be seen in Brindaban. The rolling of thunder was heard from a clear sky. Meteors were seen, though it was daylight, to shoot across the sky, and people found themselves to be trembling without any cause, as though with fear. Even in the distant pastures, Nanda and the older cowherds noticed these things, and, fearing that some evil had befallen Krishna, began to drive the cows homeward to the village. Then, taking Yasoda and Bolarama,

and following the lads, by means of the foot-
prints of Krishna, they came all together to the
shores of the Lake Kaliya.

Still Krishna was under water, and His friends
and comrades were about to abandon all hope.
Finding things at this pass, Yasoda was eager at
least to follow Him, and was about to throw
herself headlong into the fatal lake. But Bolarama, who had not been in the least discouraged,
implored her to wait, while he asked Krishna to
give them some sign. He was sure that his
Brother would defeat the serpent, and at any rate,
when they should know that it was hopeless, it
would be time enough to take desperate measures.
She consented, and he, climbing the *kodumbha* tree,
and standing on its out-stretching branch, even as
Krishna had done, put his horn to his lips and
sounded a call which would mean to Krishna,
"For the sake of your mother make some sign
that you still live!" Krishna, standing easily in
the coils of the serpent, and allowing him to
exhaust himself in blind and useless anger, heard
the call of the horn, and, as a token that He still
lived, threw His flute out of the lake to the shore.

Alas, the signal had an effect the very opposite
of that intended! All were quite sure that Krishna
would never, while He yet lived, part from His
flute. Despair, therefore, reigned supreme. But
Bolarama again blew upon his horn. "Show us

that you live!" was his message this time, and immediately on the surface of the lake they could see the peacock's feather on Krishna's crown. Again and again they saw it. For He was standing now on the serpent's head. Then He danced lightly on his neck till all the heads, save one, hung broken and powerless, and the great snake Kaliya was to be feared no more.

At this point the wives and children of the serpent lord intervened and ranged themselves before Krishna, begging Him to spare the life of His enemy. They implored Him and worshipped Him, and pleaded so well, that at last He said, "Let it then be even so! Do thou, O Kaliya, with thy one head, depart with all these thy kindred and thy subjects unto the ocean! Thou art banished for ever from this lake, whose sweet waters thou shalt defile no longer. Yet, out of My pity, do I grant thy life!"

Then Kaliya, bruised and trembling, answered, "Alas, O Lord, as I depart unto the ocean, that bird of Thine will see me. And what Thou hast spared he will assuredly destroy!"

Then answered Krishna gently, "Nay, My friend! When the Eagle sees My footprint on thy head he will bid thee go in peace!"

And so the Lord, having conquered the hundred-headed, returned to the shore, and ever after were the waters of that lake sweet as nectar.

But when Yasoda and His friends had embraced and welcomed Him, the day was already far spent, and they saw that if they attempted to return to the village, they would only be overtaken by the darkness on their way. They withdrew with the cows, therefore, within the forest, and determined to spend the night under the banyan tree near by.

Suddenly, as they slept, some one smelt fire, and with cries of " Krishna !" and " Bolarama !" they all woke one another. A terrible forest-fire had broken out, and was coming nearer and nearer, surrounding them on every side. But Krishna stood up in the midst of them smiling, and hushed their terror as if they had been children. Bidding them shut their eyes, and on no account to look at Him, He stood there and drew the fire in with His hands, drinking it up in three great mouthfuls. And none would have known it, but Yasoda, opening her eyes slightly before the time, saw through her eyelashes His last draught. So once more the cowherds slept in peace, and when morning dawned returned to their own village with the herds.

The Lifting of the Mountain

Now it came to pass, year after year, at the end of the hot weather,[1] that the cowherds of Brindaban would offer a great sacrifice to Indra, God of the Sky and King of Deities. And this sacrifice, it was believed, availed to make Him send the yearly rains, and was efficacious also to make Him restrain them, that they should not be sufficient to wash away the forests and make the Jumna overflow her banks. But on a certain year it happened that the Lad Krishna noticed the preparations that were being made for this sacrifice. And His heart was hot within Him, for He was born to put an end to the worship of Indra and the weather-deities, and to establish in its place, faith in Narayan, God Himself, Lord of the souls, not of the fortunes of men. The Youth Krishna therefore reasoned with Nanda, His foster-father, and with the other cowherds, urging them to realise that good harvests or bad came to them out of their own destiny, the fruit of causes long past,

[1] The hot weather in northern India means the months of May and June. In July begin the heavy tropical rains, which last until the beginning of October.

and could not be given or withholden by Indra
or any other of the ancient gods. " Surely, if ye
must worship," He cried, in His earnestness, " it
were better to worship this mountain under whose
shelter we dwell. Let us celebrate a feast in
honour of the forest and the priesthood and the
cows. To do this were indeed well, but to
worship Indra for the sake of harvests is but
childish nonsense and old wives' tales ! " Carried
away by His pleadings, the cowherds placed themselves entirely at his will, and that year's merry-
making was dedicated to the mountain, to which
they owed home and food and all that they en-
joyed.

But not without a struggle would the God Indra
resign His accustomed offerings. None of the
daring words of Krishna were hidden from Him.
He was present at every conference. He heard
the fiery arguments, and He saw the impression
moreover that was made on the minds of the
simple country-folk. Indra knew that if He did
not now defeat the plans of the Lord Krishna,
then were the hearts of the people lost for ever
to Him, and all the shining deities of the sky.
Therefore, to punish the presumption of the cowherds—who had dared, at the bidding of Krishna,
to enter on the rainy season without first making
sacrifices to Him—the God Indra sent down such
rain as had never been seen in Brindaban within

the memory of man. Down, down, down it poured, hour after hour, day after day, without one moment of intermission ; and the river began to overflow, and the trees to be washed away ; and it looked as if the people, and their herds, and their villages would all be lost, nay, as if the very world itself would be drowned in one great flood. But to Krishna all the anger of Indra was a very little thing. When He saw the danger of His people, He simply called them together, and, telling them to bring with them their cattle and their tools, and all their worldly possessions, He lifted up the mountain itself, and, holding it up with a single finger, He made them all take shelter beneath it ! And so He stood, protecting them, seven days and nights, till even the mighty Indra was exhausted and repentant, and ready to offer worship to Him Who was greater than all the ancient gods together. Then all the herdsmen and women came forth once more from their refuge, and the sun shone brightly upon them, and the mountain was restored to its own place, and even the spirit of the Jumna was appeased, and her flow became gentle and untroubled as before. But one by one came the old men and prostrated themselves before Krishna, saying, "Child! In sooth we know not Who You are—but whoever and whatever You be, to You be our salutation ! To You be our worship ! "

The Return to Mathura

ONE by one the seasons had gone by, and Krishna was now close on twelve years of age. One by one He had foiled all the attempts made on His life by Kansa. He had humbled the pride of Indra. He had subdued the snake Kaliya. He had swallowed the forest fire. He had wrestled with a great black bull and slain him. He had defeated every demon sent against Him. And Kansa in Mathura began to think that the time of his own danger was nigh at hand, and it were well that he should take steps to have the Son of Devaki destroyed before his eyes. The emissaries had doubtless been lax. Or they had been taken at a disadvantage in unknown places, or there had been no means of ordering the warfare by the common rules of combat. It was desirable that now all this should be reversed. Let Krishna fight the King's wrestlers in full court. Let the lists, familiar to them, be new to Him. Let the whole assembly look on and see fair play. It would be hard, thought Kansa, if, under all these conditions, he could not compass the defeat and death of the young cowherd. It was therefore

decided that a great sacrifice should be made in
Mathura, with many days' celebration of games
and feasting, and that to this the cowherds should
be bidden, with Nanda, as the King's vassals, and
Krishna and His brother Bolarama as his kinsmen.

The darkness had fallen, and all the evening
tasks were going forward, when the messenger of
the King arrived at Brindaban, carrying the invitation of Kansa to the chieftain Nanda. The cowherds were wanderers by habit, and to them it
was no great undertaking to move from place to
place, milking their cows and making butter and
curds daily on the march. Many times already
had they gone to Mathura to offer the annual
tribute, and they were familiar with the large green
reserves outside the city, which were known as the
king's parks, where they and their herds would
find abundance of room. Long before dawn,
therefore, they had set to work to prepare the gifts
which would be sent out in carts for offering to
the King, and to make themselves and their camp
ready for the removal. But first they sat for
many hours about the newly arrived guest, talking, late into the night, of the childhood and
youth of Krishna and Bolarama, and of the
dreams and thoughts that the face of the Lord
was potent to stir in the hearts of His devotees.
For the messenger of Kansa was an uncle of the
two lads, and he knew and worshipped the divine

character of his nephew. And many felt, as the
embers of the evening cooking-fires died down,
and even the logs that had been set alight afterwards turned to ashes, and the blackness of the
forest became filled with the whispers of night—
many felt in their hearts that the happiness of
those early years was over for them. The great
world without had need of the Lord, and the
hillsides of Brindaban would know Him no more.

Krishna and Bolarama were driven to the city
in state in the chariot of the royal messenger.
But on reaching the gates of Mathura they insisted
on alighting. They would like, they said, to
enjoy the sights of the city in freedom for the
rest of the day, and to spend the night with their
friends from the forests. They would not fail on
the morrow to present themselves at the tournament. Already they were attired in accordance
with their true rank, as young nobles about to be
received for the first time at court. And as they
went about the streets of Mathura, they were
everywhere treated with the respect due to
them. Thus they made their way to the place
which had been prepared for the next day's
spectacle.

All round were ranged the seats and galleries
for different sections of the spectators. One
division had been prepared for the cowherds,
another for the royal clan of the Vrishnis, a

third for the citizens and townsfolk of Mathura, and so on. High at one end of the lists towered the royal seat of Kansa, draped and garlanded and decked with banners and auspicious ornaments. Opposite were the arrangements being made for the public sacrifice. And near to the throne, in a kind of shrine, well guarded, was displayed a sacred object, no other than a great bow, said to be divine, which was regarded as the amulet and talisman of the house of Kansa. Whenever and wherever the King appeared in state, this bow was exhibited beside him, as a perpetual challenge and reminder to all the world, that if any would dispossess him of his crown, they must first bend and break this weapon of the gods. Now the bow was of such strength that no living man could bend it. And none had ever been known even to lift it alone.

None of the guards noticed anything unusual about the two youths who had entered and were strolling about the lists. Crowds were constantly coming and going, inspecting the arrangements for the next day's festivities, and not yet had the Lord signalised Himself by putting forth His divine power. Suddenly, however, before any one could prevent Him, Krishna leapt featly to the royal daïs, and went forward to seize the great bow. The guards threw themselves on Him, to snatch it back, but He lifted it lightly above them, with His left hand only, and withdrawing backwards, stood a moment to string it, and, then—closer and closer He smilingly drew the two great ends, till snap ! went the mighty weapon, even, says the chronicler, as a stick of sugar-cane is broken in two by a maddened elephant.

Rigid with terror, every one had drawn back to see the bowstring drawn, but at the sound of its breaking the whole scene changed. Even Kansa, it is said, in his distant apartments, heard the dread echo, and, guessing its cause, hastened to despatch men to seize Him Who had thus threatened his glory with defeat. But Krishna, armed only with the two fragments of the weapon, drove back all His adversaries. Some He merely repulsed, others He slew. And thus, leaving the shattered talisman behind Him, He returned to the lists by the way He had left them, and, rejoining Bolarama, went quietly out of the hall.

But Kansa lay wakeful through all the hours of that long night, or when he slept was pursued by evil dreams. Every now and then he would see as it were himself, now without a head, and again riddled with holes. It seemed to him, too, as if he walked and left no footprint. He had shivered when he heard the sound of the breaking of the bow ; but afterwards he had spoken of it lightly amongst his friends, as an unfortunate joke played by a couple of strangers. In his secret soul, however, he knew it for the sound of coming doom. He knew that the prophecies of his ancestors were true, and that with the appearance of one who could bend it, the power would depart from him and from his line.

As morning dawned, it appeared to Kansa as if he could hardly wait for the beginning of the tournament that was to decide all. Hastily, he gave orders for the completion of the preparations. The last decorations were added; drums and tabors sounded; the people began to fill their galleries, the royal guests took their places; then Kansa, surrounded by his counsellors, ascended the royal daïs, and took his seat in the very midst of the circle of kings. His appearance was full of splendour, but within, his heart was shaken with anxiety. Then the trumpet sounded the challenge, and the King's wrestlers entered the arena in order, and stood in their places, waiting to see what combatants would offer themselves. Finally, the cowherds entered in procession, headed by Nanda and other chieftains, and, offering the tribute they had brought, at the royal feet, paid public homage, and passed on to the seats arranged for them. And now, at last, all waited together for the appearance of those who might desire to try their skill with the King's fighters. But none knew that at the door by which any such must come in, Kansa had secretly stationed an elephant, who had been goaded into fury till he would rush on those who might seek to enter, and trample them to death.

With dawn that morning Krishna and His brother Bolarama had risen, bathed, and offered worship, and now, hearing the call of the drums and trumpets, they came to the hall of sacrifice to be present at the tournament. As they entered the portals, however, they saw an immense elephant rushing furiously down upon them, goaded by his keeper. Quick as lightning Krishna girded His garments tightly about Him, and stood waiting for the onset. The elephant caught Him with its trunk; but He struck it in the foot and released Himself. For a moment the angry beast lost sight of Him, then it caught Him again, and the same manœuvre was repeated. At this moment, as if the thing were a mere joke, Krishna caught the mighty creature by the tail, and dragged it backwards, as some great bird might drag a snake. Again he darted backwards and forwards, to right and left, following the turns of the infuriated elephant, even as the cowherds of Brindaban would follow the movements of a turning and wheeling calf. Now He faced it and struck it with His hands, and, again running hither and thither, He threw it to the earth with a kick from His foot. The elephant recovered its footing, however, and, again goaded by its keeper, made straight for Krishna. He, seeing now for the first time how overflowing must be the cup of

Kansa's iniquity, to have given such orders for His undoing, muttered, between closed teeth, " Tyrant ! thine end must indeed be near at hand!" and gave Himself finally to the killing of the beast and its keeper.

The great trunk would have wound itself about Him, but He vaulted lightly by its means to the creature's head, and then, placing one foot there, and one on the lower jaw, He forced the mouth open, and, bending down, drew forth its immense tusks, and with these slew both elephant and man. A few minutes later, girded as He had been for the struggle, and bearing the tusks of the creature in His hands, Krishna entered the arena, followed by Bolarama, His brother.

How different were the feelings of those who looked upon Him in that moment ! The soldiers saw in Him, it is said, a mighty general. Women saw a beautiful youth. The people saw simply a great man. Nanda and his subjects saw the beloved Cowherd of Brindaban. Devaki and Vasudeva, from their place near the King's person, saw their Babe of one stormy night twelve years before. Saints saw the Lord Himself appear on earth in human form. And Kansa, on his high seat trembled, for in the beautiful Lad before him, without armour, weapons, or followers, he, seated on his throne and surrounded by his armies, saw only his own destined Destroyer.

In that moment, all that Krishna had already done rose up before the minds of those who looked upon Him. All the fame of the demons He had destroyed, from Putana the Vampire-Nurse to Arishta the great black bull, came before them. The stories of how Indra and Brahma had done Him homage were remembered. And his great labours for the protection of men, the lifting of the mountain, the defeating of the serpent, and a dozen others—were whispered from mouth to mouth. Thus, summing up in that one instant the past and the present, Krishna stood on the threshold of the lists, awaiting the challenge.

Chanura, chief of the King's wrestlers, came forward and sounded it. It was, he announced, the royal command that the two brothers who stood before them should offer an exhibition of the famous wrestling of Brindaban cowherds, and, to gratify their sovereign in this matter, he himself was willing to give them battle.

Now Krishna well understood the trap that was laid for Himself and His brother, in the smooth and honeyed words of the challenge thus delivered. They were to make a spectacular display only, for the amusement of the onlookers, of the strange ways of wrestling in vogue amongst the cowherds. But their adversaries would have secret orders from Kansa, to put forth full strength at some unexpected moment, and kill them both, as if by accident. Instead of giving the counter-challenge direct, therefore, He answered, in the same complimentary style that the wrestler had used, that if the King really wished to see the wrestling of the cowherds, He would prove the fact by giving Himself and His brother, as their antagonists, boys of their own age.

At this Chanura lost all patience. "You say this?" he cried—"You, whose hands but now were wet with the blood of an infuriated elephant, whose strength was as that of a thousand! Your strength is not that of mere lads. You are amongst the most powerful beings in the world!"

All present understood this as a call to mortal combat, and a thrill of horror went round the assembly as they saw the two young men, little used as they must be to the methods of cities, confronted by the skill, strength, and experience of a whole bevy of famous wrestlers of the court. Devaki and Vasudeva, from their places above, made no secret of the terror which the fight inspired in them. Only in the gallery of the cowherds were there seen bright smiles and un-troubled countenances. For there alone were some who could guess the powers of the Divine Wrestlers to foil their combatants.

Chanura and Musthika then addressed them-selves to the fight with Krishna and Bolarama.

Each couple fought by all known modes of combat. Each found in his foe a worthy antagonist. At last Chanura drew back, and then, with arms out and fists clenched, came down with all his strength on Krishna, even as a hawk might swoop down on its prey. But Krishna waited calmly for his blow, and seemed to feel it no more than an elephant when struck by a garland of flowers. Then, at last, He seized Chanura by the arms, and threw him to the ground dead. And the fall of the great wrestler was as the loss of the thunderbolt from the hand of Indra Himself. As for Musthika, Bolarama slew him carelessly, with a blow of his left hand. Another pair of gladiators came forward and offered battle, and again a third, but only to be slain, each in his turn, by his chosen foe. As the third combat ended, however, all the rest of the wrestlers fled, and the cowherds could no longer be restrained. They rose from their places in a body, and, crowding round Krishna and Bolarama, embraced them, amidst mingling of laughter and shouts of triumph, and then all together, with tinkling of their ornaments, began, to the great amusement of the assembly, to dance one of the forest dances !

But the eyes of Kansa had been growing larger and larger with terror, as one by one he had seen his wrestlers slain. At the end of the third combat he had marked the sudden flight of the whole remaining staff of gladiators.   And now the fight, that to him was so serious, was degenerating into a harmless and unseemly revel, with the sympathy of all those around him, whose hearts ought, as he felt, to have been with him !

The King rose to his feet, and, at first choking with rage, but afterwards in clear, loud tones, silenced the trumpets and called to his guards— " Drive out these youths, and arrest and bind the chieftain Nanda, with all his followers !   Let Vasudeva here be slain !   Slay Ugrasena my father and his attendants, and all with them who are the friends of Krishna !   Slay !   Slay ! "

Before the King's orders had been comprehended by any other, almost before he had resumed his seat, Krishna had leapt to the royal daïs—truly, it had been foolhardy, by thus attacking all who were dear to Him, so to provoke the Protector of the Universe !   Seeing Krishna so close, and knowing that the moment long dreaded was come upon him, Kansa rose to his feet and drew his sword.   But the Cowherd grasped him by the hair of his head, and at the touch his crown fell off.   Then down from the daïs jumped the youth, bearing the King with Him, powerless in His grasp. He threw him to the ground in the arena, and a moment later dragged him all round it, even, says the historian, " as a lion might drag a dead elephant," that all his subjects might see that their

King was slain. Meanwhile, the eight younger brothers of Kansa rose in his defence, and would, if they could, have slain Krishna with their own hands. But each, as he threw himself forward, was met by Bolarama with a blow of his club that laid him dead.

Then came a scene of weeping. Even those who had hated Kansa were struck with consternation and pity, and all the royal women came, each to lament at the side of her dead husband. But Krishna and Bolarama went forward quietly to find their parents, Devaki and Vasudeva, and when they had struck off their fetters—still worn at Kansa's orders, though they sat amongst the royal guests—they touched their feet with their heads, as dutiful children. But Devaki and Vasudeva, it is said, recognising these sons of theirs as the Lord Himself, stood before them with folded hands, until there fell upon their minds once more the veil of Maya, and they could forget their greatness, to offer them the love and tenderness of long-lost parents.

Krishna Partha Sarathi, Charioteer of Arjuna

THE Lord Krishna never afterwards returned from Mathura to Brindaban. His life became that of a prince and the adviser of princes, though He never occupied the throne Himself. Henceforth He lived in the palaces and courts and council-chambers of monarchs, and sorrow dwelt eternally in the heart of Radha.

Once more, indeed, or so it is said, was He seen by His peasant friends. For they, unable longer to endure His loss, made pilgrimage to a great sacrifice announced by Him. It was that time of year when crops are harvested, and earth lies fallow for awhile, and men may rest. Then did these simple folk make bold to enter the royal *demesne* and find their Friend. And He, when He heard that they had come and were asking for Him, was glad at heart. With all state and dignity were they brought into the hall of audience, and Krishna, according to the wont of kings, dressed in the robes and jewels of a prince, came there to receive them.

But, strange to say, the country yokels would not look at Him! With eyes cast on the ground, or heads averted, stood these herdsmen and women of Brindaban, uttering not one word, casting not one glance, in the direction of the Prince Who stood before them! Then Krishna understood the desire of their hearts, and going out of their presence for a moment, He put off the robes and jewels of state, and, smiling, came back to them, clad in the simple garments of the cowherds. On His head now was the tiny circlet, with the peacock's feather in the front. In His right hand He carried the flute. And His feet were bare. And when they saw Him in this, the beloved form of earlier days, the hearts of those country-folk were glad. Calling Him again to play upon His flute to them, they romped and played and sang all day with Him amongst the royal gardens, even as of old in the meadows and woods of Brindaban. How they rejoiced in calling to mind the happy past! "Ah!" they would sing, "now we cannot see You, for You are on the elephant. But say, do You remember the grazing of the cows? Now, how can we talk with You, You who wear the diadem? But tell us, what have You to say about your stealing of the butter?" And so in a kind of hide-and-go-seek of happy memories, the hours were passed, and Krishna was once more a peasant amongst peasants. For He, the Lord, is ever the same unto His devotees, and appears unto each one of them in that very form for which His inmost heart cries out.

Those were stirring days in India, and the position of Krishna in the powerful Vrishni State, placed him in the front of affairs. Kings sought His approval and the alliance of His people. He built the splendid city of Dwarka on the sea-coast. His presence was desired at every tournament and assembly. Under his guidance the Vrishnis and their government became one of the most important factors in the life of the period. They grew indeed to such strength that Krishna Himself is said to have seen the grave danger to the national life in the existence of so strong a military class as their nobles formed, and to have sought in His own mind for means of bringing this danger to an end. It was never His way, however, to interfere in affairs, in His own proper person, and in the assertion of His own will. Rather did He look on at the world as if it were all a play which he was watching. Sometimes, at most, He would remove an obstacle, so that the will of the players might have unimpeded scope. In this way He allowed events to work themselves out, striving ever to aid the course of destiny, though this leads in the end to the self-destruction of all things.

These were the days in which the Kurus, and their cousins the Pandavas, strove for the mastery in India. The bitter-minded Duryodhana, under his blind old father, Dritarashtra, strove to make himself suzerain of all India in the capital city of Hastinapura. Unfortunately, however, this meant usurpation of the sovereign rights of his knightly cousins, the five Pandavas, who had been brought up with him and his brothers, as members of the family. Because he wished to be sole monarch, and also because the heroic accomplishments of these knights made him jealous, Duryodhana stooped to engage in many plots against the lives and possessions of the Pandavas. At one time they were compelled to hide, with their mother, in the house of a potter, and it was there that Krishna met the five brothers, and became their friend. The event happened thus.

There was a princess named Draupadi in one of the northern kingdoms, who was famous for her beauty and the greatness of her character. Now when the *swayamvara*, or bridal choice, of Draupadi was proclaimed, and all the illustrious knights in India crowded to the city of her father to compete for her hand, Krishna, who was a near relative, was amongst the kings and princes assembled as guests of the family, to look on at the marriage ceremonies.

Everything was to depend, on this occasion, on

the shooting of an arrow at a given target from a
certain great bow.   Only those who were by birth
eligible for the hand of the princess were allowed
to compete, and the victor was to be proclaimed
the chosen husband of Draupadi.   Amongst the
candidates were many of India's greatest names.
Duryodhana himself was there, eager to win the
bride of that day.   And the penetrating eye of
Krishna, from His place beside Draupadi's father,
detected in the lists five brothers, dressed as
Brahmins, whose bearing was more knightly, and
their build more heroic, than those of any others.
"What should you say," He whispered to the
bride's father, "if yon should prove to be the far-
famed Pandavas, and their Brahmin dress only a
disguise ?"   In good sooth, it was even so, and
one of these brothers it was—Arjuna, the third of
them—who shot his arrow into the centre of the
target, and succeeded in winning the royal bride.
But when the five brothers had taken her to the
potter's house, Krishna and His brother Bolarama
followed them, secretly, in the evening, and ascer-
tained that they were, as He had thought, the
Pandava heroes.   Then He gave them His blessing, saying, "May your prosperity increase, even
as fire hidden in a cave spreads outwards."
And from this time the fortunes of the Pandavas
began once more to grow.

In sooth, it was not strange that Krishna should,

at the first glance, have recognised these heroes. For Arjuna, the third brother, was that soul who had been born for the express purpose of recognising His divinity, and by this fact sharing His glory. One of Arjuna's names was Partha, and Krishna is known, in the south of India, as Partha Sarathi, the Charioteer of Arjuna.

Many times during the ensuing years did these two friends visit one another, now in the forest and again in the palace, and hold deep converse together on matters concerning the soul and God. Deep was the trust of Arjuna in Krishna's insight into those affairs of men and nations through which the higher laws find visible expression. And he, with all his brothers, and Draupadi, and their whole household, worshipped and loved the Lord Krishna, holding Him to be the Saviour of men.

It is told, indeed, of this period in their lives that a certain wicked man was the enemy of the Pandavas, and, in order to obtain power to conquer them, he went and lived for some time on the banks of the Ganges, there offering prayers and great penances to Siva, whose other name is Mahadeva, the Great God. At last the austerities practised by this man became so great and manifold that they could not fail of their accomplishment, and Siva appeared in a vision to His worshipper. "Speak!" commanded He. "Tell

me what is the boon that thou demandest
of Me!"

"Even that in battle I may defeat the five
Pandavas, standing each in his chariot of war!"
answered the man.

But Siva smiled and shook His head. "The
thing that thou askest, O mortal, is impossible.
Listen, and I will tell unto thee," said He, "who
is Arjuna."

And then the Great God revealed to His worshipper the true nature of the hero Arjuna. He
was, He said, the twin soul, Nara, of Krishna, the
incarnation of Narayan Himself. And as to
Krishna, said Mahadeva, "It is even for the destruction of the wicked and for the preservation
of religion that He hath taken His birth among
men in this warrior race. It is no other than
Vishnu the Preserver, Who goeth amongst men
by the name of Krishna. Hear, O thou mortal,
the nature of Him Whom all the worlds worship,
Him whom the learned describe as without beginning and without end, unborn and divine!
They call Him 'Krishna the Unconquerable,
armed with conch-shell, discus, and mace, adorned
with the emblem of a curl of hair, divine, clad in
silken robes of yellow hue, and chief of all those
who are versed in the art of war.' Arjuna the
Pandava is protected by this Krishna. That
glorious being, of the lotus eyes and of infinite

power, that slayer of hostile heroes, riding in the same chariot with Partha, protecteth him. Arjuna, therefore, is invincible. Even the gods could not resist his power." In such words as these did Siva Himself preach the glory of Krishna, Who was the incarnation of Vishnu the Preserver, foretelling the day when He would act on the battlefield as the charioteer of Arjuna and accord to him the divine protection.

At last there came a crisis in the affairs of the country, and between the rival branches of the royal house, and Krishna entered upon that work of restoring the true sovereign and establishing in the land the rule of righteousness, for which He had taken His birth amongst men. He chose the moment of a royal wedding, when the kings of many kingdoms were gathered together, with the Pandavas amongst them, to lay the question of the future before all. The Pandavas had a second time been exiled from their home and kingdom for some thirteen years, in discharge of a gambling debt. But now the thirteen years were ended, and it was time that the restoration of their realm should be made by Duryodhana, in fulfilment of his own promises, publicly given.

So quietly did Krishna state the case of the Pandavas and so much allowance did He make for the errors of Duryodhana, that one of His hearers took up the tale, and restated it on behalf

o

of the Pandavas, at the same time offering his
own alliance, and calling upon his friends to give
theirs also, for the re-establishment of the five
brothers.   Fired by this generous enthusiasm, it
was agreed that Duryodhana should be called
upon to make restitution, but that, if he refused,
the assembled kings should hold themselves in
readiness to form an army, for the purpose of
forcing him to do so.

The organisation of the Pandava army for this
war fell almost entirely into the hands of Krishna.
Yet so modest was His work and so restrained His
methods, that it seemed almost as if plans and
combinations made themselves.   At the very beginning of the preparations, Duryodhana and
Arjuna both went to Him to ask for His alliance,
for Duryodhana also knew His divine character.
On reaching the palace, they were told that He was
asleep.   They went forward, however, and entered
His sleeping-chamber, to await His awakening.
Duryodhana arrived first, and seated himself near
the head of the bed on a fine seat.   Arjuna stood
waiting at the foot, in an attitude of reverence.

When Krishna opened His eyes, His first glance
fell on Arjuna.   Duryodhana then spoke, ex-
pressing his desire for the help of Krishna in
the coming campaign, and adding that, as he
had entered His presence first, it would be fair
to promise it to himself.   Krishna smiled and

answered that in this matter He thought the claims were equal, since He had seen Arjuna first. He added, moreover, that, in matters of choice, it was customary to let the younger choose first. He desired to refuse no prayer that should be made to Him, but in this case He had two alternatives to propose. He could give to one of the combatants, He said, an army consisting of some tens of thousands of soldiers, ready armed and equipped. To the other He could promise only His own presence, unarmed, and resolved not to fight. Then He waited to let each of the two knights decide his own destiny ; for well did He know that one who had been so blinded by wrath and desire as to strive to keep the possessions of another, could not at the same time be so dis-criminating as to choose the Divine Person for his sole strength and stay. Even as He had fore-seen, Arjuna, in the faltering voice of devotion, begged for His presence beside him, as his un-armed charioteer, while Duryodhana was fully satisfied that his prayer had been answered when he received the promise of the services of an army of fighting men.

When the hosts of the Pandavas had been duly organised, when their friends and troops were all enrolled, and their plans made for battle, then Krishna went to the court of the Kurus to try and obtain from them overtures of peace. He failed, however, and thenceforth there was nothing before the country but the dark cloud of war.

On the great plain of Kurukshetra stood the two armies drawn up in order, and facing each other. The Pandavas were ranged under Yudisthira, their monarch, and eldest of the five brothers, over whose head waved the umbrella of pure white and ivory. Next in rank came the gigantic Bhima, whose strength was such that when still a lad he could hold any ten of the Kurus under water at the same time. Third stood Arjuna, the mighty archer, in his chariot of war, with the Divine Krishna as his charioteer ; and this chariot was regarded as the centre of the force, Krishna and Arjuna being its leaders. Fourth and fifth were the royal twins, Nakula and Sahadeva. Each of these princes was surrounded by his own section of the army. His chariot was drawn by two steeds, with flowing mane and tail, and fiery eyes. Over each warrior waved his pennon, carrying his own cognisance—Arjuna's a monkey, another an' elephant rope, a third a lion's tail, and so on. Each had with him his favourite weapons, and carried in his hand the *shank*, or conch-shell, with which to sound the trumpet of battle.

On the opposite side, in the centre of the army, Duryodhana appeared, riding on an elephant, beneath the umbrella of state. At the head of his forces, under a banner bearing the device of a palm-tree, stood Bhishma, their generalissimo, clad in white armour, driven by white horses, and looking, says the ancient chronicler, " like a white mountain." Behind them was Drona with red horses, and the heroic Karna, waiting to succeed to the command on the death of Bhishma.

For this event, Krishna and Arjuna had been born. Battle is terrible, and more terrible than any other is civil warfare. The occasion is great. Thousands of men, of different classes and countries, with their peculiar customs, dress, and armour, are gathered together, all with their attention concentrated on a single object. Music and trumpets and the noises of anger and struggle combine to exalt the spirits of all engaged in combat. The intoxication of victory comes upon men, and they die, in that mood where life and death appear as one. But on the battlefield of Kurukshetra the leaders on either side were the nearest and dearest kindred of those on the other. Bhishma, the Kuru general, was the grandfather of the Pandavas. Drona, the guardian of the forces, was their beloved teacher. On all hands could be seen one and another who in happier days had been friend, comrade, and playfellow. Yet these were the men who must be killed by them. Unless they killed them, there could be no end to the contest. It was well known, for instance, that Bhishma must die by the hand of Arjuna himself, and many similar dooms hung over the heads of different houses. Yet what would be even the empire of Hastinapura, without Bhishma, without Drona, without the hundred sons of Dritarashtra, whose friendship and energy had hitherto made its life and spirit ?

Arjuna had ordered Krishna to drive him into the space between the two armies, that he might survey the field, and there, as he looked for the last time upon all that was splendid and brilliant and still unflawed in the hosts of the enemy, these thoughts of despair came upon him with a rush ; his great bow Gandiva dropped from his hand ; and he sank down spiritless on the floor of his chariot.

Then came an instant which stands alone in history. It lasted only a few minutes. Two armies faced each other, in the second between the sounding of the trumpets and the shooting of the first arrows ; but in that one moment of expectancy the Lord Krishna revealed Himself to the soul of His worshipper, in such a way that he saw his duty clearly ; all hesitation dropped away from him, and springing to his feet fearlessly he sounded the war-cry of the Pandavas, and flung himself upon the fortunes of battle. For to see God is the only thing that can make a man strong to face the world and do his duty.

Even as of old, when the Babe Krishna had

opened His little mouth to cry, and His grieved foster-mother, bending over Him, had seen the great vision of the Universe within His lips, so now again, on the field of battle, He showed to Arjuna His Universal Form.

First in a kind of swift mystic chant came the words, " I am the soul, O Arjuna, seated in the heart of every being. I am the beginning, the middle, and the end of all things. Vishnu amongst the gods am I, amongst lights I am the Sun. I am the mind amongst the senses, the moon amongst the stars. Amongst the waters, I am Ocean himself. Amongst trees the Aswattha [1] tree am I ; amongst weapons the thunderbolt ; and Time amongst events. Of rivers I am the Ganges. Of created things I am the beginning, middle, and end. Time Eternal am I, and the Ordainer with face turned on every side ! Death that seizeth all, and the source of all that is to be. I am the splendour of those that are splendid. I am Victory, I am Exertion, I am the goodness of the good. I am the Rod of those that chastise, and the Policy of them who seek victory. I am Silence amongst things that are secret, and the Knowledge of those possessed of knowledge. That which is the seed of all things, I am that ! Supporting this entire Universe with a portion only of My strength, I stand ! "

[1] An old name for the Bo-tree, *Ficus religiosa.*

The wonderful voice died away and all the senses of Arjuna, smitten as it were for a moment, lay stilled and trembling, realising that, living or dead, all beings were equally one in God, and realising too that even what seemed his own acts were not his own, but the Lord's, done through him. Then he suddenly rose to the height of a great rapture. Before him appeared as heretofore the countless hosts of the Kurus and Pandavas, but he saw all now as a part of Krishna Himself. Each arm, each hand, each weapon, was as an arm, a hand, a weapon of the Divine Charioteer. Multitudinous were the faces and forms that appeared now as His. Fierce and terrible, like the fire that ends the worlds, was the shining energy of His glory. And like moths rushing upon a flame for their own destruction, all living things appeared to be rushing toward Him to be devoured.

But as the mortal gazed upon the great vision, the terror of the sight overwhelmed him. He could bear no more. And he shrank back, crying, "O Thou that art Lord of all the gods, Thou that art the refuge of the Universe, be gracious unto me! Have mercy! Show me once more, I pray, Thy common from!" At these words, like a dream, the mighty splendour passed, and Arjuna, strong and alert, with mind braced, and muscles and nerves made firm as steel, found himself once more with his Charioteer, about to engage in the awful battle of Kurukshetra. But what he had understood in those few seconds, it took all his after-life to express. Nay, when it came to be written down, it took many words. And what was taught in a single flash of insight and knowledge has stood since, through all the ages, as one of the world's Scriptures, under the name of " Bhagavad Gita, the Song of the Blessed One."

The Lament of Gandhari

THE sun itself was pale that rose over the battle-field of Kurukshetra, when the combat was ended. The eighteenth day had seen the slaying of Duryodhana, and the last night of all had witnessed a massacre in the sleeping camp of the Pandavas, wherein children, grandchildren, friends, and confederates of the victors had all alike been put to the sword. To add to the horror of this carnage, it was known that many of the destined victims, wakened from sleep by cries and sounds of struggle coming out of the dark-ness, and believing that an army had taken them by surprise, had struggled to their feet and slain each other. Morning dawned on scenes of deso-lation and despair. True, the Pandava heroes and Krishna stood uninjured and victorious, but about them lay the death of all their hopes. Theirs was henceforth the empire, but without any heir to whom it could be left. The throne was secured to them, but their homes were empty.

Around them on every hand lay the flower of the Indian knighthood, silent for ever. Those who had marched to battle with colours flying, those whose chariots had been foremost, their steeds most spirited, and their trumpets loudest, those whose seats had been veritably on the back of the elephant, lay now on the cold earth, at the mercy of kites and jackals, of vultures and wolves. Even amongst the mighty hosts of Duryodhana, their foe, three officers alone were left alive.

In the distance was seen the woe-stricken procession of the royal women of the Kurus, coming to mourn their dead. And the Pandavas trembled as they gazed at them, for those whose reserve had been hitherto so impenetrable that the gods themselves might scarcely look on them, walked now, absorbed in their great grief, in utter indifference of the public eye. The hundred sons of Dritarashtra all lay dead upon that field.

Somewhat withdrawn from the rest, and made venerable, not only by their rank, but also by their manifold bereavements, their great age, and their blindness, Gandhari the Queen and Dritarashtra the King were seated in their car of state. They were the heads of the defeated house, and heads even, by blood kindred, of the family of the victors. For them, by reason of the respect due to them, the meeting with the Pandavas must necessarily seem more like the submission of Yudisthira than his triumph. To them, therefore, came the young King—Dharmma-Raja, King of Righteousness, as his people called him henceforth—with his four brothers, and Draupadi, and Krishna, and, touching their feet, stood before them in deep silence.

Right queenly was the aged Gandhari in her sorrow. Dritarashtra her husband had been born blind ; but she, out of wifely devotion, of her own accord had darkened her eyes with a bandage, and worn it faithfully all the years of their union. And by this had come to her deep spiritual insight. Her voice was as the voice of fate. That which she had said would happen, could not fail to come to pass. Day after day of the battle, when Duryodhana had come to her in the morning, asking for her blessing that he might return triumphant from that day's fighting, she had said only, "Victory, my son, will follow the Right !" From the beginning she had known that Kurukshetra would see the end of all her house. Even now, such was the sternness of her self-control, her heart was weeping rather for her husband, in his sorrow and desolation, than for her own loss of "a century of sons." And this was the more true, since she knew well that had it not been for Dritarashtra's own weakness and desire, the disaster of this day need never have been theirs. Her own inflexible will had never wavered. Never for one moment had she cast longing glances towards empire, preferring it in her secret heart to righteousness. But this very fact, that her husband was being

crushed, under the doom he had himself brought
down upon himself, was calling out her deepest
tenderness in this sad hour. Proud and stern
to the whole world beside, to him Gandhari was
all a wife, gentle and loving and timid in sight of
his pain. She knew well that from her in these
terrible moments might go out the force that
destroys, and lest she should bring harm thereby
upon Yudisthira as he approached to make salutation, she restrained her powers forcibly, and bent
her eyes downward, within their enfolding bands,
upon his foot ; and immediately, it is said, at that
point where she was looking, a burn appeared, so
terrible was her gaze.

But when she had spoken kindly with Draupadi
and the Queen-mother of the Pandavas, Gandhari
turned away from all others and addressed herself
to Krishna. With Him alone there was no need of
self-control. With Him she might even let the
battlefield, with all its fearful details, rise point by
point before the eyes of her mind. Hand in hand,
as it were, with the Lord, she might gaze on all,
think of all, and tell out her whole heart.

"Behold, O Lotus-Eyed," she cried, "these
daughters of my house ! Widowed of their lords,
with locks unbound, hear Thou their cries of woe!
Brooding over their dead bodies, they call to mind
the faces of the great Bharata chiefs ! Behold
them seeking out their husbands, their sires, their

sons and brothers! The whole field is covered with these childless mothers, and widowed wives, of heroes. Here lie the bodies of great warriors, who in their lifetime were like to blazing fires. Here are scattered their costly gems and golden armour, their ornaments and garlands. The weapons hurled by heroic hands, spiked clubs and swords, and darts of many forms, lie in confusion here, never again to speed forth on dread errands of slaughter. And beasts of prey roam hither and thither at their will, amongst the dead. How terrible, O Krishna, is this battle-field! Beholding these things, O powerful One, I am on fire with grief!

"How empty is now become the Universe! Surely, in this dread contest of Kurus and Pandavas, the elements themselves have been destroyed! Desolate, like ashes of dead fires, lie now those heroes who took the part of Duryodhana in this fray. On the bare earth sleep they who knew all softness. Hymned by the cries of jackals are they whose glory was chanted by the bards. Embracing their weapons, they lie low amidst the dust of battle. And the wailing of women mingles with the roar of hungry beasts, singing them to their rest. What was that destiny, O Krishna, that has pursued us? Whence came this curse that has fallen upon us?" Weeping and lamenting in this fashion, the Kuru queen

suddenly became aware that the dead body of her
son Duryodhana lay before her. This sight was
too much for the doom-smitten woman, and all
her grief burst forth afresh. She remembered her
own terrible blessing, " Victory, O my son, will
follow the Right !" pronounced every morning
over the head of the kneeling prince. She saw now
realised that same vision that had been present
with her daily, since the battle began. All these
days she had been treading a path of anguish
under the shadow of the coming woe. She had
become as it were the companion of judgment and
sorrow, and there was no room for appeal. A
great queen was Gandhari, wife of Dritarashtra,
sovereign of the Kuru clans, yet she was woman
and mother also, and her mourning that was half
wail, half prayer, rose suddenly to a new note.

"Behold, O Krishna !" she said. " Behold my
son, wont in battle to be irresistible, sleeping here
on the bed of heroes ! Terrible are the changes
wrought by Time ! This terror of his foes, who
of old walked foremost amongst crowned persons,
lies now before us in the dust. He for whose
pleasure the fairest of women would vie with one
another, has none now to bear him company save
hungry jackals. He who was proudly encircled
by kings, lies slain now, and encircled by the
vultures.

"Fanned now is he by noisome birds of prey,

with the flapping of their wings. Prince as he was and soldier, my son lies slain by Bhima, even as the elephant may be slain by the lion. Behold Thou him, O Krishna, lying on the bare ground yonder, stained with his own gore, slain in battle by the club of Bhima ! Not long since, beheld I the earth, full of elephants and cattle and horses, ruled by Duryodhana without a rival. To-day do I behold her destitute of creatures, and ruled by another.

"Ah, why breaketh not my heart into a hundred fragments, at the sight of these my beloved slain in battle ? What sin have I and these other weeping daughters of men, committed, that Time should have brought upon us this disaster ?"

Passing then from the contemplation of Duryodhana and the sons of her own household, the mourning chant of the Queen proceeded. Dwelling upon each hero in turn, Gandhari passed the whole history of the battle in review. Again and again, her mind took note of the impossibility of having stayed the great catastrophe at any point. Again and again she dwelt on the inevitableness of fate. Every now and then would her sobs break out afresh, "How early, O Blessed One, how early, have all these my sons been utterly consumed !"

The voice of Gandhari failed and broke, and she ceased for a moment from the wildness of her sorrow. In that moment, all that had happened passed swiftly before her mind. Like one who had risen a step on a mountain side, she saw suddenly also the Pandava bereavement. The battle appeared before her as a play, in which two armies had destroyed each other. Who had been the mover of all these puppets? Who, that could have prevented, had allowed such evil to befall? With one swift glance, Gandhari saw the truth, and, in the thunder-like tones of the prophet, gazing at a vision of far-off doom, with the voice of the judge instead of that of the mourner, she turned slowly round and addressed herself once more to the Lord of All.

" Two armies, O Krishna, have been here consumed. Whilst they thus put an end to each other, why were Thine eyes closed? Thou who couldst have done either well or ill, as pleased Thee, why hast Thou allowed this evil to come upon all? Mine is it then, Thou Wielder of discus and mace, in virtue of the truth and purity of womanhood, to pronounce Thy doom! Thou, O Govinda, because Thou wast indifferent to the Kurus and Pandavas, whilst they killed each other, shalt Thyself become the slayer of Thine own kinsmen. In the thirty-sixth year from now, O slayer of Kansa, having brought about the destruction of Thy sons and kindred, Thou shalt Thyself perish by woeful means, alone in the wilderness. And

P

the women of Thy race, deprived of sons, kindred and friends, shall weep and wail in their desolation, as do now these of the race of Bharata!"

And lo, as Gandhari ended, the Lord looked upon her and smiled! "Blessed be thou, O Gandhari," said He, "in thus aiding Me in the ending of My task. Verily are My people, the Vrishnis, incapable of defeat, therefore must they needs die by the hands of one another. Behold, O mother, I accept thy curse." And all who listened to these words were filled with wonder and fear.

Then the Holy Knight bent down to the aged Queen. "Arise, arise, O Gandhari," He said, "and set not thy heart on grief! By indulging in sorrow man increaseth it two-fold. Bethink thee, O daughter, that the Brahmin woman bears children for the practice of austerities? The cow bringeth forth offspring for the bearing of burdens. The labouring woman addeth by child-bearing to the ranks of the workers. But those of royal blood are destined from their birth to die in battle!"

The Queen listened in silence to the words of Krishna. Only too well did she know their truth. Desolation was spread around and within. Nothing appeared before her save the life of austerity, to be spent in the forest. With vision purified by great events, she looked out upon the world, and found it all unreal. There was nothing further to be said, and she remained silent. Then she and Dritarashtra, together with Yudisthira and the other heroes, restraining that grief which rises from folly, proceeded together to perform the last rites for the dead by the Ganges side.

The Doom of the Vrishnis

MANY years had gone by, and men had almost forgotten the great warfare of their youth, on the Battlefield of Kurukshetra. Under the long reign of Yudisthira, the land had reposed, growing daily in prosperity. And the different peoples, living in different parts of India, looked up to their suzerain and were content. Amongst others none had waxed richer or more powerful than those clans who owned the sway of Ugrasena, King of Mathura, and his powerful Minister Krishna. Their country, from the city of Mathura on the Jumna, to Dwarka—that Krishna had built—on the sea-coast, was filled with abundance of good things. As soldiers and knights the people had come to enjoy life daily more and more. Their cities were beautiful, their mode of living was splendid, they possessed great treasures, and they themselves were fine and strong, and full of health, and love of manly pleasures.

Suddenly, in the midst of all this prosperity, strange rumours began to be whispered about amongst them. Certain great lords of the court were said to have angered three divine sages who

kittens were fathered by dogs, and mice by the
mungoose. Fires, when first lighted, bent their
flames toward the left. Sometimes they threw
out a blaze whose splendour burnt blue and red.
The sun, at his rising and setting over the doomed
city, seemed to be encircled with headless bodies
of men. Those who kept silence, for prayer or
thought, immediately became aware of the heavy
tread about them, of marching hosts, yet never
could they find out what had caused the sound.
The constellations were again and again seen to
be struck by the planets. The wives of Vrishni
heroes dreamt nightly of a witch who came and
snatched from their wrists the auspicious thread.
And the guards of the royal armoury suddenly
discovered that the place where the weapons and
standards of State should be were empty.

Then the Vrishnis, in their fear of what seemed
to be coming upon them, felt the need of
some opportunity for public prayer and penance
for the averting of evil destiny. But Krishna,
pondering alone upon all these portents, understood that the thirty-sixth year was come, and
that the words of Gandhari, burning with grief at
the death of her sons, and deprived as she had
been of all her kinsmen, were about to be fulfilled.
And seeing all things, and understanding that what
was to be would surely come to pass, He did not
attempt to turn aside the course of destiny, but

rather set Himself calmly and cheerfully to make
the path of events easy. He sent heralds therefore throughout the city, to command the Vrishnis
to make a pilgrimage to the sea-coast, there to
bathe in the sacred waters of the Ocean.

The command agreed well with the feeling of
the nobles themselves, that they would do wisely,
as a people, to appoint an occasion of public
devotion and sacrifice, by which to avert the
divine anger threatening them. Preparations were
immediately begun, therefore, for the journey of
the great knights, and all their households and
retainers, to the sea-side. This could not be done
without laying in large supplies of all kinds of
provisions. And now also came the opportunity
to break the command of Ugrasena, and the self-
restraining ordinance of the whole city. Great
stores of wines and spirits were made ready, along
with all kinds of costly meats and other viands,
and the vast procession, with its carriages and
elephants and horses, and its contingents of
servants journeying on foot, was organised for the
march. Little did these turbulent warriors, heads
of powerful houses, and skilled in the wielding of
sword and bow, suspect that their time was come !
Only the Lord Krishna, of infinite energy, knew the
character of the hour and stood unmoved.

The coast was reached, the place of encamp-
ment chosen, and tents were pitched. But then,

instead of worship and fasting, the Vrishnis, impelled by the blindness of fate, entered upon high revels. Wine flowed at every banquet. The field echoed and re-echoed with the blare of trumpets. On every hand were actors and dancers plying their vocations. Plays, tournaments, and feasts followed each other in rapid succession.

A spark will cause a conflagration when the forest is dry. Perhaps it began with a word said in drunken jest. Perhaps it was some indiscreet reminiscence, called up by confused brains. In any case, a terrible quarrel broke out suddenly amongst these banqueters. Anger led to fierce recrimination, and the challenge was followed on every side by blows. In a few brief moments the scene of pleasure had become a field of slaughter. Those of the same blood stood ranged against one another. Son killed sire, in that awful day, and sire killed son. And men whisper to this day of a terrible thunderbolt of iron, seeming as if it were hurled by invisible hands, that worked havoc of death on that dread field. The Vrishnis, having reached the day of their doom, rushed upon death, even as insects rush into the flame. No one amongst them thought of flight. And the Wielder of discus and mace stood calmly in their midst, holding raised in His hand an iron thunderbolt, which He had formed out of a blade of grass.

The sound of the strife died away in silence, for all the clansmen—save one who was sent to call Arjuna from Hastinapura—had been destroyed. Krishna, then, leaving the camp in charge of servants and men-at-arms, and knowing well that the time for His own death had come, returned hastily to the city and called upon His father to assume the direction of affairs, holding the women of the Vrishnis under his protection till the arrival of Arjuna at Dwarka. For Himself, He said, having witnessed again a scene as terrible as the slaughter of the Kurus, and being robbed of His kinsmen, the world had become intolerable to Him, and He should retire to the forest for the life of renunciation. Having so spoken, Krishna touched with His head the feet of Vasudeva, and turned quickly to leave his presence. As he did so, however, a loud wail of sorrow broke from the women and children of His house. Hearing this, the merciful Lord retraced His steps, and, smiling upon them all for the last time, said gently, " Arjuna will come and will be your protector. And all your need shall be met by him." Then He departed from the palace, and made His way to the forest, not to return.

Never again was the Lord Krishna seen of the world He had left behind. Reaching the lowest depths of those wild places, He established Himself there in meditation. Deeply pondered He on all that had passed, grasping in His mind the curse of Gandhari, and the nature of Time and Death. Then did He set Himself towards the restraint of all His senses. Seated firmly beneath a tree, He steadied His own mind upon itself, and drew in all His perceptions, one after another. At last He became all stillness and all silence, reaching the uttermost rest. . . . Then, it is said, that all might be fulfilled, wrapped thus in self-communion as in an impenetrable mantle, Krishna laid Himself down upon the bare earth. Nothing in His whole body was vulnerable save the soles of His feet. And as He lay thus, a fierce huntsman came that way, and mistaking the feet of the Lord for a crouching deer, aimed at them an arrow, which struck Him in the heel.

Coming quickly up to his prey, the huntsman, to his dismay, beheld One dressed in the yellow cloth, and wrapped in meditation ; and he knew Him moreover to be divine, for behind Him he beheld the shining-forth of innumerable arms. Filled with remorse, not untouched with fear, that huntsman fell to the earth and touched the feet of Krishna. And He, the blessed Lord, smiled upon His slayer, and blessed and comforted him. Then, with these words of compassion upon His lips, He ascended upwards, filling the whole sky with His splendour. Reaching the threshold of the divine region, all the gods and their attendants advanced to meet Him, but He, filling all Heaven with His glory, passed through the midst and ascended up into His own inconceivable region. Then did the abodes of blessedness resound with His praises. All the divinities, and the sages, and the celestial hosts, bending before Him in humility, worshipped Him. The gods made salutation, and exalted souls offered worship, to Him Who was Lord of All. Angelic beings attended on Him, singing His praises. And Indra also, the King of Heaven, hymned Him right joyfully.

TALES OF THE DEVOTEES

The Lord Krishna and the Broken Pot

Now, the Lord Krishna was bidden by a certain rich man to a feast. And they set before Him many dishes. But His eye took note of a cup that by chance was blemished, and first this imperfect one He drew to Himself, and out of it began to eat. Which when that rich man saw, he fell at His feet and said, "O Lord, dealest Thou even thus with men? Choosest Thou always the broken vessel first?"

The Lord Krishna and the Lapwing's Nest

IT was the battlefield of Kurukshetra. The white conch-shells were about to sound, the elephants to march forward, and the attack of the archers to commence. The moment was brief and terrible. Banners were flying, and the charioteers preparing for the advance. Suddenly a little lapwing, who had built her nest in the turf of a hillock in the midst of the battlefield, drew the attention of the Lord Krishna by her cries of anxiety and distress for her young. "Poor little mother!" He said tenderly, "let this be thy protection!" and, lifting a great elephant-bell that had fallen near, He placed it over the lapwing's nest. And so, through the eighteen days of raging battle that followed, a lapwing and her nestlings were kept in safety in their nest, by the mercy of the Lord, even in the midst of the raging field of Kurukshetra.

The Story of Prahlad

THERE is a strange old Hindu notion, according to which a very young child is said to be like a fish. Then comes a time when all the baby's eagerness is for food, and his little arms and legs and head are like so many small appendages, almost always kicking. This stage of development suggests the tortoise. Next the baby creeps on all-fours. How like a boar! Then it begins to leap upwards and fall down—half-man, half-lion. After this it becomes a dwarf or little man. At last comes the age of the heroes, Rama and Krishna, who make it possible to be a Buddha. Altogether, Hindus count ten of these degrees, or steps, and call them the ten incarnations of the God Vishnu. Gradually each stage has come to have its own wonder-tale attached to it, and perhaps the story of Prahlad is simply the legend that grew up about the idea of a Man-Lion.

Hiranyakasipu was the king of the Daityas, or demons. Now these demons are the cousins of the Devas or gods, and the two parties are always at war with each other. The gods rule the three worlds,—their own, the upper ; the middle, where men dwell ; and the nether, or abode of the demons. But occasionally the demons gain control, seizing the thrones of the gods and usurping their power. Then the gods have to go to Vishnu the Preserver, and pray to Him to help them out of the difficulty, and sometimes He does it in a very curious way.

In such an epoch, Hiranyakasipu lived and was king. He defeated all the gods, and seated himself on the throne of the three worlds, declaring that nowhere in the universe was there any god but himself, and that both demons and men must worship him alone. Then, in fear of a coming catastrophe, the gods themselves began to walk the earth in the form of men ; and, doubtless, they appealed also to the Lord Vishnu, imploring His aid. In any case, soon after the king's victory, a little son was born to him, in the city of Moultan in the Punjab, and he named him Prahlad.

Curiously enough, with such a father, the little Prahlad proved a very religious child. He seemed to have inborn ideas about worship and about the gods. And his father, who had determined to drive the thought of the deities out of the world, was very much troubled about him. At last he made up his mind to put him into the hands of a very stern teacher, with strict orders that he was never to be allowed to worship any

one but his own father. The teacher, to have
him better under his control, took the prince to
his own home. It was all to no purpose. When
they taught him his alphabet, showing him the
letter *K*, "Yes, that is for Krishna," the child
would reply, and learn it eagerly. *G*, — "For
Gopala," said Prahlad, and everything that they
could teach him, he applied at once in this way.
Not only did he himself talk of nothing but
Krishna; he spent much of his time also in teaching his worship to the boys around him. This
was too much. After struggling in vain to reform
his pupil, the distressed schoolmaster felt that he
must appeal to Hiranyakasipu, or the mischief
would soon spread too far to be set right. The
King's anger was great, and he sent for his son. " I
hear that you have been worshipping Krishna!"
he thundered, when the little boy, who had
been brought away from his books, stood before
the throne. " Yes, father!" said Prahlad bravely,
"I have." " Are you going to promise me that
you will never do it again?" asked the King, and
he looked very terrible, while the royal jewel in
his turban shook with rage.

" No, father, I cannot promise," said poor little
Prahlad.

" You cannot promise!" shouted his father, in
amazement at his daring. " But I can have you
killed!"

"Not unless it is the will of Krishna!" said the child firmly.

"We'll see about that," said Hiranyakasipu. And he ordered his guards to take Prahlad and throw him, though he was his own son, down to the bottom of the ocean, and there pile up rocks on top of him.

He hoped up to the last minute that the little one would be frightened, and run back to give the promise he required. But Prahlad did not come.

The fact was, he was worshipping Krishna in his own heart with such a feeling of love and happiness, that he had scarcely heard his father's words, and did not even notice when they put him on a stone slab, and piled huge blocks up on top of him, and threw the whole great mass out into the ocean.

He never noticed! He had forgotten all about himself. That was the secret of it. But no rocks could keep down one who forgot himself like this. So everything fell aside, and he rose again to the surface of the water. Then Prahlad remembered, and at once he found himself kneeling on the shore, face to face with the Lord Krishna Himself. The Lotus-Eyed smiled gently. Light seemed to be streaming out round Him in all directions. And He put His hand on Prahlad's head to bless Him, saying, "My child, ask of Me what thou wilt!"

"O Lord!" said Prahlad, "I don't want long life, or riches, or anything like that! But do give me a love of God that shall never change in my heart, however much other things may come and go around me ; that in the midst of this change-ful world I may cherish unchanging love, for Thee, O Thou Unchangeable! This alone is my whole wish!"

"Prahlad," said the Lord Krishna solemnly, "you shall be always My soldier and My lover."

Then everything that was beautiful disappeared, for the King's guards had found Prahlad again, and were carrying him once more into his father's presence.

"Who brought you out of the sea?" said the King, scarcely believing his own eyes.

"Krishna," said the child.

"What name dared you to utter?" said his father, growing purple with fury.

"Krishna's," replied Prahlad.

"Where is this Krishna of yours?" asked Hiranyakasipu.

Prahlad's eyes opened wide in wonder. "Why," he said, "He is everywhere!"

"Even in this pillar?" said the king mockingly.

"Yes, even in that pillar!" answered his little son.

The King uttered a loud jarring laugh. "Let Him appear to *me*, then," he cried, "in whatever form and deed best please Him!"

Terrible words ! and wonderful prayer of Hiranyakasipu ! Great beyond that of common men must have been his power, for at this demand, ringing out into the ears of the Lord Himself, the pillar cracked from side to side, and out sprang One, half like a man and half like a lion, who leapt upon him and tore him into pieces !

So the demons were driven out, and the devas took their own places once more. But some say that the soul of Hiranyakasipu was glad of this release. And these hold that he was the same who in some former birth had been Ravana, King of Lanka, and who yet again was to come into the world as Shishupal.

For once upon a time, long before, they say, a great sainted soul had been driven back to birth by some evil fate. But a choice had been offered him. He might pass out of this bondage, it was said, after seven births as the friend of God, or three as His enemy. Without a moment's doubt he chose three births as the enemy, that he might the sooner return to God. Wherefore he became Ravana and Hiranyakasipu, and yet again that Shishupal whose story is still to tell.

The Story of Druwa—A Myth of the Pole Star

THE poetry of the world is full of the similes devised by poets to suggest the midnight sky. The great multitude of the stars shining and quivering, as it were, against the darkness, have been likened to many things—to a swarm of golden bees, to golden apples on a tree, to a golden snowstorm in the sky, to fireflies at evening, holes in a tent-roof, distant lamps moving in the darkness, jewels on a blue banner, and so on, and so forth. But only in India, so far as I know, have they ever been compared to white ants, building up a vast blue anthill!

For the fact that seems most deeply to have impressed the Hindu mind, was not the appearance of the starry dome, so much as the perfect steadiness in it, of the Polar Star. Wonderful star! the only point in all the heavens that stayed unmoved, while round it came and went the busy worlds. And this stillness moreover must have characterised it from the very beginning of things. It was never for the Pole Star to learn its quietude.

It came by no degrees to its proper place. Rather has it been faithful and at rest since the very birth of time. Surely in all the world of men there could be nothing like this, unswerving, unerring from beginning to end, the witness of movement, itself immutable. Unless indeed we might imagine that some child in his heart had found the Goal, and remained thenceforth, silent absorbed and stirless, from eternity to eternity, through all the ages of man.

In India, the mystic land of the lotus, was born the child Druwa. His father was a king, and his mother, Suniti, the chief of all the queens. Yet even on a lot so fortunate as this, may fall the dark shadow of disaster. For long before the birth of Druwa, the son of one of the younger queens had been promised the throne, and the coming of the new child would undo this claim, since the son of the principal queen was undoubtedly the King's true heir. It is easy, therefore, to understand the anger and fear of the lesser wife at the child's birth. She was jealous of the new baby, on behalf of her own son, and did not fail to show her feeling in many ways ; till at last the King, in very anxiety for their safety, ordered his wife and little one to be exiled from the court, and sent them to live in a simple cottage, on the distant edge of a great forest.

It was a humble cottage enough, yet charming

in its own way. It was built of grey mud, and
thatched with brown palm-leaves. In front, there
was a deep verandah covered by the wide eaves ;
and here even a queen could rest, and receive
her village-friends, without a screen, for facing it,
instead of the city, was the impenetrable forest,
whence at night-fall could be heard the roaring of
wild beasts.

More and more, as time went on, did the
occasional visits of holy men, on their way
through the forest to distant shrines, become the
great events of their woodside life. For the hush
of the green woods brought with it healing, and
the thought of God. And a great peace entered
gradually into the heart of Suniti the Queen.
Thus, under her calm influence, the child Druwa
would linger, towards sunset, near the lotus-ponds,
dreaming of the beauty of the great flowers that
rocked to and fro with every movement of the
waters, yielding but untouched. They came by
degrees to mean for him all holiness, all tenderness, all purity, these large pink and white lotuses,
lying against their wide green leaves, as if the
gods had passed that way across the waters, and
left them blossoming in their footsteps. Or he
would lie awake at night, and listen to the sobbing
of the palm-leaves, rustling and swaying in the
darkness, far above him, wondering, wondering,
what was the story they were telling. Or he

would stand quietly, watching the peasants in the rice-fields that stretched to the horizon behind them, sowing the seed, and, when the rains lay deep on the earth, transplanting the crops.

So the years passed, and the brooding silence of nature was all about them. Only in the sad heart of Suniti, all the joy of life was centred in her son.

At last, when Druwa was seven years old, he began to ask about his father. "Could I not go to see him, Mataji, honoured mother?" he said one day.

"Why, yes, my child!" said the poor Queen, full of startled pleasure at the thought, yet so accustomed to sorrow, that she trembled at any change in the even tenor of their life, lest it should end by robbing her of the one thing that was still hers. "Oh yes, thou shalt go, little one, to-morrow!"

And so, the next day, Druwa set out, in the care of a guard, to seek his father, and tell him that he was his son. Beautiful was the road by which they went. High over their heads spread the boughs of the shady trees, and on each side lay the wide fields. Every now and then they would pass a great pond, with its handsome bathing-steps on one side, crowned by an arch, and near by would see the children of the village playing. For each village had its own bathing-pond and its own temple. And in the streets, as they passed through them, it being still early in the morning, they would see the jeweller working over his little stove, the potter turning his wheel, and the cowherds taking the cows to pasture in the distant meadows. Sometimes the child walked, and sometimes he was carried. At last they arrived at the royal gates, and Druwa went in, past the sentinels, and entered the palace itself. On and on he went, till he reached the hall of audience, then he came to the steps of the throne, and there, at last, he saw the King himself. At this point, he ran to his father's arms.

The King was overcome with joy. Not one day had gone by, of all those seven years, without his longing for his wife and son, and here was suddenly the little one himself, come of his own accord, full of love and trust. He felt as if he could never caress him enough, or distinguish him enough, to make up for those long years of neglect.

At this very moment, however, Druwa's stepmother entered the hall. If only this lady had been the Queen, her son would have had the right to be King some day, and she would not have needed to claim the succession for him. But as it was, she could never forget that her rival Suniti was the real Queen, and that Druwa therefore was the rightful heir. And her whole heart was full of jealousy. Now, therefore, her anger knew no bounds. She taunted her husband with the memory of his early promise, and spoke words so wicked about the child on his knee, that in haste he put him down, and turned to plead with her, as if afraid that her evil prayers might come to pass.

But even a child knows that a strong man or woman is the greatest thing in the whole world, and when his father put him away, Druwa felt as if his heart had broken within him, at finding him weak. Silently, all unnoticed, he touched his feet, and kissed the steps of the throne before him. Then he turned, beckoned to his guard, and went.

It seemed a long way home. But at last they reached the doorway, where the Queen had watched hour after hour, not able to rest, in her terrible fear that something might have happened to her boy. The servant disappeared, and the child lifted the long lath-curtain, and bounded into her presence. Ah, how glad she was to see him ! Here, at least, he was at home.

Then they went out into the verandah together, and Druwa began to eat the fruits and cakes that were laid in readiness. While he ate, his graceful young mother watched him anxiously. Yes, it was as she had feared it might be. There was a difference. Something sad had come into the little face, as if in that one short day it had grown much older. And Suniti sighed, for she knew that all the happy years of his childhood were behind them. He would never be her baby any more.

But when he had finished his meal—for to speak while eating would have been grave disrespect!—Druwa told her · exactly what had happened, and the two sat sad and silent for awhile. Then he asked a strange question: "Mother! is there any one in the world who is stronger than my father?"

"Oh yes, my child!" she answered, thinking of the Lord Krishna, and half shocked at Druwa's ignorance, "Oh yes, my child, the Lotus-Eyed!"

The solemn little face grew all eagerness. "And mother, where dwells He?" he asked. "Oh, far far away!" she answered vaguely, and then, seeing that she must give a reply,—"Deep in the heart of the forest, where the tiger lives, and the bear, there dwells the Lotus-Eyed, my son!"

Druwa said little more. A voice seemed to be sounding in his heart. It was so loud that sometimes he wondered if his mother did not hear it. From far far away in the depths of the forest it called, "Come to me! Come to me!" and he knew that it was the voice of the Lotus-Eyed, in Whom was all strength.

About midnight, he could bear it no longer. He rose up from his little bed, and stood over his sleeping mother for a moment. She did not wake. "O Lotus-Eyed, I leave my mother to Thee!" he said in his heart. Then he stole quietly out, and stood on the verandah, looking at the forest.

It was bright moonlight, and the trees cast long black shadows. He had never been allowed to go even a little way into the forest alone, and now he was going down to its very heart. But it must be right, for he could hear the voice calling, "Come to me!" louder than ever. "O Lotus-Eyed, I give myself to Thee!" he said, and stepped off the verandah, and over the grass into the forest.

He was barefooted, but the thorns were nothing. He had been weary, but that was all forgotten. On and on without resting, he went, seeking the Lotus-Eyed.

At last he reached the heart of the forest. Then came one with great fiery eyes, and hot breath, and swinging tail. Druwa did not know who it was. He went up to him eagerly. "Are you the Lotus-Eyed?" he asked. And the Tiger slunk away ashamed. Next came something with heavy footsteps and deep dark fur. "Are you the Lotus-Eyed?" asked Druwa. And the Bear, too, slunk away ashamed. Still the child heard the

voice of the Lotus-Eyed in his heart, saying,
"Come! Come!" And he waited. All at once,
out of the darkness of the forest there appeared
before him a holy man, whose name was Narada,
and he laid his hands on his head, saying "Little
One, you seek the Lotus-Eyed! Let me teach
you the way by which you shall find Him, and
where!"

And then he showed him how to sit down on
the earth, without moving, and to say over and
over again, "Hail, Blessed One, Lord of the
Worlds! Hail!" And he said that if his whole
thought could fasten without wavering, in perfect
steadiness, on the words he spoke, he would find
the Lotus-Eyed, without a doubt.

The boy sank down on the ground, as he was
told, and began to repeat the sacred text. Like a
rock he sat there, moving not a muscle. Even
when the white ants came to build their anthill,
and raised it up around him, he never stirred.
For deep in his own heart Druwa had found the
Lotus-Eyed, and he had come to rest for ever.

So the Pole Star was given him for his home,
and is called to this day Druwa-Lok.

But some say that away beyond it is another,
larger and just as true, and that there Druwa's
mother, Suniti, was placed, that her child might
be always at her feet, and joy be hers, throughout
the countless ages of those stars.

Gopala and the Cowherd

FIRST I must tell you that Gopala had the best mother that ever lived. His father, too, had been a good man. He had not cared about money. All he had wanted was to be good, and read the holy books, learning all the beautiful things he could, and teaching them to other people. The village folk regarded him as their learned man, so they gave him a little field in which he could grow corn, and there was a patch of ground near his house which produced fruit and vegetables, and this had always been enough. When he lay dying he said to his wife, " Beloved, I am not very anxious about you and Gopala. I know that our Lord Himself will take care of you. Besides, the field will bring you corn, and our kind neighbours will dig the garden for you, that you may have food." And the mother said, " Quite right, my husband. Have no care about us. We shall do well." Thus she cheered him, with all her strength, that he might die in peace, fixing all his thought on God.

And when all was over, the neighbours came and carried the dead body away. And they put it on a pile of wood, and set lighted straw to it, and it was burned until only a few ashes were left. Then they took the ashes and threw them into the river, and that was the end of Gopala's father.

So now the child and his mother lived all alone in the forest, and the only thing she was waiting for was the day when she also could die and rejoin her husband. But she wanted to be quite sure of being allowed to go to him. So she said many many prayers, and bathed three times every day, and tried to be hardworking and good. And the neighbours were indeed kind. Her corn was sown and harvested with that of the village, and they came and helped in the gardening, so that there was always food enough.

By-and-by, when Gopala was four or five years old, his mother felt that it was time he went to school. Only before that could happen, he must have new clothes ; and a little mat to carry under his arm, and unroll for a seat at school ; and inside the mat, a number of palm-leaves for a copy-book, and a pen-box with an inkstand in it, and some reed pens. He would not need a slate just yet, for very little boys have sand strewn over the floor, and make their first letters and figures, with their fingers, in that. I wish you could have seen the new clothes he wanted ! Poor little Gopala ! India is such a hot country

R

that two long pieces of cotton are all a little boy needs. One, called the chudder, is thrown over the left shoulder like a kind of shawl. And the other, the dhoti, is folded round him below, and fastened in at the waist. I suppose he would want four of these, two for to-day, and two for to-morrow, when to-day's suit would be washed in the stream.

Of course all these things together cost very little, but to the poor mother it seemed a great deal, and she had to work hard for many days at her spinning-wheel, to earn the money.

At last all was ready, and, carefully choosing a lucky day, she blessed her little son, and stood at the cottage door, watching him go down the forest-path to his first lessons.

As for Gopala, he went on and on. The road seemed very long, and he was beginning to wonder if he had lost his way, when at last the village came in sight, and he could see numbers of other boys going in to school. Then he forgot that he had been a little frightened, and hurried up with the others and presented himself in class.

It was a long and delightful day. Even when lessons were over, there were games with the other boys, and when at last he set out to go home, it was almost dark. It was a long time before Gopala could forget that first walk home through the forest, alone. It grew darker and darker, and he could hear the roars of wild beasts. At last he was so frightened that he did not know what to do, and so began to run and never stopped till he was in his mother's arms.

Next morning he did not want to go to school. "But," said his mother, "you had such a happy day yesterday, my child, and learnt many beautiful things! You said you loved your lessons. Why do you not wish to go to-day?"

"School is all very well, mother," he replied, "but I am afraid to go alone through the forest."

And then he stood there, so ashamed! But how do you think his mother felt? Oh, such a terrible pain came into her heart, because she was too poor to send any one with him to school. It was only for a minute though, and then she remembered the Lord Krishna. She was one of those who worship Him as a young child, almost a baby, and she had called her own little one after Him, for the word Gopala means "Cowherd."

So she told her little boy a story. She said, "You know, my child, there lives in these woods another son of mine Who is also called Gopala. He herds cows in the forest yonder. He is always somewhere, near the path, and if you call out to him, 'Oh, Cowherd Brother, come with me to school!' He will come and take care of you, and then you will not be frightened, will you?"

And Gopala said, "Is it really true that my Brother will come and take care of me?"

And his mother said, "Yes, it is true—just as true as it is that you are God's child, and that He loves you."

"Good-bye, mother," said Gopala; "I love to go to school."

He set out bravely enough, but a little way down the forest path it was rather dark, and he began to feel afraid. He could hear his own heart go pit-a-pat. So he called out, "O Brother Cowherd, Brother Cowherd, come and play with me!"

The bushes first began to rustle, and then parted, and out peeped a boy's head, with a little gold crown on it, and a peacock's feather in the crown. Then a big boy jumped out and took the child's hand, and they played all the way to school.

But when they came near the village, the young Cowherd, telling His little brother to call Him again, on his way home, went back to his cows. There was something so lovely about this boy, He was so full of fun, and yet so kind and gentle and strong, that Gopala grew to love Him as he had never loved any one before.

And as, day after day, he told his mother all about it, words could not express her gratitude. But she was not in the least surprised. It seemed to her quite natural that the Child Krishna should comfort a mother's heart.

So time went on. And then something happened. The schoolmaster announced that he must give a feast—a wedding-party, or something of the kind.

Now people in India practically never pay a schoolmaster for keeping a school. It is quite easy for him, all the same, to obtain food. For his field, like the widow's, is part of the village-lot, and the villagers plant and dig for him also.

But on a special occasion, such as the present, when it becomes known to his pupils that he must provide a feast, each boy will go home to his parents and say, " My noble teacher "—for so the master is called—" my noble teacher is about to give a party. What gifts can I take to him ? "

Then some mothers will set to work and cook quantities of sweetmeats, cakes, and puddings; some will prepare great trays of fruit ; one will buy beautiful silk cloth for him and his wife to wear at time of worship, and others will send cotton and muslin for daily clothing. In this way the school-master and his wife are amply provided for.

And now, like others of course, Gopala said to his mother that night, " Mother, to-morrow is our noble teacher's party. What can I take to him ? "

Again her child's words made the poor mother

very sad for a moment. She knew that she was not rich enough to give her little boy anything for his master. But it was only a moment, and she brightened up again, for she thought of the Child Krishna, and knew that He would help them.

"I cannot give you anything to take to your teacher, but ask your Brother in the forest for something as you go to school in the morning," she said.

So in the morning Gopala and the Shepherd Boy played all the way to school ; but just as He was leaving, Gopala said to him, "O Brother, I almost forgot. Will you give me something for my teacher to-day? He is going to have a party."

"What can I give you? What am I but a poor Cowherd? Oh, but I know"——and away He ran for a moment, and came back with a little bowl of sour milk. In India they eat the thick part of sour milk, and call it curds. And He said, "That is all I can give you, Gopala. It is only a poor Cowherd's offering. But give it to your teacher."

Gopala thought it was a beautiful present, the more so because it came from his woodland friend. So he hastened to the master's house, and stood eagerly waiting behind a crowd of boys, all handing over what they had brought. Many and varied were the offerings, and none thought even of noticing the gift of the fatherless child.

This neglect was disheartening, and tears stood in the eyes of Gopala, when, by a sudden stroke of fortune, his teacher chanced to look at him. He took the tiny pot of curd from his hands, and went to empty it into a larger vessel, but, to his wonder, the pot filled up again. Again he poured, again the little pot was full. And so he went on, while it filled faster than he could empty it. Then the master gave them all curds to eat, and went on pouring and pouring. Still the little cup was full. Every one said, "What does this mean?" And Gopala, as much astonished as the rest, understood for the first time Who his Brother in the forest was. Never till this moment had he even guessed that the Child Krishna Himself had come to play with him. So when the master turned to him with the question, "Where did you get this curd?" it was very reverently that he answered, "I got it in the forest, from my Brother, the Cowherd."

"Who is He?"

"One who comes and plays with me on my way to school," said Gopala. "He wears a crown on His head, with a peacock's feather in it, and carries a flute in His hand. When I reach school He goes back and tends His cows, and when I am going home He comes again to play with me."

"Can you show me your Brother in the forest?"

"If you come, Sir, I can call."

So hand in hand the master and Gopala went along the path together. At the usual place the child called, "Cowherd Brother! Brother Cowherd! Won't you come?" But no voice answered. Gopala did not know what to do, and he saw a look of doubt on his teacher's face, so he cried once more, "O Brother Cowherd, if you do not come, they will think I do not tell the truth!"

Then came a voice, as if from far away within the forest, "Nay, little one, I cannot show My face. Thy master still has long to wait. Few sons indeed are blest with mothers like to thine!"

A CYCLE OF GREAT KINGS

The Story of Shibi Rana ; or, The Eagle and the Dove

THERE was a certain king whose name was Shibi Rana, and his power was so great, and grew so rapidly, that the gods in high heaven began to tremble, lest he should take their kingdoms away from them. Then they thought of a stratagem by which to test his self-control, and humble him by proving his weakness. For in the eyes of the gods only that man is invincible who is perfectly master of himself.

One day, as Shibi Rana sat on his throne in his pillared hall, with the open courtyard and its gardens and fountains stretching far before, there appeared high up in the air, flying straight towards him, a white dove, pursued by an eagle, who was evidently trying to kill it. Fast as the dove flew in its terror, the eagle flew faster. But just as it was on the point of being captured, the smaller bird reached the throne of Shibi Rana ; the King opened his robe, and without a moment's hesitation it fluttered in, and nestled, panting and trembling, against his heart.

Then the eagle's flight came to a stop before the throne, and his whole form seemed so to blaze with anger, that every one trembled except the monarch, and no one felt the slightest surprise at hearing him speak.

"Surrender my prey!" he commanded in a loud voice, facing the King.

"Nay," said Shibi Rana quietly; "the dove has taken refuge with me, and I shall not betray its trust."

"This, then, is your vaunted mercy?" sneered the eagle. "The dove that you have sheltered was to have been my food. Show your power by protecting it, and you starve me. Is such your intention?"

"Not at all," said the King; "in fact, I will give you in its place an equal quantity of any other food you choose."

"Of any other food?" said the eagle mockingly. "But suppose I asked for your own flesh?"

"My own flesh should be given," said Shibi Rana firmly.

A harsh laugh sounded through the hall, startling those who were standing about the throne; but when they looked again at the face of the bird, his eye was steady and piercing as before.

"Then I require," said he, speaking slowly and deliberately, "that this dove be weighed in the balances against an equal weight of the King's flesh."

" It shall be done," said Shibi Rana motioning for the scales.

" Stay ! " said the eagle. " The flesh must be cut from the right side of the body only."

" That is easily granted," said the King with a smile.

" And your wife and son must be present at the sacrifice ! "

" Bring the Queen and my son into our presence," said the King to an officer.

So the witnesses took their places, the balances were brought, and the dove was placed on one side, while the executioner prepared to carry out the horrible order. As he proceeded, however, it was found, to the dismay of the whole court, that with each addition of the King's flesh the dove grew heavier, and the weights of the two could not be made equal.

Then at last, from the left eye of Shibi Rana there fell a single tear.

" Stop ! " thundered the eagle, " I want no unwilling sacrifice. Your tears destroy the value of your gift."

" Nay, my friend," said the King gently, turning on the eagle a face radiant with joy—" nay, my friend, you are mistaken ; it is only that the left side weeps, because, on behalf of the weak and unprotected, it is given to the right of the King alone to suffer ! "

At these words, startling all who heard them, the forms of the eagle and the dove were seen to have vanished, and in their place stood Indra, the Chief of the Gods, and Agni, the God of Fire.

And the voice of Indra was hushed with reverence as he said, "Against greatness like that of Shibi Rana, the gods themselves shall struggle but in vain. Blessed be thou, O King, Protector of the Unprotected, who burnest with the joy of sacrifice ! For to such souls must the very gods do homage, yielding to them a place above themselves."

Bharata

ONCE upon a time, in those bright ages when India was young, there lived a great king, Bharata, and so famous was he that even now the people speak of their country amongst themselves as Bharat Varsha, or Bharata's Land ; and it is only foreigners who talk of it as " India."

In the days of this ruler, it was considered the right thing for every man, when he had finished educating his family—when his daughters were all married, his business affairs in order, and his sons well-established in life—to say farewell to the world and retire to the forest, there to give the remainder of his life to prayer and the thought of God. This was considered to be the duty of all, whatever their station in life, priest and merchant, king and labourer, all alike.

And so in the course of events the great King Bharata, type of the true Hindu sovereign, gave up his wealth and power and withdrew. His family and people woke up one morning, and he was gone. That was all. But every one understood that it meant that he had passed out of the city during the night in the garb of a beggar, and the news spread through the country that his son was king. Just as the water of a lake closes over a stone thrown into it, and leaves no trace, so society went on its usual course, and the loss of Bharata made no mark.

And he made his way to the forests and plunged into meditation. He had had enough of riches and dignity. So they were easy to give up. He thought that he wanted nothing more that the world could give, save only peace.

But one day, as he sat under a great tree, repeating the name of God, a mother deer with her little one came down to the stream close by to drink. Just at that moment a lion roared in the forest, and the poor mother, startled, tried to jump the stream, carrying her fawn. But the shock had been too much for her. As she reached the opposite bank she died, and her babe slipped back into the river, and was carried down by the current. Bharata, the hermit, saw the whole occurrence, and, full of mercy to all living things, broke through his devotions to run and save the fawn. He waded into the stream, and catching it in his arms, bore it into his hut and lighted a fire, by whose warmth he fondled it back to life. Alas, this beautiful deed became the saint's stumbling-block! For all his hope grew to be centred on this foster-child, and he who could give up crown and kingdom and money, like so much dross, forgot God for a baby deer! When night drew on and his whole mind should have been concentrated in meditation, he would be wondering why his little one had not come home, and agonising lest some tiger had eaten it.

So, when the time came for him to die, it was on the tearful eyes of the fawn that his eyes looked, and of his love for it that he thought last, instead of thinking of God.

Now we know that the last thought of the dying determines his next life. We begin again just where we left off. Naturally, therefore, in his next birth, Bharata himself became a deer.

But his prayers and devotion also could not fail to bear their fruit. So this deer remembered all that had happened to him in the past, though he had not the gift of speech. Therefore he wandered always near the hermitages, ate the remains of the offerings whenever he had a chance, and listened to the readings of the sacred texts. In this way he exhausted the results of his sin, and was born once more in a human body.

This time he was the son of a Brahmin, which was a great advantage. For the Brahmin caste is the highest and most religious amongst the Hindus. Hence in it the greatest amount of bathing is done ; the greatest pains are taken that food shall be clean and simple, and of the proper kinds ; and

S

every man has a right to learn Sanskrit, and read the holy books.

But Bharata had forgotten nothing of his last two lives, and this time he determined to finish the struggle, and rid himself of this bondage of birth. For we must always remember that in the Indian religion these bodies of ours are held to be prisons, where we are subject to many tortures, to pain and need, and separation from those we love. And the great object of the struggle of life is to be free, and reach the place where we may chose what we shall do, whether to come back into them or not. This was what Bharata wanted, so he made up his mind that in this birth he would be quite silent, and dwell upon God in his heart, thus avoiding all temptation to further sin. And this vow he kept. Only he spoke once, and this was how it happened :—

He was supposed by his family to be dumb and an idiot. It did not occur to any one then that he ought to marry. So when his father died his brothers divided the property amongst themselves, and regarding him as good for nothing they divided his share also, and allowed him to make himself useful, and live upon their charity. During the day, the wives of his brothers would use him in lifting and carrying, and he would perform patiently whatever labour was imposed on him. Sometimes they would be angry, and then he would go out and sit under a tree, waiting till their anger had cooled. One day this had happened as usual, and Bharata had withdrawn, when a royal palankeen came in sight, borne by three coolies instead of four. Seeing this strong-looking fellow—whom they soon discovered to be dumb—seated by the roadside, the bearers insisted on putting down their burden till he had been forced to join them. Now the occupant of the palankeen was a king, who was proud of his learning, and he looked out and commanded the Brahmin to help in carrying him. Perhaps that one glance was enough to show Bharata that he had a message to that soul. He jumped up, took one pole of the chair, and began to walk. But he was curiously unsteady! Hop! jump! jolt! he went; jolt! jump! hop! It was terrible to be carried in this way. For Bharata was full of mercy to every living thing, and he had to move aside for each ant and beetle and worm, lest his foot should kill it. At last the King put out his head. "Art thou too weary, O boor, to walk straight?" he said. "If so, put down thy burden and rest once more." His new servant looked at him, smiling, and spoke for the first time in his life, and his voice was as sweet as liquid honey, and his words were as the words of kings—

"Whom, O Friend, do you address as 'thou'? And whom do you call by the name of 'boor'?

Is there anything in the whole world that is not yourself? And to that Self can there be either weariness or rest?" Such a light of greatness beamed about the man, that all who heard were overawed, and the King got out of the palankeen and prostrated himself, putting the dust of his feet on his own head.

"What, O Mighty One, art thou?" he said. And sitting down by the roadside, Bharata instructed him for many hours, till the desire for freedom was lighted also in the King's heart, and he never rested till he had given up his kingdom and become a wanderer. But the Brahmin went back to his own people, and never spoke again. And when at last there came to him the hour of death, then was he indeed free. Bharata endured the bondage of re-birth no more.

The Judgment-Seat of Vikramaditya

FOR many centuries in Indian history there was no city so famous as the city of Ujjain. It was always renowned as the seat of learning. Here lived at one time the poet Kalidas, one of the supreme poets of the world, fit to be named with Homer and Dante and Shakespeare. And here worked and visited, only a hundred and fifty years ago, an Indian king, who was also a great and learned astronomer, the greatest of his day, Rajah Jey Singh of Jeypore. So one can see what a great love all who care for India must feel for the ancient city of Ujjain.

But deep in the hearts of the Indian people, one name is held even dearer than those I have mentioned — the name of Vikramaditya, who became King of Malwa, it is said, in the year 57 before Christ. How many, many years ago must that be ! But so clearly is he remembered, that to this day when a Hindu wants to write a letter, after putting something religious at the top —"The Name of the Lord," or "Call on the Lord," or something of the sort—and after writing his address, as we all do in beginning a letter,

when he states the *date*, he would not say, " of the
year of the Lord 1900," for instance, meaning
1900 years after Christ, as we might, but he
would say " of the year 1957 of *the Era of
Vikramaditya.*" [1] So we can judge for ourselves
whether that name is ever likely to be forgotten
in India. Now who was this Vikramaditya,
and why was he so loved? The whole of that
secret, after so long a time, we can scarcely hope
to recover. He was like our King Arthur, or like
Alfred the Great—so strong and true and gentle
that the men of his own day almost worshipped
him, and those of all after times were obliged to
give him the first place, though they had never
looked in his face, nor appealed to his great and
tender heart—simply because they could see that
never king had been loved like this king. But one
thing we do know about Vikramaditya. It is told
of him that he was the greatest judge in history.

Never was he deceived. Never did he punish
the wrong man. The guilty trembled when they
came before him, for they knew that his eyes
would look straight into their guilt. And those
who had difficult questions to ask, and wanted
to know the truth, were thankful to be allowed to
come, for they knew that their King would never
rest till he understood the matter, and that then
he would give an answer that would convince all.

[1] The name of this era is *Samvat*.

And so, in after time in India, when any judge pronounced sentence with great skill, it would be said of him, " Ah, he must have sat in the judgment-seat of Vikramaditya ! " And this was the habit of speech of the whole country. Yet in Ujjain itself, the poor people forgot that the heaped-up ruins a few miles away had been his palace, and only the rich and learned, and the wise men who lived in kings' courts, remembered.

The story I am about to tell you happened long, long ago ; but yet there had been time for the old palace and fortress of Ujjain to fall into ruins, and for the sand to be heaped up over them, covering the blocks of stone, and bits of old wall, often with grass and dust, and even trees. There had been time, too, for the people to forget.

In those days, the people of the villages, as they do still, used to send their cows out to the wild land to graze.

Early in the morning they would go, in the care of the shepherds, and not return till evening, close on dusk. How I wish I could show you that coming and going of the Indian cows !

Such gentle little creatures they are, with such large wise eyes, and a great hump between their shoulders ! And they are not timid or wild, like our cattle. For in India, amongst the Hindus, every one loves them. They are very useful and precious in that hot, dry country, and no one is allowed to tease or frighten them. Instead of that, the little girls come at daybreak and pet them, giving them food and hanging necklaces of flowers about their necks, saying poetry to them, and even strewing flowers before their feet! And the cows, for their part, seem to feel as if they belonged to the family, just as our cats and dogs do.

If they live in the country, they delight in being taken out to feed on the grass in the daytime ; but of course some one must go with them, to frighten off wild beasts, and to see that they do not stray too far. They wear little tinkling bells, that ring as they move their heads, saying, " Here ! here ! " And when it is time to go home to the village for the night, what a pretty sight they make !

One cowherd stands and calls at the edge of the pasture and another goes around behind the cattle, to drive them towards him, and so they come quietly forward from here and there, sometimes breaking down the brushwood in their path. And when the herdsmen are sure that all are safe, they turn homewards—one leading in front, one bringing up the rear, and the cows making a long procession between them. As they go they kick up the dust along the sun-baked path, till at last they seem to be moving through a cloud, with the last rays of the sunset touching it. And so the

Indian people call twilight, cowdust, "the hour of cowdust." It is a very peaceful, a very lovely moment. All about the village can be heard the sound of the children playing. The men are seated, talking, round the foot of some old tree, and the women are gossiping or praying in their houses.

To-morrow, before dawn, all will be up and hard at work again, but this is the time of rest and joy.

Such was the life of the shepherd boys in the villages about Ujjain. There were many of them, and in the long days on the pastures they had plenty of time for fun. One day they found a playground. Oh, how delightful it was! The ground under the trees was rough and uneven. Here and there the end of a great stone peeped out, and many of these stones were beautifully carven. In the middle was a green mound, looking just like a judge's seat.

One of the boys thought so at least, and he ran forward with a whoop and seated himself on it. "I say, boys," he cried, "I'll be judge and you can all bring cases before me, and we'll have trials!" Then he straightened his face, and became very grave, to act the part of judge.

The others saw the fun at once, and, whispering amongst themselves, quickly made up some quarrel, and appeared before him, saying very humbly,

"May your worship be pleased to settle between my neighbour and me which is in the right?" Then they stated the case, one saying that a certain field was his, another that it was not, and so on.

But now a strange thing made itself felt. When the judge had sat down on the mound, he was just a common boy. But when he had heard the question, even to the eyes of the frolicsome lads, he seemed quite different. He was now full of gravity, and, instead of answering in fun, he took the case seriously, and gave an answer which in that particular case was perhaps the wisest that man had ever heard.

The boys were a little frightened. For though they could not appreciate the judgment, yet his tone and manner were strange and impressive. Still they thought it was fun, and went away again, and, with a good deal more whispering, concocted another case. Once more they put it to their judge, and once more he gave a reply, as it were out of the depth of a long experience, with incontrovertible wisdom. And this went on for hours and hours, he sitting on the judge's seat, listening to the questions propounded by the others, and always pronouncing sentence with the same wonderful gravity and power. Till at last it was time to take the cows home, and then he jumped down from his place, and was just like any other cowherd.

The boys could never forget that day, and whenever they heard of any perplexing dispute they would set this boy on the mound, and put it to him. And always the same thing happened. The spirit of knowledge and justice would come to him, and he would show them the truth. But when he came down from his seat, he would be no different from other boys.

Gradually the news of this spread through the country-side, and grown-up men and women from all the villages about that part would bring their lawsuits to be decided in the court of the herd-boys on the grass under the green trees. And always they received a judgment that both sides understood, and went away satisfied. So all the disputes in that neighbourhood were settled.

Now Ujjain had long ceased to be a capital, and the King now lived very far away, hence it was some time before he heard the story. At last, however, it came to his ears. " Why," he said, " that boy must have sat on the Judgment-Seat of Vikramaditya ! " He spoke without thinking, but all around him were learned men, who knew the chronicles. They looked at one another. " The King speaks truth," they said ; " the ruins in yonder meadows were once Vikramaditya's palace ! "

Now this sovereign had long desired to be possessed with the spirit of law and justice. Every day brought its problems and difficulties to him, and he often felt weak and ignorant in deciding matters that needed wisdom and strength. " If sitting on the mound brings it to the shepherd boy," he thought, " let us dig deep and find the Judgment-Seat. I shall put it in the chief place in my hall of audience, and on it I shall sit to hear all cases. Then the spirit of Vikramaditya will descend on me also, and I shall always be a just judge ! "

So men with spades and tools came to disturb the ancient peace of the pastures, and the grassy knoll where the boys had played was overturned. All about the spot were now heaps of earth and broken wood and upturned sod. And the cows had to be driven further afield. But the heart of the boy who had been judge was sorrowful, as if the very home of his soul were being taken away from him.

At last the labourers came on something. They uncovered it — a slab of black marble, supported on the hands and outspread wings of twenty-five stone angels, with their faces turned outwards as if for flight—surely the Judgment-Seat of Vikramaditya.

With great rejoicing it was brought to the city, and the King himself stood by while it was put in the chief place in the hall of justice. Then the nation was ordered to observe three days of prayer and fasting, for on the fourth day the King would ascend the new throne publicly, and judge justly amongst the people.

At last the great morning arrived, and crowds assembled to see the Taking of the Seat. Pacing through the long hall came the judges and priests of the kingdom, followed by the sovereign. Then, as they reached the Throne of Judgment, they parted into two lines, and he walked up the middle, prostrated himself before it, and went close up to the marble slab.

When he had done this, however, and was just about to sit down, one of the twenty-five stone angels began to speak. "Stop!" it said: "Thinkest thou that thou art worthy to sit on the Judgment-Seat of Vikramaditya? Hast thou never desired to bear rule over kingdoms that were not thine own?" And the countenance of the stone angel was full of sorrow.

At these words the King felt as if a light had blazed up within him, and shown him a long array of tyrannical wishes. He knew that his own life was unjust. After a long pause he spoke. "No," he said, "I am *not* worthy."

"Fast and pray yet three days," said the angel, "that thou mayest purify thy will, and make good thy right to seat thyself thereon." And with these words it spread its wings and flew away.

And when the King lifted up his face, the place of the speaker was empty, and only twenty-four figures supported the marble slab.

And so there was another three days of royal retreat, and he prepared himself with prayer and with fasting to come again and essay to sit on the Judgment-Seat of Vikramaditya.

But this time it was even as before. Another stone angel addressed him, and asked him a question which was yet more searching. " Hast thou *never*," it said, " coveted the riches of another ? "

And when at last he spoke and said, " Yea, I have done this thing ; I am not worthy to sit on the Judgment-Seat of Vikramaditya ! " the angel commanded him to fast and pray yet another three days, and spread its wings and flew away into the blue.

At last four times twenty-four days had gone, and still three more days of fasting, and it was now the hundredth day. Only one angel was left supporting the marble slab, and the King drew near with great confidence, for to-day he felt sure of being allowed to take his place.

But as he drew near and prostrated, the last angel spoke : " Art thou, then, perfectly pure in heart, O King ? " it said. " Is thy will like unto that of a little child ? If so, thou art indeed worthy to sit on this seat ! "

"No," said the King, speaking very slowly, and once more searching his own conscience, as the judge examines the prisoner at the bar, but with great sadness ; "no, I am not worthy."

And at these words the angel flew up into the air, bearing the slab upon his head, so that never since that day has it been seen upon the earth.

But when the King came to himself and was alone, pondering over the matter, he saw that the last angel had explained the mystery. Only he who was pure in heart, like a little child, could be perfectly just. That was why the shepherd boy in the forest could sit where no king in the world might come, on the Judgment-Seat of Vikramaditya.

Prithi Rai, Last of the Hindu Knights

(THE INDIAN ROMEO AND JULIET)

Now in the days of the old Hindu knighthood of India, there were four great cities where strong kings lived, who claimed that between them they ruled the whole of the country. And some of these cities you can find on the map quite easily, for three of them at least are there to this day. They were Delhi, Ajmere, Guzerat, and Kanauj, and one of them, Guzerat, is now known as Ahmedabad.

The King who sat on the throne of Delhi was the very flower of Hindu knights. Young, handsome, and courageous, a fearless horseman and a brave fighter, all the painters in India painted the portrait, and all the minstrels sang the praises, of Prithi Rai ; but loudest of all sang his own dear friend, Chand, the court-bard of Delhi.

Prithi Rai's life had not been all play by any means. His duty, as a king, was greater than that of other knights, since he had of course to defend his people. And already he had had

to fight great battles. For across the border
lived a Saracen people under a chief called
Mahmoud of Ghazni, and six times this chieftain
had invaded India, and six times Prithi Rai
had met and overcome him. Only, fighting as
a good knight should, for glory and not for
greed, each time he had conquered him he had
also set him free, and Mahmoud had gone home
again. And the last of these battles had been
fought at Thaneswar, where the Afghan was badly
wounded.

Just at this time, it very unfortunately happened
that the King of Ajmere died, and left no son or
grandson to succeed him. But he had had a
daughter who had married the King of Delhi,
and Prithi Rai was her son. So, as the old
man had no son's son to leave his throne to,
it seemed natural enough to leave it to his
daughter's son, Prithi Rai, who thus became King
of Delhi and Ajmere, and in this way the most
powerful monarch in India. But this made one
man very angry. The King of Kanauj claimed
that *he* ought to have had Ajmere, for he had been
married to a sister of the old King. Probably he
had always been jealous of Prithi Rai, but now he
began to hate him with his whole heart.

In all countries always it has been believed
that the bravest knight should wed the fairest
lady. Now in the India of that day it was

T

accepted on all hands that Prithi Rai was the bravest knight, but, alas, every one also knew that the most beautiful princess in the world was the daughter of Kanauj! She was tall, graceful, and lovely. Her long, thick hair was black, with a blue light on it, and her large eyes were like the black bee moving in the petals of the white lotus. Moreover, it was said that the maiden was as high-souled and heroic as she was beautiful.

So Prithi Rai, King of Delhi, determined to win Sanjogata, Princess of Kanauj and daughter of his mortal foe, for his own. How was it to be done?

First he went to his old nurse who had brought him up. He prostrated himself before her and touched her feet, calling her "Mother," and she, with a smile, first put her fingers under his chin, and then kissed her own hand. For so mothers and children salute each other in India. Then the King sat down on the floor before her, and told her all that was in his heart.

She listened, and sat without speaking for a few minutes when he had finished. "Well," she said, after a while, "give me only your portrait. I shall send you hers. And I can promise you, that when you win your way to the girl's side, you will find her just as determined as yourself, to marry no one but you."

That evening the old nurse left Delhi with a

party of merchants bound for another of the royal cities. And in her baggage, unknown to her humble fellow-travellers, was a tiny portrait on ivory of the King. It was a week or two afterwards, that the ladies of the King's household, at Kanauj, took an old woman into their service who claimed that she had been born at the court of Ajmere, and had waited, in her childhood, on the late Queen of Kanauj. This old lady soon grew specially fond of the Princess, and was gradually allowed to devote herself to her. In the long, hot hours she would sit fanning and chatting with her, or she would prepare the bath, with its scents and unguents, and herself brush the soles of Sanjogata's feet with vermilion paint. Or at night, when the heat made it difficult to sleep, she would steal into some marble pavilion on the roof, and coax the Princess to come out there into the starlight, while she would crouch by her side, with the peacock's fan, and tell her tales of Delhi, and of Prithi Rai, and his love for her. And often they gazed together at a miniature, which had been sent, said the old woman, by her hand, to ask if the Princess would deign to accept it. For as we all have guessed, of course, it was the old nurse of Prithi Rai's mother, and of Prithi Rai himself, who was here, serving the maiden whom he hoped to make his bride.

In a few months, came the time when the King

of Kanauj must announce his daughter's marriage. And he determined to call a *swayamvara*, that is, a gathering of princes and nobles, amongst whom the princess might come and choose her husband. She would carry a necklace of flowers in her hand, and heralds would go before. At each candidate's throne as they came to it, the praises of that prince, and all his great deeds in battle and tournament, would be declared by the heralds. Then the Princess would pause a moment, and if she decided that this was the knight whom she desired to choose for her husband, she would signify the fact by throwing her garland round his neck. And then the *swayamvara* would turn into a wedding, and all the rival princes would take their places as guests. This was a ceremony only used for a royal maiden, and naturally no one was ever asked whom it would not be desirable for her to choose.

In this case, invitations were sent to the kings and princes of all the kingdoms, save only of Delhi, and all India knew that the most beautiful princess in the world was about to hold her *swayamvara*.

This was the time for Prithi Rai to act. So he and his friend Chand, the court-bard, disguised themselves as minstrels, and rode all the way to Kanauj, determined to be present at the *swayamvara*, whatever it might cost.

At last the great day dawned, and Sanjogata made ready for the bridal choice. Very sad at heart was she, for she knew not what the day might bring forth, only she was sure that of her own free will she would marry none but Prithi Rai, and he had not even been asked to the ceremony.

The insult thus done to the knight of whom she dreamed, burned like fire in the heart of the Princess, and she wondered contemptuously which of the princes whom she would meet in the hall of choice, could dare to stand before the absent King of Delhi on the field of battle. And something of her father's own pride and courage rose in her against her father himself, as the hour drew near for the *swayamvara* to open. Yet behind all this lay the dull misery of the question, What could she possibly do to announce her silent choice in the absence of the hero ? A princess might choose amongst those present, but to speak the name of one who was absent would be a fall unheard of from the royal dignity ! How the brow of the Rajput maiden throbbed as they bound on it the gold fillets of her marriage-day ! How the wrists burned, on which they fastened the bridal ornaments ! And the feet and ankles, loaded with their tiny golden bells, which would tinkle as their owner walked, like " running water " in the bed of the streamlet, how glad they would have been to carry Sanjogata away into seclusion, where she might do anything rather than face the ordeal before her !

At last, however, the dreaded hour had come. Seated on thrones in the hall of choice, the long array of knights and princes held their breath as they caught the first distant sounds of the blare of trumpets preceding the princess. Nearer and nearer came the heralds, and so silent was the company that presently, underneath all the noise and clang of the procession without, could be heard distinctly, throughout the great hall, the tinkle of anklets, and they knew that the queen of that bridal day was approaching.

As for Sanjogata herself, as with slow footsteps and bent head she paced along the pathway from the castle to the doorway of the hall, she saw no one amongst the many thousands, on foot and on horseback, beside the path. Had she but once looked up, the whole scene would have been changed for her, and in a moment she might have made her choice. But this was not to be. Lower and lower bent the head of the royal maiden beneath her long rich veil. Tighter and tighter were clasped the hands that with their firm hold on the marriage-garland, hung down before her. And slower and slower were the footsteps with which she drew near to the hall of choice, till she had reached the door itself. But there the proud daughter of kings raised her head high,

to lower it never again. For one moment she
paused, startled, dismayed, incredulous, and then,
with flushed cheeks and haughty air, drawing
herself up to her full height, she entered the
hall of choice with perfect calm. For here at
the entrance to the pavilion stood a grotesque
wooden figure of the King of Delhi, made to
stand like a doorkeeper, to wait at the marriage
of the chosen knight. At first Sanjogata could
not believe her own eyes. The image was
hideous, mean, and dwarfish, but it was un-
mistakably intended for Prithi Rai. Had it not
been insult enough to the gallant knight that his
name had been omitted from the list of guests,
that Kanauj should add to this the madness of
mockery? Yet so it was. And as soon as she
had realised it, the daughter of the King knew also
her own part in the day's great ceremonies, and
whatever might be the outcome for herself, she
would play it to the end. The princes rose to
their feet as the veiled maiden entered, and then
sat down once more on their various thrones.
The heralds fell back at the entrance, making
room now for the Princess to precede them. And
then, with slow firm steps, she, whose each footfall was music, passed on from throne to throne,
waiting quietly for the questioning cry of her own
heralds, and the answering salutation of those
about the enthroned prince, before she could

listen to the tale of brave deeds by which each
bard sought to glorify his own master in the eyes
of the fair lady. But at each throne, after
patiently listening, after giving every opportunity
to its adherents to urge their utmost, the veiled
Princess paused a moment and passed on. And
something in her bearing of quiet disdain told each
whom she left behind her, that she required more
of the knight she would choose than he had yet
attained. But the sadness of disappointment gave
place to astonishment, as Sanjogata drew near to
the last throne, and stood listening as patiently
and as haughtily as ever. This prince, as all
thought, she must perforce accept. Round his
neck she must throw the marriage-garland. With
veil knotted to his cloak, she must at his side step
forward to the sacred fire. These things she must
do, for now there was no alternative. Yet none
of these things did the daughter of the King
attempt. Her slender form looked right queenly,
and even beneath her veil her courage and
triumph were plain to be seen as she turned her
back on the whole assembly, as if to pass out of
the hall of choice, and then stood a moment in
the open doorway, and—threw the garland round
the neck of the caricature of Prithi Rai!

Her father, seated at the end of the hall, high
above the guests, sprang to his feet with a
muttered oath! From the marriage-bower to

the darkness of the dungeon, was this the choice
that his daughter would make ? What else could
she mean by such a defiance ? But scarcely had
he strode a foot's length from his place when a
tall horseman from amongst the crowd was seen to
stoop down over the form of the Princess, and,
lifting her to his saddle, gallop off out of sight,
followed by another. For Prithi Rai and his
friend Chand had not failed to be present at
Sanjogata's *swayamvara*, knowing well that though
the King of Delhi was not amongst the guests, yet
no other than he to whom her heart was given
would be chosen by the peerless daughter of
Kanauj.

And then the festive hall became the scene of
a council of war. The King of Kanauj swore a
mighty oath that to the enemies of Delhi he would
henceforth prove a friend. The outraged princes
added their promises to his, and runners were sent
across the border with letters to Mahmoud of
Ghazni, offering him the alliance of Kanauj in his
warfare against Prithi Rai. The day that had
dawned so brightly went down in darkness
amidst mutterings of the coming storm. For
the wedding day of Sanjogata was to prove the
end of all the ages of the Hindu knighthood.

A year had passed. To Prithi Rai and his
bride it had passed like a dream. Amongst the

gardens and pavilions of the palace they had
wandered hand in hand. And Prithi Rai, lost
in his happiness, had forgotten, as it seemed,
the habits of the soldier. Nor did Sanjogata
remember the wariness and alertness that are
proper to great kings. It was like a cup of rich
wine drunk before death. Yet were these two
right royal souls, and knew well how to meet the
end. Suddenly broke the storm of war. Suddenly came the call to meet Mahmoud of Ghazni
on the field of action. And then, without a tear,
did Sanjogata fasten her husband's armour, and
buckle on his sword, and kiss the royal jewel that
she was to place in the front of his helmet. And
while the battle raged around the standard of
Delhi, she waited, cold and collected in the palace.
What had she to fear? The funeral fire stood
ready, if the worst news should come. Not for
her to see the downfall of her country. Was she
not the daughter and the wife of kings?

Hours passed away, and ever on and farther
onwards rolled the tide of battle—on one side
the infuriated Kanauj, fighting by the side of the
alien in faith and race, and on the other Prithi
Rai with his faithful troops. Splendidly fought
the adherents of the King of Delhi. But in the
end the advantage of numbers prevailed, and
Prithi Rai fell, pierced to the heart, at the foot of
his own banner.

It was dark when they brought the news to Sanjogata, waiting in the shadows of the palace. But red grew the night with the funeral fire, when she had heard. For her eye brightened when they told her, and her lips smiled. "Then must I haste to my lord where he awaits me," said this Rajput queen gaily, and with the words she sprang into the flames.

So passed away the old Hindu kings and queens of Delhi, and all things were changed in India, and Mohammedan sovereigns reigned in their stead.

A CYCLE FROM THE
MAHABHARATA

The Story of Bhishma and the Great War

FOR sixty miles outside "the rose-red walls" of modern Delhi, the plain is strewn with ruins. Broken columns and huge masses of masonry lie there, as if they had been tossed about by giants in their play. Here and there is some stone pillar or other monument of special importance. Such is the marble - screened enclosure where a gentle Moslem princess sleeps her last sleep, amidst the bright sunlight and the chasing shadows. Such is the lofty pillar of Asoka, with its inscription, and such is the old walled town of Indraprastha, three or four miles from the gates of the present fortress.

It is a strange old place. The few inhabitants of to-day live, something like the cream in a bowl of milk, in a top layer of streets and houses. The cottage-yard in which one watches rice parching, or clothes being hung out to dry, is made on the roof of an older dwelling, and that perhaps on another. So that after one has rambled awhile through Indraprastha it becomes easy to believe that the city is ancient, and even to imagine that it may first have been built by King Yudisthira, four or five thousand years ago.

For that is the claim,—that Indraprastha was first built before the Great War broke out, by the Pandava heroes, Yudisthira and his four brothers, and that it was their capital until the day when all their enemies were slain, and they went in state to Hastinapura, near the modern Meerut, to reign as sovereigns over the whole country.

What a district it is! Rome, with all her ruins, is not so old, nor so imposing. From Thaneswar, fifty miles to the west of Delhi, to Meerut, thirty miles to the north, the whole country is covered with the remains of ancient buildings, and the memories of ancient war. Many times has the supremacy of India been decided on this spot, once by Yudisthira, in the battle of Kurukshetra, again by Prithi Rai and Mahmoud of Ghazni, and many times since then, even down to the other day.

But it is far away from these last, back into the twilight of time, that we wish to go—back as far as those early days of the Pandava knights, and their cousins the Kurus, when the country was known as " Maha Bharata," Great India, because she was the mother of heroes, and their deeds were the deeds of the great. In those days, the chief of both clans alike was Bhishma, " the

Grandsire," as he was called, and he was equally
loved and respected by all. He was not the King,
but, greater still, the maker and director of kings, and
amidst all the events of that stirring time his form
looms large on his great battle-charger, like that of
some mystic Arthur of an earlier age. Bhishma was
not the King, but he had been born to the throne,
and of his own free-will had given up his right.

It had happened in this wise. When he was still
young, having been brought up in great splendour,
as the only son, and heir-apparent, of Shantanu the
King, a strange thing befell. His father, the sovereign
of the country, fell in love with a beautiful maiden,
who was nothing but a fisherman's daughter !

This fisherman, however, was very fine and
proud, and would not hear of his daughter
marrying out of her proper rank. If she did
this, he said, it would only be to bring un-
deserved humiliation upon herself.   It was true
that she would live for the rest of her life in a
palace, but in that palace who would she be ?
None would look upon her as the Queen, for no
son of hers would ever be considered fit to inherit
the throne. Only if her son could be made crown-
prince, instead of Bhishma, would he consent to
her wedding the King. This meant that the fisherman could not take the proposal seriously. So
strong were all men, in the days of the heroes !

Of course the condition named was out of the

question, and as soon as King Shantanu understood that the girl's father really meant what he
said, he withdrew his suit. But it was impossible
to forget the beautiful maiden herself, and every
one saw that the King was sad at heart. Even
the Prince began to notice it, and to inquire the
reason why, and after a while he found some
member of the court to tell him the story.
How unexpected was the result! No sooner
did Bhishma understand the cause of his father's
sorrow, than he called for his chariot, and set out
to visit the house of the fisherman. On arriving
there, he inquired carefully whether there were
not some reason for the refusal of marriage,
other than that which had been assigned. But
the fisherman assured him that there was not.
If it had been possible to make his daughter the
mother of future kings, he would by no means
have objected to her entering the royal household.

"Then," said the Prince, "the matter should be
easily settled, for I am perfectly willing to give up
all right to the throne, in favour of the children of
your daughter Satyâki."

"Ah, Sir," said the fisherman, "it is easy for
you to promise, and easy for *you* to keep! I
believe in your good-will. But you will marry
some day, and what about your sons? *They*
will not be willing to forego a crown, simply
because such was your intention!"

The Prince saw the truth of these words, and quietly determining that his father's happiness was dearer to him than all the world besides, he made up his mind to another great vow. "I promise you," he said, "that I shall never marry. So I can never have a child to lay claim to the succession. And now, will you allow me to take your daughter to my father?"

The fisher-maiden was led forth veiled, and the Prince saluted her as his mother, and placed her in his own chariot. Then, taking the place of the charioteer, he gathered up the reins, and drove straight to the doorway of the palace.

Shantanu could hardly believe his eyes, when the bride that he had desired was led before him, by the son for whose sake he had silently renounced her. But when he understood how and why she had come, he felt a sudden awe of the selflessness of his own child, and named him for the first time "Bhishma, the Terrible," blessing him with a wonderful blessing. "Go forth, my son," said the King, "knowing that as long as thou shalt desire to live, none can ever endanger thy life. Death himself shall never be able to approach thee, without first obtaining thine own consent." The blessing of father or mother always creates destiny, and long, long afterwards Bhishma, on his lonely death-bed beside the lake of

Kurukshetra, was to prove the truth of the King's words.

From this time on the life of the Prince was half that of a monk. Full of knightly deeds he was, but, like some great knight-templar, no act was performed for his own benefit, but always for the safety of his order or the commonwealth. It was his part to crown kings and then serve them, protecting their kingdoms for them. Satyâki the Queen had two sons, but one died young, in the early years of her widowhood, and it seemed as if the royal line might become extinct. With tears, then, she, now the Queen-mother, but once a simple fisher-maiden, implored Bhishma the Prince to marry, releasing him over and over again from his promise.

But nothing would induce him to break his vow. Instead, he went, like a monk clad in armour, to the *swayamvara* of the princesses of a neighbouring kingdom, and challenged all the other guests to fight. Then he won each duel in turn, and ended by carrying off the three daughters of the King, to be the wives of Satyâki's son. With breathless pride and admiration had the royal maidens watched the prowess of the strange knight. His strength was indeed terrible. Every antagonist went down before him. And his armour shone in the sunlight with gold and jewels. But the eldest of the three sisters turned pale, as one after another each combatant was beaten, and it became evident that they were to have no choice at all at their *swayamvara*.

.   .   .   .   .   .

At last they all set out for Hastinapura, and the warrior, who at the tournament had been invincible in his might, came riding beside their litters, and chatting gaily with them through the curtains. So gentle and so courtly was he in his bearing, that presently, with many blushes and some sighs, the eldest princess turned to speak with him of a secret sorrow. She and a certain king had long, she said, felt love for one another, and had secretly plighted their word to choose and be chosen at the bridal feast. But now the strong arm that had won them all, to be the brides of Hastinapura, was parting her and her betrothed for ever.

The knightly Bhishma did all he could to offer comfort to the poor bride, and secretly sent messengers to summon her lover to the court. So, a few days later, when the wedding was commencing and brides and bridegroom were bidden to take their first look at each other, for the lucky moment was come, it was only the two younger sisters, who, opening their eyes shyly, found the King of Hastinapura before them. But, alas, the affianced husband of the eldest princess was not there, as Bhishma had hoped and striven to have him. For he regarded his betrothed as now wedded to another, and refused to come and take her to himself. And she, poor lady, feeling unspeakably dishonoured by this refusal, but unable to be angry with the prince whose name she loved, prayed earnestly to the gods to let her, girl as she was, become a knight, that she might some day meet Bhishma face to face on the field of battle, and bring about his death. And her prayer was granted. And so, from this day onwards, the dark shadow of destiny lay ever across the path of the great and knightly warrior, and the footsteps of death were never far off from him.

Now the young King of Hastinapura lived happily with his two queens for seven years. Then he died, and they were left widows. But they had three sons — Dritarashtra the Blind, Pandu the Pale, and Vidura the Just. So once more Bhishma was left with the education of princes who were not his sons, and the care of a kingdom that was not his own, upon his hands. He found wives for Dritarashtra and for Pandu, and bestowed the royal domains on them.

It is told of Gandhari, the princess of Gandhara, or Afghanistan,[1] bride of the blind King Dritarashtra, that, when she heard of his infirmity, she bound her own eyes also with many folds of cloth, and vowed to remain thus sightless through-

---

[1] Gandhara was a country bordering on, and in part including Afghanistan.

out her life.   For she could not bear to enjoy the light from which her husband was shut out.

The wife of Pandu the Pale was known as Pritha or Kunti, and she became the mother of the five Pandavas, as they were called, Yudisthira, Bhima, Arjuna, and the twins Nakula and Sahadeva. Every one loved these boys, for they were full of great qualities, and the heart of Bhishma was glad, for he saw that Yudisthira, the eldest of all the princes, had in him the making of a perfect king.   Prince Pandu, the father, died suddenly in the forest, and Dritarashtra declared that the young Yudisthira should be regarded henceforth as the heir to both kingdoms.

But, alas, amongst the two families of Pandavas and Kurus, that called Bhishma Grandsire, there was one false heart—that of Duryodhana, head of the Kurus and eldest of the hundred and one children of Dritarashtra the King!

All the princely cousins had grown up side by side ; they had had the same lessons ; they had played together.   But the strength of Bhima, second of the Pandavas, was so great that, un-aided, he could hold any ten of the Kurus under water at the same time.   This of itself angered Duryodhana, and he could obtain no redress, for Bhima always won the victory again.   But it was not only Bhima.   The young Yudisthira was specially beloved for his gentleness and heroic

uprightness, and Arjuna threw himself with such
devotion into every task that he was the most
skilful archer of them all, and the favourite of
their tutor, Drona, the Brahmin.

Perhaps it was natural that the young chief of
the Kurus should be made jealous by all this
brilliance. But it was not knightly. Duryodhana,
indeed, had courage and skill and princely daring,
but not the sunny temper and generous heart of
the true knight. There was a vein of treachery
and skilful cunning in him, and he was too
remorseless an enemy to be a perfect friend.

Long, long afterwards, when Bhishma lay dying,
and when all his life was passing in review before
him, as it does before the eyes of dying men, he
could look back on the youth of these children of his
house, and trace clearly the growth of the hatred that
had led to the Great War. Every year of Duryodhana's life had added to its bitterness, and he had
been unscrupulous in striving to satisfy his enmity.

Once he had tried to poison Bhima, and had
almost succeeded, but the Prince had recovered,
after eight days of a deathlike swoon. Again, he
had formed a dastardly plot to entrap the Pandavas
and their mother into a lonely house and set it on
fire. This conspiracy also had seemed to succeed,
yet by the warning of Vidura, their uncle, the
little company had escaped and taken shelter in
the cottage of a village potter.

It was at this very time, when all things were against them, that the real greatness ot these princes had been proved.   For they had attended the *swayamvara* of the daughter of Drupada, King of Panchala, and, beggars as they seemed, had carried off the Princess, in face of all the splendour and wealth of India's sovereigns.

The bride, Draupadi, proved, as does always the perfect wife, to be the good star of the house into which she had thus entered.   Amongst other things, at the bridal tournament itself, they had for the first time become aware of one whom to know and love was like winning the vision of the Holy Grail.

High up amongst the royal guests, beside His Uncle, the King of the Vrishnis, stood a form, dark almost as the midnight sky, and clad in yellow. It was the Lord Krishna—the Holy Knight.   And He, looking down upon the five brothers, was not deceived by their humble garb, but knew at once who and what they were.

Above all, He saw in Arjuna that one soul destined to behold the wondrous vision of Himself as the Universal Form.   Already there sounded in His ears the words of the hymn of adoration, that would be associated with his name through all ages.

" Hail to Thee ! hail ! a thousand times, hail ! and again and again, hail to Thee ! " Arjuna would sing, in the midst of illumination on the battlefield.   " Victory to thee in the east, and victory in the west! Victory through all the Universe be Thine! For infinite in power, and infinite in will, pervading all, Thou art the All." And then, faltering with excess of memory, the chant would tremble and change, and the worshipper would cry—"What in the past I have ignorantly uttered, from irreverence or from love, calling upon Thee as 'O Krishna! O Yadava! O Beloved!' looking upon Thee merely as a mortal friend, unlightened of this, Thy divine greatness, all such I implore Thee, O Ineffable, to forgive!" . . .

And Krishna, to whom past, present, and future were all alike an open book, threw the mantle of his friendship over the Pandava heroes, from this first hour of Draupadi's *swayamvara*. All these things passed before the eyes of the dying grandsire, like a play seen in a dream.

Shielded by the relationship now existing between Draupadi's kindred and themselves, and protected by their alliance with Krishna, the powerful minister of the Vrishni State, Yudisthira and his brothers had next proceeded to resume their name and dignities. Then the news had been carried to Hastinapura, that they still lived, and Bhishma himself, full of thankfulness that the stain of the blood-guilt was wiped off his nephew's name, had insisted on Dritarashtra's recalling the Pandavas, and assigning to them half the kingdom.

Those were the days of the building of Indra-

prastha—for that part of the realm that was
given to Yudisthira was wild and covered with
jungle, lying towards the Jumna. Yet such were
the patience and industry of the young heroes,
and such the skill of the eldest in good government, that it was not long before they had erected
this mighty city, with foundations so deep, that
ages would pass and leave the walls still standing ;
with fortifications so strong that armies would
never be able to destroy it ; and with a site so
well chosen that over it, or some city near by,
should always float the standard of India's rulers.
All these things did Bhishma remember.

And when they were well established in their
new capital, the Pandavas had laid all the surrounding kings under tribute, and proclaimed the
Royal Sacrifice, where fealty should be sworn.
And Bhishma smiled, as the imperial pageant
passed before his eyes.

But the splendours of Indraprastha, and the
proud ceremonies of the Homage of Vassals, had
inflicted countless new wounds on the jealous
heart of Duryodhana, so that he determined in
his wrath to compass the ruin of his cousins.
And the cheeks of the dying chieftain were
crimsoned with shame and sorrow, as he remembered how the son of Dritarashtra had consulted eagerly with the false-hearted and cowardly
as to the method of his treachery. At last a

brother of Gandhari the Queen, suggested that he should challenge Yudisthira to a game of dice with himself, he being skilful at play—and that the Kuru dice should be loaded, that he might lead the Pandavas to the loss of all their possessions under the semblance of a game. It was well known that the young Emperor loved gambling, though he showed little skill, and that a formal challenge to throw for the stakes was deemed by him as sacred as the call to battle.

The message was duly issued and received, and the Pandava heroes, with Draupadi, set out for Hastinapura, to play the fatal game. For a moment, Yudisthira was startled, to find, on his arrival, that Duryodhana himself would not be his antagonist. Then he recalled the form of the challenge, and realising that honour demanded acceptance of any odds, he staked and threw. Staked, threw, and lost, alas! Again he tried, with larger risks. Then the fever of the gamester came upon him. It never occurred to him that the play was false. Again and again he threw, always with odds increased—and always the game went against him. till in one short hour he who had entered Hastinapura as Overlord of all India, stood beggared and a bondsman, beside four brothers, who, with his wife, were all alike the slaves of Duryodhana.

It was now that the first of the Kurus committed his most unknightly deed. A younger

brother was sent to the Queen's apartments, to
bring Draupadi into the presence of the gamblers.
Insulting hands were laid upon her beautiful hair,
and she was dragged, resisting, into the Court.
The head, it must be remembered, is always sacred,
and surely doubly inviolable should Draupadi's
have been, having so lately been sprinkled with
anointing water, in her husband's coronation.

The riotous scene progressed. Thinking to
complete the degradation of the Pandavas, but
really working to invoke ruin on themselves, the
same rude hands that had just been laid in
sacrilege on the hair of the Queen, now attempted
to snatch away her *sari*, that she might stand in
this public place unveiled. But Draupadi called
on Krishna in her heart, and clung to His name,
and lo, the scarf and veil that were being plucked
from her, were miraculously multiplied, and
hundreds upon hundreds of such garments were
thrown aside by the despoilers, yet was not the
Queen for one moment disrobed ! Against their
own will, these disorderly men of the royal household stood covered with shame, while the wrathful
Pandavas touched the depths of silent misery and
defeat, bound by the pledges of Yudisthira.

At this very moment there was a sudden hush,
and all rose to their feet, for the old blind
Dritarashtra, summoned by Bhishma, was being
led, trembling, into his son's presence. Tears

rained from his sightless eyes, as he stretched out his hands in appeal to Duryodhana.

"My son! my son! is this madness?" he cried. "Forget you that as a mother's blessing works a man's greatest good, so a woman's sorrow brings him supreme woe? Why should you out-rage this proud and helpless queen, unless, indeed, ye be wearied of the good days, and desire to bring destruction on your father and his house?" And then, as if in a vain desire to mitigate the force of the coming doom, by winning some measure of goodwill from the hapless woman, the old man turned himself to Draupadi, "Speak, my daughter!" he commanded tremulously. "Name three boons that I can grant to you. This at least remains, that *I* am free to restore whatever *you* may ask!"

The heroic consort of the Pandavas drew her-self up to her full height, and the clear cold tones of her wonderful voice rang through the hall. "I speak, O King, as a free woman," she began, "for he who has sold himself into slavery has no power over the free to make them bondsmen. Yudisthira first bartered his own freedom, there-fore could he claim no control over his wife's!" The King nodded his assent, and Draupadi went on. "I demand, then, the freedom of Yudisthira, that no son of mine henceforth may have to claim a slave for his father!"

"Granted," said Dritarashtra briefly. "Ask again."

" Next," said Draupadi, " I beg the same for his four brothers, with all their weapons."

" This I also grant," said the blind King ; " and what is your demand in gold and other wealth ? "

" Nay," said the stately Draupadi, with a flash of mingled scorn and pride, " I ask no more ! The Pandavas, being free, can right themselves— they need owe no man anything ! "

Dritarashtra shuddered, as if a cold blast had swept over him, even while he bent before the courage of the Queen. For her refusal to accept his amends seemed to him as a terrible curse upon his house. But Duryodhana's soul had become blinder by reason of his enmity, than were the bodily eyes of his two parents. He pressed forward eagerly.

" Nay, O my father ! " he cried, thrusting himself before Dritarashtra, " I also will consent to this restoration if thou wilt grant me but one condition more ! Let these Pandavas and their wife go forth free, but let them live in the forests, as a forfeit, for twelve years, and spend their thirteenth year in disguise, wherever they will. At the end of these thirteen years, if they are not discovered by me or by my friends, let them be indeed free. But if in their thirteenth year we track them out, another twelve years of exile pays the penalty. One throw more of the dice to settle it ! "

All waited, breathless, for the King's answer.

What would he do ? Which side would he take ? But a moment before it had seemed as if, with Draupadi's help, he might break the spell of disaster that Duryodhana's licence was about to cast over the royal house. Now the shadow of evil, bringing woe behind it, threatened to enwrap them all again. Where, and on which side, would the King be found?

Alas, overborne by his son's impetuosity, Dritarashtra nodded consent. Yudisthira accepted the challenge, and the fatal dice were once more thrown and lost !

The Pandava princes saluted the King, and turned to go. " But," said Dritarashtra, raising a warning hand to detain them, and speaking loudly in the hearing of all the nobles present, " But,—if my son fail to discover your hiding-place, then, on the day that ends the thirteen years, know, O Heroes, that yours is the right to return to your home and to your empire, free men and princes as but yesterday ye came forth."

Duryodhana and the little group of lawless courtiers gathered round him, bit their lips in anger at what they considered his father's needless generosity. But the promise was already spoken, and could not be recalled. The five knights were gone. And in her distant chamber Pritha was saying farewell to her sons for thirteen years.

These scenes also passed before the eyes of Bhishma. He remembered all.

Twelve years of forest life went by, and but for Draupadi's mortified pride of womanhood, they might have been years of unclouded happiness. Great sages, and Krishna Himself, came to visit the heroes in their retirement, and often they wandered forth on delightful pilgrimages. Once, indeed, Duryodhana and his guard, visiting the neighbourhood where they chanced to be, fell into trouble, and were made prisoners of war. Then the Pandava brothers, hearing of their plight, sallied forth on a raid of liberation, and enabled them to go back to Hastinapura.

Oh, with what bitterness had Duryodhana come home from this expedition ! Bhishma smiled sadly to himself, as the picture of the return passed before him. How the Prince had sat upon the ground, refusing food, and how at last he only rose, as it appeared to onlookers, when new hopes and plans for vengeance were matured within his heart!

There was a lonely place in the jungle, where men's feet never trod. Here, as the twelve years drew to an end, Yudisthira and his brothers came, with their weapons all wrapped up to look like corpses, and hung them on the trees ; for so it was the fashion of those days to do oftentimes with the bodies of the dead. Then they sought menial employment in the household of a neighbouring king, and in this concealment the last year passed away.

x

And now at last the thirteen years were ended, and the Pandavas demanded the restoration of their kingdom. Alas! the chief place amongst Dritarashtra's counsellors had long been held by that false knight, his son. The weakness that had always had place in Dritarashtra's character had grown with the years, and he was now completely under the influence of Duryodhana. Justice called for the cession of Indraprastha and half the kingdom. The King's own words were fresh in all memories. Krishna Himself pleaded in person that right should be done. Bhishma, as chief of the kingdom, pointed out sternly the peril that lay in breaking a pledge, and declaring war on the allies of Krishna. But the awful fate that works in the affairs of men had borne everything before it. Even now it would seem as if Duryodhana might have saved himself and his fortunes by the simple right. But, infatuated, he refused to listen, and proceeded with his organisation of the army and other warlike preparations. Bhishma himself was compelled by his allegiance to take the part of commander-in-chief.

The dying minister and warrior must have covered his eyes as he came to this point in his reverie. For the panorama of destruction was still so fresh that it could scarcely present itself in pictures: the trumpets of battle, the neighing of horses, the trampling of elephants, and

Scorning to shoot at one who had been a girl, Bhishma would laughingly aim a shaft at Arjuna, whenever a sudden turn of the wheels gave him a chance. As so much play seemed to him those darts which clustered thicker and thicker on his own person. But when sunset drew near, the hour for the mortal wound being come, he received an arrow straight in his heart, and fell from his chariot to the ground.

Even now, however, Death could not draw near to Bhishma. In the moment of his fall, the thought flashed into his mind that he was about to die in the dark half of the sun's year, a time most unfortunate for great souls, and he determined to remain alive six months, that he might die in the summer solstice.

The leaders of both sides crowded round him, having doffed their armour in token of truce. They would have carried him away to comfortable quarters, but he would have none of it. "The hero's bed," he said, "is where he falls. I desire no other. But I need a pillow!" He had fallen on the broad ends of those arrows which had struck him behind, and his shoulders being thereby lifted, his head hung down. One and another ran and brought him cushions. Their luxury was fit for kings. But the old saint-warrior shook his head. "Arjuna, child!" he said, looking towards him who had provided him with

his hard bed, standing now speechless with grief.
Arjuna understood the request, and shot three arrows
downwards into the earth, with such sure aim that
they made the support the mighty bowman required.

Bhishma gave a sigh of relief, and ordered that
a trench should be dug about him, and he be left
without tent or furnishings, to spend the remaining
months in solitary worship.   Next day, however,
needing water, he had recourse again to Arjuna
and his arrows, and a great spring burst forth at
that place where the soldier shot his bolt into the
earth, so that the ear of Bhishma was soothed
with the sound of running water, until the day of
his actual departure.   Such at least is the legend
of the people concerning the great pond that
sparkles still on the lonely plain of Kurukshetra.

Of the remainder of Bhishma's life, men speak
to this day with bated breath.   Eight long days
more the battle raged beside him, and at the end,
the Doom-cloud of the Kurus had broken, and
carried all away with it, and the Triumph of the
Pandavas was established.   For the five brothers
stood victorious, with all their foes lying slain
about them.   Then the tide of war ebbed away
from Kurukshetra, and Bhishma, through sunny
days and starry nights, kept his long vigil, while
months passed by for the victorious Pandavas, in
the business entailed by victories and the government of kingdoms.

At last, however, Yudisthira—again a new-crowned monarch, but of a wider realm than ever—was free to turn with his brothers, and follow Krishna to where their dying clansman lay. The young sovereign desired that he, who had seen three generations of kings, should give him his blessing, and pass on to him his long-garnered lore of statecraft.

And the Holy Knight Himself laid healing hands of coolness and peace on the burning frame and anguished wounds of the warrior-saint, so that his mind grew as clear and his speech as strong as in former years, and he revealed all his wisdom to these adopted sons of his old age.

Fifty days later the Pandavas once more drew near to Bhishma, knowing that the time had come that he would die. Before he passed away, his last whispered blessing was still for Yudisthira, left to fulfil the heavy task of kings. But he died, fixing all his thought on Krishna, and so united himself with the Eternal, to live for ever in the love and memory of India as Bhishma the Terrible, her great and stainless knight, who lived as he had died, and died as he had lived, without fear and without reproach.

The Ascent of Yudisthira
into Heaven

To Arjuna, when Krishna passed away, the whole earth became a blank. He could no longer string his great bow, Gandiva, and his divine weapons failed to come to his hand at need, for he could not concentrate his mind upon them. Therefore he understood that his time was ended. He and his brothers had accomplished the great purpose of their lives. The moment had come for their departure from the world.

For to all is it known that understanding and courage and foresight arise in us, only so long as the days of our prosperity are not outrun, and all alike leave a man, when the hour of his adversity strikes. Such things have Time only for their root. It is Time, indeed, that is the seed of the Universe. And verily it is Time who takes back all at his own pleasure. Arjuna saw therefore that to the place whence his invincible weapons had come to him, thither had they been withdrawn again, having, in the day given them, achieved the victories that had been theirs. He realised, moreover, that when the time for his use of them should again approach, they would return of their own accord into his hands. Meanwhile, it was for himself and his four brothers to set their faces resolutely, towards the attainment of the highest goal.

Yudisthira fully agreed with this thought of Arjuna. " You must see," he said to him, " that it is Time who fastens the fetters, and Time who loosens the bond." And his brothers, understanding the allusion, could utter only the one word, "Time! Time!" The Pandavas and Draupadi, being thus entirely at one in the decision that the empire was over for them, the question of the succession was quickly arranged. The entreaties of citizens and subjects were overruled ; successors and a protector installed in different capitals ; and farewell was taken of the kingdom. Having thus done their duty as sovereigns, Yudisthira and his brothers, with Draupadi, turned to the performance of personal religious rites. Donning coverings of birch bark only, they fasted many days and received the blessings of the priests. Then each took the fire from his domestic altar,——that fire which had been lighted for him on his marriage, and kept alight, worshipped, and tended ever since by his wife and himself in person,——and threw it into consecrated water. This was the last act of their lives in the world, and as it was performed, and the brothers turned themselves to the east, all the women in the assembled court burst into tears. But for the great happiness which shone now in their faces, it would have seemed to all as if the Pandavas were once more leaving Hastinapura poor, and defeated at dice, for their exile in the forest. Followed for some distance by a crowd of citizens, and by the ladies of the royal household, the little procession went forward—none, however, daring to address the King, or to plead with him for a possible return. After a time, the citizens went back, and those members of the Pandava family who were to be left behind, ranged themselves about their new king as a centre. Those of the royal consorts who were daughters of reigning houses, set forth, accompanied by travelling escorts, for their fathers' kingdoms. Those who were related to the succeeding sovereign took their places behind him ; and so, receiving fare-wells and benisons from all, Yudisthira, Bhima, Arjuna, and the twins Nakula and Sahadeva, looked their last on the world they were leaving, and went onward, followed by Draupadi. But Yudisthira was in fact the head of a party of seven ; for hard upon their footsteps followed a dog, whose affection for them all was so great that he would not desert them.

Long was the journey and arduous, and it was

made barefooted, and clad in simple birch bark, by
these who had but yesterday had at their command
all the resources of earth. It was their intention
to practise the life of renunciation in the mountains of the far north, but first they would worship
the land that they were leaving, by travelling
round it in a ceremonial circle. Nothing had they
left, save their garments of birch bark. Only
Arjuna, reluctant to part from them, carried his
mighty bow Gandiva, and his two inexhaustible
quivers of arrows. Thus many days passed.
Suddenly, as the little procession of pilgrims
reached the shores of the great sea that lies on
the east, they found their road barred by one
whose presence was like unto a veritable mountain. Closing the way before them stood the
God Agni, Divinity of the Seven Flames, and the
Pandavas waited with folded hands to receive his
commands.

"From Ocean brought I Gandiva, O Arjuna,"
said the Devourer of Forests, "to thine aid. To
Ocean again, then, let thy weapons be here restored. Along with the discus of Krishna, let
Gandiva vanish from the world. But know that
when his hour shall again strike, he of his own
accord will come once more into thine hand!"
Thus adjured, and urged also by his brothers,
Arjuna came forward, and standing on the shore,
hurled into the sea with his own hands his price-

less bow Gandiva, and his two inexhaustible quivers. And the God of Fire, satisfied with this supreme renunciation, disappeared from before them.

On and on went the pilgrims, until the circle of their worship was complete. From the salt sea, they proceeded south-west. Then they turned north, and passing Dwarka, the city beloved of Krishna, they saw it covered by the waters of the ocean. For even so had it been prophesied, that all the things they had known should pass away, like a dream. At last they reached the Himalayas, home of meditating souls. Here were the great forests, and here the mighty snow-peaked mountains, where the mind could be stilled and quieted, and centred on itself. And beyond, in the dim north, lay Meru, Mountain of the Gods. And here it was, as they journeyed on, with faces set ever to the goal, that all the errors, of all their lives, took shape and bore fruit. They had been but small, these sins of the Pandavas,—a thought of vanity here, a vain boast, unfulfilled, there! Yet small as they were, they had been sufficient to flaw those lives that without them would have been all-perfect, and one by one the heroic pilgrims turned faint with a mortal faintness, and stopped, and fell. Only in the clear mind of Yudisthira— "the King of Justice and Righteousness," as his subjects had loved to call him—in that clear mind,

with its trained sense of human conduct, rose
knowledge of its cause, with each disaster that
befell.

Even he himself, it is said, could not altogether
escape the common lot of imperfection, and as
he felt the very pang of death shoot through one
foot where it touched the earth, he remembered
a shadow that had fallen once, upon his own
unstained truth.

But with him there could be no rebellion
against the right. He shed no tear, and uttered
no sigh. Rather did his own purpose shine
clearer and stronger before him, at each defeat
of his little party. And thus Yudisthira, not even
looking back, proceeded alone, followed by the
dog.

Suddenly there was a deafening peal of thunder,
so overwhelming that the two stood still on the
mountain-side. Then came towards them, as it
were, a cloud of light, and when this had become
clear, the hero beheld in the midst of it Indra, the
God of Heaven, standing in his chariot.

"It is ordained, thou chief of the race of
Bharata, that thou shalt enter the realm of
Heaven, in this thy human form. Wherefore do
thou herewith ascend this chariot," said the god.

"Nay, Lord of a thousand Deities!" answered
the King, "my brothers have all fallen dead, and
without them at my side, I have no desire to enter

Heaven. Nor could any one of us, indeed, accept felicity, if the delicate Draupadi, our Queen, were banished to regions of hardship. Let all therefore go in with me."

"But thou shalt behold them all when thou reachest the abodes of blessedness," said the god. "Verily they have but ascended there before thee. Wherefore yield thee not to grief, O Chief of the Bharatas! But rise with me in this thy mortal form."

The King bowed his head in acceptance of the invitation, and stood aside to let the dog go first into the chariot.

But Indra intervened. "To-day, O King, thou hast won immortality! Happiness and victory and a throne like unto my own, are thine. But send away this dog! Enjoy what thou hast achieved!"

"How difficult is it to an Aryan," said Yudisthira, "to do a deed unworthy of an Aryan! How could I enjoy that prosperity for which I had cast off one who was devoted?"

Said Indra, "For men with dogs there is no place in Heaven. Thou art the Just! Abandon thou this dog! In doing this will be no cruelty."

But Yudisthira answered slowly, "Nay, great Indra, to abandon one who has loved us is infinitely sinful. Never till my life ends shall I give up the terrified, nor one who has shown me devotion, nor those who have sought my protection or my mercy, nor any who is too weak to protect himself. Never have I done this. Never shall I stoop to do it. Therefore do I refuse, out of mere desire for my own happiness, to abandon this dog!"

In the King's voice there was no possibility of reconsideration. Yudisthira had made up his mind. He would not be moved.

Yet still the Deity argued with him. "By the presence of a dog, Heaven itself would be made unholy! Thou knowest that his mere glance would take away from the consecrated all its sacredness. Wherefore, O King, art thou then so foolish? Thou hast renounced thine own brothers and Draupadi! Why shouldst thou not renounce this dog?"

"It is well known," replied Yudisthira, "that one cannot but renounce the dead! For them there are neither enemies nor friends. I did not abandon my brothers and Draupadi so long as they were alive! I only left them, when I was unable to revive them. Not even the frightening of one who had sought our protection, nor the slaying of a woman, nor stealing from a Brahmin, nor treachery to a friend, would now appear to me a greater sin than to leave this dog!" And lo, as he finished speaking, the dog vanished, and in his place was the radiant presence of

Y

Dharmma, the God of Righteousness. "Hail, O Yudisthira!" said he, "thou who hast renounced the very chariot of the celestials on behalf of a dog! Verily, in Heaven is none equal unto thee! Regions of inexhaustible happiness are thine!"

Then, surrounded by the chariots of the gods, Yudisthira the Just, the King of Righteousness, seated on the car of glory, ascended into Heaven in his mortal form. And entering, he was met by all the Immortals, eager to welcome him to their midst, eager to praise him as he deserved. But Yudisthira, looking round and seeing nowhere his brothers or Draupadi, said only, "Happy or unhappy, whatever be the region that is now my brothers', to that, and nowhere else, do I desire to go!" "But why," remonstrated Indra, "dost thou still cherish human affections? Thy brothers also are happy, each in his own place. Verily, I see that thou art but mortal. Human love still binds thee. Look, this is Heaven! Behold around thee those who have attained to the regions of the gods!"

But Yudisthira answered, "Nay, Conqueror of the Demons! I cannot dwell apart from them. Wherever they have gone, thither, and not elsewhere, will I also go!"

At this very moment the King's eyes, sweeping Heaven again, in his first eager search for those he loved, caught sight, first of Duryodhana, then of

his foe's brothers, and finally of the whole hundred
and one sons of Dritarashtra, blazing like the sun,
wearing all the signs of glory that belong to heroes,
and seated on thrones like gods. At this sight,
Yudisthira was filled with rage. "I will not," he
shouted in anger, "dwell even in the regions of
happiness with the vain and reckless Duryodhana!
For him were our friends and kinsmen slaughtered.
By him was the Queen insulted. Listen to me,
ye gods! I will not even look upon such as
these. Let me go there, whither my brothers
are gone!"

"But, Great King," said one of those about
him, smiling at his fury, "this should not be. In
Heaven do all feuds cease. By pouring himself,
like an oblation, on the fire of battle, by remaining unterrified in moments of great terror, has
Duryodhana attained to celestial joys. Do thou
forget thy woes. This is Heaven, O Lord of men!
Here there can be no enmity!"

"If such as he could have deserved this,"
answered Yudisthira, no whit appeased, "what
must not my friends and kindred have deserved!
Let me go to the company of the righteous!
What are the celestial regions to me without
my brothers? Where they are, must in itself be
Heaven. This place, in my opinion, is not so."

Seeing the King so determined, the gods turned
and gave orders to the celestial messenger, saying,

"Do thou show unto Yudisthira his friends and kinsmen," and, turning his face away from the regions of blessedness, yet keeping still in the world of the gods, the divine guide made to do their bidding, and went forward, followed by the King.

Dread and terrible was that road by which they now journeyed. Dark and polluted and difficult, it was noisome with foul odours, infested with stinging insects, and made dangerous and fearful by roaming beasts of prey. It was skirted on either side by a running fire. In its strange twilight could be seen sights of a nameless terror. Here and there lay human bones. It seemed to be full of evil spirits, and to abound in inaccessible fastnesses and labyrinthine paths.

On went the messenger of the gods, and on behind him followed the King, his mind every moment sinking deeper and deeper into thoughts of anguish. At last they reached a gloomy region, where was a river, whose waters appeared to boil, foaming, and throwing up clouds of vapour. The leaves of the trees, moreover, were sharp like swords. Here also were deserts of fine sand, luminous to the sight and heated to white heat. The very rocks and stones were made of iron. There were terrible thorns also, and innumerable cauldrons filled with boiling oil. In such forms did they behold the tortures which are inflicted upon sinful men.

Seeing this region of night, abounding thus in horror, Yudisthira said to his guide, "How much further must we travel along paths like these? What world of the gods is this? I command thee at once to disclose to me where my brothers are!"

The messenger stopped. "Thus far, O King, is your way! It was the command of the denizens of Heaven that, having come to this point, I was to return. As for yourself, if you, O Yudisthira the Just, should be weary, you have the right of return with me!"

Stupefied by noxious vapours, and with his mind sunk in heaviness, the King turned round, and took a few steps backwards. As he did so, however, moaning voices and sobs broke out in the thick darkness about him. "Stay! stay!" sighed the voices. "Our pain is lessened by the presence of Yudisthira. A sweet breeze, a glimpse of light, come with thee. O King, leave us not this instant!"

"Alas! alas!" said Yudisthira in his compassion, and immediately stood still amongst these souls in Hell. As he listened, however, the voices appeared to be strangely familiar. "Who are you? Who are you?" he exclaimed to one and another, as he heard them, and great beads of sweat stood on his brow as their unbodied groans shaped themselves out of the darkness into answers, "Arjuna! Draupadi! Karna!" and the rest.

A moment passed. " Duryodhana in Heaven !" he pondered, " and these my kinsmen fallen into Hell ! Do I wake, or dream ? Or is all this some disorder of the brain ? What justice can there be in the Universe ? Nay, for this crime shall I abandon the very gods themselves !" At these words, uttered within himself by his own mind, the wrath of an all-powerful monarch awoke in the heart of Yudisthira. " Go !" he thundered in anger, turning himself to his guide. " Return thou to the presence of those whose messenger thou art, and make known to them that I return not to their side. Here, where my brothers suffer, here, where my presence aids them, here and no other where, do I eternally abide !"

The messenger bowed his head, and passed swiftly out of sight. Up to high Heaven passed he, carrying this defiance of Yudisthira, to Indra, Chief of Gods and Men. And the King stood alone in Hell, brooding over the unspeakable sufferings of his kinsfolk.

Not more than a moment had passed, when a cool and fragrant breeze began to blow. Light dawned. All the repulsive sights disappeared. The boulders of iron, the cauldrons of oil, and the thorny plants vanished from sight. And Yudisthira, raising his eyes, saw himself surrounded by the gods.

" These illusions," said they, " are ended.

Ascend thou to thine own place! Hell must indeed be seen by every king. Happy are they whose good deeds have been so many that they first suffer and afterwards enjoy. To thee and to these thy kindred, Yudisthira, has Hell been shown only by a kind of mirage. Come, then, thou royal sage, behold here the heavenly Ganges. Plunge thou into this Milky Way, and casting off there thy human body, divest thyself with it of all thine enmity and grief. Then rise, O thou of never-dying glory! to join thy kinsmen and friends and Draupadi, in those blessed regions wherein they already dwell, great even as Indra, enthroned in Heaven!"

THE END

Printed by T. and A. CONSTABLE, Printers to His Majesty
at the Edinburgh University Press, Scotland